FOREVER MINE

Also by Elizabeth Reyes:

<u>Moreno Brothers Series</u>
Always Been Mine
Sweet Sophie
Romero
Making You Mine

<u>5th Street Series</u>
Noah
Gio
Hector
Abel

<u>Fate Series</u>
Fate
Breaking Brandon (Fall 2013)

FOREVER MINE

The Moreno Brothers #1

Elizabeth Reyes

Forever Mine

The Moreno Brothers #1

Elizabeth Reyes

Copyright © 2010 Elizabeth Reyes

I dedicate this to my wonderful family for their love and support and for putting up with endless days and nights of me sitting in front of the computer, writing. A special thanks to all the friends and other family members who have been listening to me ramble on and those who have read the entire book and provided excellent feedback.

PROLOGUE

Sarah went numb. This could not be happening. She gripped the phone, her knuckles going white. The knot in her throat was unbearable.

"Sarah, are you still there?"

In an almost inaudible whimper, Sarah answered, "Ah huh."

"I know this is hard, honey, but it's not the end of the world. We talked about this already, and you knew it was a possibility. I tried, Sarah. I really did, but there's no way around it. We've gone over all the other options, but anything else is too much of a risk. It's for the best."

"But, senior year ..." Sarah felt the anger building and the tears burning in her eyes. She felt ready to blow up—lash out. Then she heard her mom again. Her voice choked up as well.

"I know, honey. I'm *so* sorry. I really screwed things up this time."

Her mom took a long, trembling deep breath, and it broke Sarah's heart. She wanted to be with her to hug her and to comfort her.

"It's okay, Mom. I'll be fine."

Her mom cleared her throat and lowered her voice. Sounding very determined, she spoke again, "I am going to make this up to you. I promise, okay?"

"Okay."

"I've already called Aunt Norma. She and Uncle Alfred will be here this weekend. They wanna help us pack, so you and I will have time to spend together. Then I'll have to be in court on Monday."

Sarah gasped. "Monday?"

"Yeah, babe, Monday."

Sarah covered half her face with her free hand and shook her head. Not wanting to make her mother feel any worse, she choked back a sob.

"All right, mom," she whispered.

"I'm gonna be here a while, honey, so don't wait up for me. We'll talk more about this tomorrow."

She hung up and looked at her best friend Sydney who'd been sitting on the bed next to her the whole time. Sydney stared at her anxiously.

"She's pleading guilty and gonna do at least three years. I have to go live with my Aunt Norma in California." Sydney kept a strong front, but Sarah fell into his arms crying.

CHAPTER 1

ONE MONTH LATER

La Jolla High School, California

Even as she stood in the middle of a bustling hallway with noisy students rushing by her, Sarah felt utterly alone. One month wasn't nearly enough to prepare her for a new school, new friends—a new life.

God, how she missed Sydney. This wasn't at all how she'd imagined her first day as a senior in high school would be. She had so many plans at her old school, and now she stood here completely lost.

Clenching her backpack in her hand, she walked off in no particular direction. She wanted to get out of the middle of the human traffic jam. Where in the heck was her cousin, Valerie? She *had* said the main entrance hall just outside the counselor's office, hadn't she?

They'd been dropped off together by her aunt, but Sarah had to go to the counselor's office. Since she'd enrolled so late, her schedule hadn't come in the mail like Valerie's. No sooner than the moment they had walked into school together had Valerie started socializing, promising she'd be right there when she got back from the office.

The bell rang, and Sarah tried not to panic. She glanced at her schedule but had no idea where her first class was. She backed up slowly until her back was against a wall. Had Valerie really abandoned her? No, she wouldn't. She took in some of the faces around her and wondered if she should just ask someone for directions to her first class.

High-pitched squealing got her attention, and she turned to the front entrance to find some girl had her arms wrapped around one of the guys that had just walked in. Sarah rolled her eyes. She'd always hated those types of girls. The guy was obviously a jock because he wore a letterman's jacket and so did his two friends.

Deciding she was on her own, she walked back toward the office and frowned when she realized a map of the school had been just outside the office the entire time. There were a few kids standing in front of it, examining their schedules and then looking up at the map. Apparently, she wasn't the only newbie at this school—not much of a consolation. Sarah looked around for Valerie, feeling more than a little annoyed at her.

Male laughter erupted just behind her, and she turned to find the same jocks she'd seen walk in earlier with a few more guys horsing around. The tall one who had been greeted at the door by the squealing girl was smiling when their eyes met. The smile on his face seemed to dissolve slowly. She stood there frozen, her lips slightly opened. For a moment, she thought he might say something, and then she heard Valerie.

"There you are!"

Sarah snapped out of her daze and watched as Valerie, who'd already taken Sarah's schedule, smiled wickedly. "We have two classes together!"

"We do?" Sarah's cheeks still felt warm, but she quickly walked alongside of Valerie, incredibly grateful for her timing.

Valerie talked about the classes just until they were far enough away and around the corner of the building. "Oh, my God, Sarah, do you know who that was staring at you?"

Surprised, and not sure why, Sarah pretended not to understand. "Who?"

Valerie gasped. "That was Angel Moreno! Don't you remember? I've told you about him and his brothers."

"No," Sarah lied. Of course she remembered, that was part of the reason she could hardly breathe when she recognized him.

The bell rang again.

"Oh, shit," Valerie looked at her watch. "We're gonna be late on our first day."

She grabbed Sarah's arm, and they were off on a foot race to their first class.

TWO WEEKS LATER

Angel took long, rapid strides around the science building. His stomach tensed up as the bell rang. He was late to practice again, and he knew his coach wouldn't be happy. It was the second time this week, but he had to stay after class to get the extra credit assignment. He was failing Spanish II, again. *Spanish!* His parents owned a Mexican restaurant, for crying out loud. The only reason he had taken it was because he needed two years of a foreign language to even have a prayer of getting into a four-year college. And now it may cost him time on the field.

Apparently, he was only good at the curse words, and the teacher called his Spanish, *Spanglish.* It was a Catch 22 though, if he didn't stay late to get the extra credit assignments, he wouldn't be able to make up some of the lousy scores he'd been getting on the quizzes. If he didn't make them up, he wouldn't have the grades to play on the team. Not picking up his grade also meant staying after school for tutoring. Just the thought made him groan.

He made it to the weight room just as they were starting warm ups. The coach barely looked at him and pointed to the bleachers outside in the hot sun.

"Twenty," he said. "Make 'em fast."

Running bleachers was the worst. As he began to sprint toward them, he heard Dana call out to him from the track area where the cheerleaders were warming up.

"Bleachers again, Angel?"

He nodded, barely looking her way. Some of the other girls laughed and joined in. His dimples made their appearance as usual, although his smile was anything but genuine. The catcalls had stopped making him uncomfortable a long time ago, especially from this group of girls.

At seventeen, Angel was already an impressive six-foot-two. He was very much following in his two older brothers' footsteps. Although it was nice to have the instant admiration as soon as he started high school, there were times he resented having to live up to his brothers' legacies. He had the looks, the build, the popularity but, unfortunately, not the grades.

He frowned at the thought of his two older brothers being on full sports scholarships in college, and here he was struggling to stay eligible to play high school football. It was embarrassing, but he wasn't going to give up. As his father and lately his oldest brother Sal always said, "Failure is not an option."

Lost in his thoughts, and still annoyed with himself, Angel ran slowly and pensively up the bleachers for the fourth or fifth time; he'd lost count. Sweat trickled down his face, and he struggled to keep his breathing steady. He usually could get a rhythm going, but not today. Someone ran right past him a little too closely. Startled, he almost lost his balance. He caught himself and was about to give the guy an earful when he heard her apologize and realized he was a *she*.

"I'm sorry, did I bump you?"

"No, I'm good." Angel bent over with his hands on his knees, trying to catch his breath.

"You sure you're okay?" she asked again.

He looked up at her for the first time, still breathing hard. The sun was directly behind her. Angel squinted at a petite silhouette. She shifted slightly, blocking the sun for a moment. The first thing he noticed was her eyes. They were an amazing light green. A startling contrast to her dark features. She stared at him as she too stood there, breathing hard.

Her hair was up in a ponytail, except for a few strands dampened by her perspiration that stuck to the sides of her face and forehead. It surprised Angel that he didn't recognize her from anywhere. He thought he knew everyone in the school. But there was something familiar about her; he just couldn't place it.

"I'm fine," he said.

"Good." She started untangling the earphone wire. Apparently, she'd taken it out of her ear when she stopped to check on him. She didn't smile back or ask anything else but seemed eager to be on her way. He watched as she adjusted it in her ear and got ready to go back to her running.

With his heart pounding and palms sweating, to his own surprise, he stammered, "So, you like to run?"

Stupid, stupid, stupid.

She turned and looked at him without responding. Maybe she hadn't heard him—he hoped.

"I'm Angel. What's your name?"

"Sarah."

All he could manage was a smile as the name sunk in.

"Well, have a good one," she said and ran off.

He watched as she ran up and across the bleachers. From a distance, she looked very small with little to no curves. Then it hit him—lost girl—from the first day of school. That's where he'd seen those eyes. He'd noticed them even then. He remembered feeling struck, but he hadn't seen her since and had almost forgotten about it. Almost.

He started his bleachers again, and his thoughts went back to his grades. Was he really gonna need to be tutored? He shook his head in disgust and picked up his pace.

***

Sarah ran, concentrating hard. She had a feeling he was still watching her and would die if she fell or tripped. The butterflies in her stomach were out of control. How could she almost knock him over? Of all people, it had to be *him*. She should've said more to him, but she'd been at a loss for words, thoughts—just like the first day of school when he'd caught her gawking at him like an idiot. Ever since then, she'd avoided coming face-to-face with him again. Any time she even thought she saw him, she'd run in the opposite direction.

Her legs almost gave out when she realized who she'd bumped. *Damn him and his smile.* As sure as she was that he probably didn't even remember her, she hadn't wanted to chance making a fool of herself again.

Sarah knew all about the great Moreno brothers. Valerie had lived here her whole life and had gone through grade school and middle school with them. Since Valerie had a huge crush on Angel's older brother, Alex, she told Sarah about them all the time.

Sarah thought back to the first time she'd seen Angel two summers ago. She and her mother had come out to visit her mother's sister, Valerie's step mom, Aunt Norma. Valerie had taken her along to a beach party with her.

It was an all-day party, but Valerie, being self-conscious about her body, decided they'd show up late, after all the swimming was done. They arrived when everyone was just hanging around the bonfires and listening to music. Sarah had never really grasped everything Valerie had told her about Angel and his brothers. She made them out to be like movie stars—drop-dead gorgeous. Valerie had poked her when he and his friends arrived. "There he is. That's Alex's little brother."

Sarah had looked up in time to see him in all his glory. He was anything but little, even back then. He and his friends seemed to move in slow motion toward a group of girls. The girls waited, their anxious smiles enormous. He wore denim shorts and a tank top that showed off his muscles. Sarah had never seen a finer-looking smile. His dimples were incredible. She watched as one of the girls practically jumped into his arms, hugging him, and then looked around casually to make sure everyone was watching.

"Is that his girlfriend?" she'd asked Valerie.

Valerie had immediately huffed, "She wishes. That's Dana, the one I told you about. She's forever throwing herself at him and tries to convince anyone that will listen that the two of them are an item. Everyone knows he's never had a girlfriend. Why should he when he can have all the girls he wants—whenever he wants?"

Sarah remembered watching him and fantasizing that day. It was all she could do. The girls he hung with seemed so experienced and cool around him and his friends. They laughed, sometimes a little too exaggeratedly, but still at least they could hold a conversation around him. She had barely been able to breathe the first day of school when he looked at her. And now she had almost knocked him down. If he did remember her as the gaping fool from the first day, he'd now have yet another asinine memory of her. She was hopeless.

None of that mattered anyway. Making friends was not on her agenda. She didn't plan on sticking around long enough for that.

She picked up the speed and tried to get him off her mind. She remembered Sydney's birthday. It was this weekend, and she had to make sure she finally emailed the gift. She'd put a slideshow together with pictures of the good times they had had, along with all of the songs that held special meaning to just the two of them. She knew Sydney would appreciate it much more than any store-bought gift.

If it hadn't been for Sydney, she didn't know how she would've gotten through the past year, and she wanted to show her appreciation. Sydney meant the world to her. They'd been through so much over the years, last year especially when the nightmare with her mom started.

When Sarah was forced to move to California with her aunt, she and Sydney made a pact to always keep in touch. So far, they had swapped emails, and since Sydney's parents had offered to get her a cell phone that had unlimited minutes, they could talk every day. No matter how far away, Sarah was determined to keep Sydney and his family in her life forever.

Aunt Norma didn't know about Sarah's plans. She would be eighteen in January, and once she was, no one, not even her mom, would be able to stop her from going back to Arizona. She would save enough money to be able to pay Sydney's parents to let her stay with them. She already had several babysitting gigs lined up. Between that and school, there was no room for a social life.

Sarah could hardly wait. Just the thought made her smile. Next semester she'd be running for her home track team at Flagstaff High, where she belonged, and her life would go back to the way it should be.

She glanced up from her feet as she made her way down the bleachers and saw Jesse Strickland waiting for her at the bottom, arms crossed, smiling from ear to ear. *Oh, God, what now*? She fought the urge to roll her eyes. As she reached the bottom, Jesse stood in front of her, deliberately blocking her way. He reached over to pull an earphone out of her ear, but she stopped his hand from getting any closer and did it herself.

"You know what today is?" he asked, smirking.

"Nope."

He stared at her in disbelief. "Valerie didn't tell you?"

Sarah shook her head, not the least bit interested. She was getting hotter, and already sweating. She knew she'd soon be drenched if she didn't start running again.

"Is this gonna take all day?" she said. "I'm in the middle of my run here."

"It's my birthday." He opened up his arms. "I'm here to collect."

Sarah's eye's narrowed, and she stepped back. "Collect what?"

He stepped forward grinning big. "Well, being that we're here in school. I'll take a hug for now." He leaned in and began putting his arms around her small waist.

Sarah scowled, pushing him away. "I don't owe you anything!"

Obviously amused, he lifted an eyebrow and proceeded to move forward and force a hug. "Oh, come on, Sarah, we've done so much more before, what's a hug now?"

"That was a long time ago and a mistake, so get over it!" She struggled to undo his hands that had clasped behind her waist. She felt his weight on her, heavy at first, pushing her against the fence. And then just like that, the weight was gone. It took her a moment to understand what had happened. Then she realized someone had pulled him off of her and saw Jesse slammed against the side of the bleachers.

Her legs went limp. She held on to the fence for support with one hand; the other lay flat on her chest, feeling the hard thud of her heart against it. It was *Angel.*

CHAPTER 2

"You have a problem, asshole?" Angel demanded, his face inches from Jesse's, his forearm at Jesse's neck.

Jesse's face reddened as he struggled to get the words out. "I-I'm was jus' messin' with her."

Angel turned to face Sarah, without loosening his grip on Jesse. She stood there wide-eyed, a hand over her chest. "Are you okay?"

Sarah nodded. "Yeah."

Angel turned back to Jesse's face which by now was a nice shade of deep crimson. He pushed him one more time against the bleachers, slamming his head against the wood siding.

"Get some fucking manners," he snarled.

Released, Jesse fell to one knee, coughing and gasping for air. Again, Angel turned to face Sarah. He took a few steps her way. She still held her hand to her chest, and her eyes remained on Jesse who, now on his feet, continued to cough. She finally looked at Angel, with those eyes that were beginning to haunt him.

He was determined not to clam up again. "Are you sure you're okay?" He fought back the urge to pull a strand of hair away from her face. She smiled at him for the first time.

"Yeah, thanks," she replied. "You didn't have to do that. He was just being a little pushy. I could've handled it." She stood up straight, putting her hand to her waist.

"Yeah, maybe you could've. I just don't have patience for idiots."

A few people had noticed the scuffle and slowed as they walked by, but not enough to call the attention of any teachers.

Again, she turned to watch Jesse huff away embarrassed, still coughing and rubbing his throat.

"He'll be fine."

Sarah shrugged, and they started back slowly toward the gym.

Walking so close, side by side, Angel was distracted when their hands touched for just a second. He refocused on his reaction to seeing Jesse push himself on her. It was typical of him to want to help, but he had gone a little overboard. He could've just pushed him off. Instead, he really wanted to see Jesse hurt.

He stared at her now, eyes narrowing. "Is he a friend of yours?"

Sarah glanced his way but turned away quickly. "That's not what I would call it."

Angel tightened his jaw and stared straight ahead. "What does that mean?"

She focused on the cheerleaders, who were now staring at them, especially Dana. Angel was oblivious to them, his eyes fixed on Sarah now.

She finally looked back at him. "We hung out once a long time ago."

Hung out? "You dated him?"

"Not exactly."

She never completely looked him in the eye, and the frustration was getting heavier. Jesse was one of the biggest assholes he knew. He couldn't imagine her being involved with him in any way.

They reached the gym before he could push further, and she gazed at him. She put her hand on his arm and every hair on his body stood at attention.

"Thanks again for what you did back there."

Angel couldn't help staring at her eyes.

"I'll see you around." She took her hand off his arm and began to walk away.

What? That's it? No way was he letting her get away so fast. He grabbed her hand as she turned from him. It was soft and small in his big brawny hand. His heart raced.

She turned to look at him. He tried focusing on something other than her eyes, but it was impossible.

"Are you going to the game on Friday?"

She studied him for a moment and then cleared her throat. "I can't. I'm working."

A few guys turned the corner and strolled toward them. She tugged her hand, but he held it tight. He glanced at the guys and back at her.

"Work, huh? 'Til what time?"

"Not sure yet, I'm babysitting, so it depends on what time their parents get home."

She tugged her hand again, this time just hard enough that Angel let go, and she started to walk away again.

Angel frowned. "Well, there's a party after. Maybe you can go to that, if they get home early?"

She was at the locker room entrance when she turned back to face him.

"Maybe." She waved and disappeared behind the door.

Angel stood there, staring at the locker room door. This was ridiculous. Why was he so bad at this all of a sudden? Then it dawned on him. He'd never actually asked a girl out. The irony made him chuckle. He'd always just hook up with someone at a party or dance and then ended up parking with her somewhere. Even with all the girls he'd been with, he'd never been inclined to actually ask any of them out. And now that he was trying to, he sucked at it.

***

Sarah sat on her bed, staring at the phone. She'd been home for a few hours already and hadn't told anyone about today.

She couldn't wait to talk to Sydney. She'd already left two messages for him, and he still hadn't called her back. Sarah glanced at the clock. She hoped he called before seven. That's when her mom called on Wednesdays, and they only had a miserable fifteen minutes to talk. Sarah jumped when the phone rang. She grabbed it and flipped it open.

"Hey."

"Lynni?" Sydney had always called her by her middle name—said she just didn't look like a Sarah.

"Yeah, it's me."

"You sound different," he said.

"No, just happy to hear you." She was almost giddy. "Listen, I've been dying to talk to you. You're never gonna guess what happened today."

"Really? Let's hear it."

Good ole Sydney, he sounded just as excited as she felt.

She made herself comfortable on the bed. "Okay, remember I told you about Angel?"

"You mean, *the* Angel?"

She eagerly brought him up-to-date about her afternoon. When she mentioned the party, Sydney asked, "You gonna go?"

"No, I can't. I'm working."

"Are you kidding me, Lynni? This is your chance to have some fun out there. You can't pass it up!"

"I've already committed," she said. "And the Salcidos pay really well. Besides, I wouldn't know anyone, well, except for Valerie."

"And Angel," Sydney reminded her.

Sarah smiled. God, she wished Syd were here. If he went with her, everything would be so perfect. "You don't understand. I've seen the girls he hangs out with. They're so sophisticated, and popular and, rich looking."

She stood up with the phone against her ear then walked over and stood in front of the mirror. She put her hand on her waist and smiled big, batting her lashes like the girls she'd seen around Angel, and immediately felt stupid. Her breasts had filled in somewhat, making her feel a little sexier, but she just didn't feel well put together like those other girls. She looked at her less-than-exciting clothes and winced. *No way is Angel interested in this.*

"Who cares? Let me tell you something, Lynni. It amazes me that you still think so little of yourself. I can guarantee you this guy would die for a chance with you. So, he's Mr. Popular, Mr. Football player, who gives a shit? Have you looked in the mirror lately?"

"Yes! I'm looking right now. I just wish you could be here to see the kind of girls he normally dates. Then you'd know what I'm talking about."

"I don't have to see them. I've seen you."

Sarah sighed and plopped back down on her bed. "What does it matter anyway? It's not like I'm gonna be here long. Remember?"

"You're doing it again." She could hear the annoyance in Sydney's voice.

"Doing what?" But she knew exactly what he was talking about.

Before she left Arizona, Sydney's parents offered to let her stay with them, so she could finish out her senior year there, but her mother refused. She insisted Sarah be with family. Sarah had argued Sydney's family was more like family to her than Aunt Norma. They only visited Aunt Norma once or twice a year. And she felt so close to Sydney's parents. All those late nights and holidays her mother had to work, they'd gladly taken her in as one of their own.

She was so devastated when her mother refused that she swore she'd never leave her room at Aunt Norma's, except to go to school. So the first few weeks in California, before school started, she just sat around feeling sorry for herself. Sydney had made her promise that she'd make the most of it. He hated the idea of her being out here alone and miserable.

"Remember?" he'd said. "You love the ocean, Lynni. It's all you talked about when you got back from your visits to your aunt's. Now you'll get to be near it for months."

Sydney encouraged, demanded, at one point even threatened to stop calling and taking her calls if she didn't try to make the best of it. So she had. She started running every day at school, instead of coming straight home. She promised to try to get out on the weekend when she got a chance. So far, she'd made sure all her weekends were booked babysitting.

"It's not like he asked me out, Syd. He just asked if I was going to be there." She stood up and looked at herself in the mirror again and frowned.

"Will you promise me something?"

Sarah hesitated. "What?"

"If he does ask you out, you'll say yes. Hell, if anybody asks you out, you'll say yes."

"Syd, I can't even talk when he comes near me. I can barely get a sentence out. I've made such a stupid couple of first impressions. I seriously doubt he'll be asking."

"You're kidding me, right? Man, you must have it bad for this guy 'cause you don't even have to try to be likable—I know!" He paused. "Tell him a joke." She heard him laugh, and she knew why. "He'll love how you can't get halfway through it without cracking yourself up."

Sarah started laughing and threw herself on the bed. "Shut up!"

Sydney was still laughing. "Just be yourself, Lynni, no more, no less. I promise you can't go wrong."

He was right about one thing. She did laugh a lot. Even though sometimes she thought she did it too much. Lately, the only one that could make her laugh was Sydney. She sucked in a deep breath.

"Okay, *if* anyone asks, I promise I will." She wasn't too worried about it. "Oh, except for Jesse."

"Well, yeah, of course."

Sarah had met Jesse the very night she'd first laid eyes on Angel two summers ago. One of Valerie's friends was going out with Jesse's friend, so they had hung out with them. Sarah agreed to go for a walk on the beach with Jesse that night, away from the crowd, and they sat down to talk. She had never kissed a boy back then, so when he asked if he could kiss her, she let him. Before she knew it, they were making out, and when it started getting heavy, she got scared and made him stop. He called her a tease, and they walked back to where the rest of the crowd was in silence.

Later, when she was back in Arizona, he called her to apologize and had called her off and on ever since. Now that she was going to school here, he'd been a constant pest: asking her out, cornering her by her locker, and insisting on walking her to class. After today's incident, she hoped he'd back off.

She'd been talking to Sydney for about an hour when Sarah heard her other line click. She couldn't tell who it was by the caller ID, but she was getting ready to wrap it up with Sydney anyway. She said goodbye to him, and clicked over to the other line.

"Hello?"

"Hi, Sarah, this is Mrs. Salcido. Listen, hon, Mr. Salcido is going to have to work late Friday night, so our plans are shot. We won't need you to babysit after all, but maybe next week?"

After she hung up, she sat there contemplating whether or not to call Sydney back. There was no need to call. She knew exactly what he'd say. She lay back on her pillow. What's the big deal? It was just a party; she'd been to plenty. She laid her hands that still gripped her cell phone on her pounding chest and stared at the ceiling. She could do this.

CHAPTER 3

They'd won their game and were all in good spirits as they waited outside of the party. Eric still sat behind the wheel. Angel, who stood outside of the car, leaned in the driver side window. "Pass me a water."

Eric grabbed one from the ice chest and took one for himself.

"C'mon, let's go in." Romero stood in the middle of the street.

Angel made a face. As good as he felt about the way the game had gone tonight, he was tired and not really in the mood for partying. He'd never admit it to anyone, but the only reason he was there at all was for the possibility of seeing Sarah. He'd been thinking about her ever since the day they had talked. Hell, he'd thought about her during the game. He kept glancing up at the stands every chance he got, prompting several disgusted hollers from his coach of, "Get in the game! What the hell's the matter with you, Moreno?"

He hadn't seen her at the game, but then she did say she had to work. There was still a chance she'd make the party. Looking across the street at the lights coming from the DJ in the backyard, anxiousness crept up his spine. "Hold on, give me a sec." He downed some of his water.

"Just take it in with you," Romero said. "I'm ready to get my groove on."

Angel turned to Eric who shrugged. He took another long swig. "All right, I'm ready."

Romero did his famous violent pelvic thrust a couple of times. "Let's do this."

Angel and Eric laughed. Angel grabbed what was left of the twelve pack of beer in the backseat. "You're a moron," he chuckled.

They went down the long driveway and turned the corner. There were a lot more people than they'd expected. They started making their way through the crowd. Angel was just beginning to scope the place when he saw her. He had to do a double take, because he almost didn't recognize her. The second he turned away though, it hit him. His body was suddenly overheating.

Angel gulped hard. Her long hair flowed more than halfway down her back. It was darker than he remembered, and it curled at the bottom. Her jeans hugged her body, and she wore a pair of strappy heels. Her black blouse tied around her neck and was backless, except for the bottom part that draped delicately around the small of her back.

He reached for a beer and could feel how clammy his hand had become. *For God's sake, she's just a girl.* He cursed under his breath. He intentionally placed himself facing Sarah's direction. He took a short swig of his beer but was careful not to drink too much. Romero was a perfect example of how he might act if he drank too much, and that was the last impression he wanted to make on her.

Romero had walked away for a while to talk to some of the regular girls. He came back to announce they had after-party dates. Usually Romero got high fives all around, but tonight both Angel and Eric seemed out of it.

Angel just nodded his head and half smiled. Eric hadn't even heard. He was staring out into the crowd but at no one in particular.

Romero frowned and tapped Eric. "Hey, man. Did you hear what I just said?"

Eric quickly came back to earth. "Sorry, man. No, what was that?"

"I said Stacey and her friends are down for later tonight. We get dessert, and hey, Natalie is over there." He winked.

Eric and Natalie had hooked up regularly last year, though not nearly as often as Angel and Dana.

Eric shook his head. "I'm gonna have to pass. I gotta get up early tomorrow."

Romero's eyes grew wider. "You're gonna pass up a piece of ass 'cause you have to get up early?" He was obnoxiously loud.

"Easy." Eric looked around. "I'm right here. Lower your voice."

Romero shook his head and turned toward Angel. "What about you? Are you in?"

"Well, yeah," Angel lied. "But Eric's my ride. How's that gonna work?"

Romero kept shaking his head. "Unbelievable, hold on— let me see what I can do."

Romero shot Eric a disgusted look and grabbed another beer. He walked toward the girls, stumbling a little. "Dude, he's getting wasted." Eric turned to Angel.

"Yeah, he is." Angel shook his head.

Romero put his arms sloppily around two of the girls.

"Who's he kidding?" Eric chuckled. "He's gonna be passed out in my back seat in an hour. How'd he get drunk so fast?"

"He drank the whole way here, and you know he's a lightweight," Angel said.

They'd all only started drinking about a year ago. Then when a senior last year had almost killed himself driving drunk, it scared them so much they'd all cut back. Even when they did drink, like tonight, it was just a few beers, and they designated a driver. Tonight it was Eric.

Angel took his attention away from Romero for a second to look in Sarah's direction. She had a cup in her hand. He wondered what she was drinking. He could hear Romero calling for Eric.

"Aw shit, dude, he's calling me." Eric looked in the other direction, pretending not to hear.

"You might as well go. Before his drunk-ass comes over here and drags you over."

"Me? What about you?"

"He ain't calling me," Angel laughed.

"You're gonna stay here by yourself?" Eric raised an eyebrow.

"No, there's someone I wanna go say hi to."

Romero was getting louder. Eric finally acknowledged him. He checked the box with the beer. "There's four more in here. You want one?"

"Nah, I'm good." Angel held up his bottle to show he still had plenty. Eric picked up the box and walked away toward Romero, muttering under his breath.

Strolling in Sarah's direction, Angel recognized the short blond girl holding a beer bottle with her as the ex-girlfriend of his teammate, Reggie Luna.

As he approached Sarah, he could feel his heart pick up speed and his stomach clench up. Despite his attempts to calm down, he felt completely unnerved. It annoyed the hell out of him.

He walked around behind her and moved in closer. She smelled heavenly: a soft delicate fragrance. Not overpowering, like some of the girls he'd hugged earlier.

He wanted to put his arm around her waist and pull her up against him. Instead, he leaned over and talked in her ear. "Hey, you made it."

She spun around, nearly losing her drink. Her expression went immediately from startled to pleased. "Yeah, they cancelled."

Angel couldn't get over how amazing she looked. If he gazed at her all night, it wouldn't be long enough. "I almost didn't recognize you with your hair down." His eyes took it all in.

She nodded. "Yeah, it's too long, especially when I'm running. It gets all over my face."

Angel wanted it all over his face. "It's beautiful though. You should wear it like that at school."

She hesitated for a second. "Thank you." She avoided eye contact again.

He didn't want to, but he decided it would be better to change the subject before she got uncomfortable and made an exit. He had no intention of letting her run away again, not this time. He glanced at her cup. "What are you drinking?"

She smiled timidly. "Wine."

"Wine?"

She laughed. "Why does everybody say it like that?"

Her smile somehow had a calming effect on him. "Out of a cup though? You can't drink it straight out of the bottle?"

"It's not a cooler." Her expression challenged him. "It's the good stuff."

She turned to her friend and then glanced into her cup. It was almost empty. "As a matter of fact," she said, "I need more."

She bent over to a medium-sized ice chest and pulled out a small jug of wine.

"Nooo!" Angel put his hand over his mouth in disbelief. "Oh, you're sick. You come to a party with a jug of wine in an ice chest?"

She laughed even more now. Her friend laughed with her. Sarah caressed the jug lovingly. "How else am I supposed to keep my little Precious cold?"

Her demeanor was refreshing, especially since she had seemed so apprehensive at school. Maybe it was the wine. Whatever it was, he loved it. He watched as she poured the wine in her cup, noticing how little she poured in before stopping. She put the jug back in the ice chest and pointed at her friend. "She brings one too."

Her friend opened her mouth wide, as if Sarah had just snitched on her. Angel raised his eyebrows in exaggerated disbelief. "You too? But you're drinking beer. You don't need an ice chest."

Her friend smiled and tapped her bottle. "I can't drink beer unless it's ice cold."

"By the way, Angel, this is my cousin, Valerie," Sarah said.

Angel nodded. "Yeah, I know Valerie."

Valerie's eyes widened slightly in surprise.

"Sure," he acknowledged her surprise, glad that Sarah had said her name. *That*, he would've never remembered.

"So, why don't you just put your drinks in the same ice chest?"

Valerie rolled her eyes at Sarah. "Sarah doesn't like her *Precious* to be disturbed."

"She's very fragile." Sarah held her cup close to her.

Angel nodded, and then put his hand up. "It's a *she?* Okay, well, now that makes sense."

Sarah smiled, as she took another quick sip of her wine. Valerie got pulled away by another girl.

Angel took his last swig of beer and threw the empty bottle in a trashcan nearby.

"Are you out?" Sarah asked.

"Yeah, that was my last one."

"Well, here." Sarah bent over to Valerie's ice chest. She giggled, pretending to be sneaky. "Let's steal one of Valerie's."

Angel turned to see if Valerie was watching. "No, it's cool. I don't wanna take her beer."

Sarah shook her head. "She's not gonna finish all this. She never does, and then we're gonna end up throwing it out later tonight."

"Throw out beer? Are you nuts?"

"Well, we can't take it home. My aunt would kill us."

"Oh, well, in that case, let me help the cause." He held out his hand.

Her finger brushed his hand as she passed him the bottle. That's all it took to ignite him. His hand trembled as he took a swig of his beer. He watched her the whole time. Her eyes were so big, her lashes so dark and heavy—everything seemed to slow down when she blinked. His insides smoldered, and he gulped his beer hard.

"So, are you here alone?" she asked.

He looked around. He had to. If he stared at her any longer, he was afraid he'd freak her out.

"Nah, my friends are here somewhere. We just got split up." He turned back to her. "How 'bout you? Is it just you and Valerie tonight?"

She sipped on her wine again. "Yeah, well, I came here with just Val, but we're supposed to meet up with friends later."

Angel took another swig of his beer and looked around casually. "Guys?"

"No, some of her girlfriends—they're not here yet though. That's why I'm here. I really don't like these kinds of parties, but none of her friends could get here until later, so she talked me into coming with her."

Angel smiled, unable to look away from her eyes. "I'll have to thank her later for that. So, where *do* you like to go?"

She held his gaze for a moment and then smiled, making Angel's legs weak. "I love the beach," she sighed. "I just moved out here a few months ago from Arizona, so the beach is new to me. I could spend every night there watching the sunset. I mean, don't get me wrong, the sunsets in Arizona are just as beautiful. It's just the newness of the cool salty air and watching while listening to waves crash and the birds … quack?"

Angel was puzzled. "Quack?"

She burst into laughter. "Squawk? You know what I mean!"

"God, you were doing so well," he teased, pretending to gaze out into the sky. "I mean, I could almost hear the waves crashing and everything."

Sarah still laughed. Angel wondered if she was getting tipsy, but he continued to tease her. He loved hearing her laugh. "I mean peep would've been closer, but quack? Really?"

Sarah's hand was over her mouth, but there was no muffling her laughter. "I got the point across, didn't I?"

"I'm just saying. The wind was blowing in my hair and everything. Look." He pretended to hold his hair down.

"Stop!" she squealed.

He couldn't help laughing with her. It was such a cute laugh and so contagious. She was refreshing. It wasn't just that she was enjoying his jokes, but that she didn't mind laughing at herself. So many other girls would've been too busy trying to be seductive. She didn't even have to try. He could tell being seductive was the last thing on her mind.

She wiped the corners of her eyes. She'd literally laughed that hard. "Is my mascara all messed up?" She opened her eyes wide.

He stepped forward to get a better look. Her makeup had smeared slightly on the bottom corner of her right eye. "Hold still." He moved closer to her.

He wiped the bottom of her eye very slowly and gently with his pinky. He was so close to her face he could smell the wine on her breath. She held her cup right in front of her, and he felt her tense up when his body touched her hand. He examined her other eye.

"Your eyes are amazing," he said without moving back.

Their eyes locked for just a second, and then she backed up slightly. "Thanks."

She turned away, and Angel watched as she took a very long sip of her wine. It surprised him how uncomfortable compliments made her. With eyes like those, you'd think she'd be used to them. Still, she broke the silence as only she could.

"Where's my Precious?" she said in a coddling voice then bent over and opened her ice chest. Angel watched as she poured herself less than a quarter of a cup.

He enjoyed teasing her. "Maybe if you'd fill the cup, you wouldn't have to refill so often."

"Ah, to deal with lower society," she smirked. "This isn't beer, Angel. You sip, so if I fill it, by the time I'm halfway through, it'll be warm. I don't like warm wine, okay?"

"Oh no, you didn't just call me lower society!"

"Oh, yes, I did."

Angel held his pointer finger up in front of her, and she began to giggle again. "One word."

"Bring it." She took a sip.

"Quack!"

She covered her mouth with the cup to avoid spitting and turned her back on him, so he couldn't see it leak out the side of her mouth. She turned back to face him and kept laughing. "You had to go there." She wiped around her cleavage.

His eyes were fixated on her hands. "I had to." Gulping hard, he watched her continue to wipe the wine from the front of her blouse. "I can help you with that."

She smiled at him, half rolling her eyes. "That's okay." She returned her attention to her blouse, and he couldn't look away.

He was still standing there gaping when he felt a tap on his shoulder. It was Eric. "Hey, dude, you ready?"

Angel turned around. Eric was holding Romero up. "Damn, is he that wasted?"

Eric shot him a sarcastic look. Angel turned to Sarah. "This is my ride."

She glanced over at Eric holding Romero up and giggled a little. Angel could see she was lightheaded from the wine.

She seemed so small and delicate and incredibly vulnerable. "I won't leave though. Where's Valerie?"

She smiled at him. "Go ahead. I'm fine."

Like hell. "Yeah, you are fine. But I'm not leaving you until Valerie gets back."

The party was beginning to end and Valerie, Sarah's ride, was nowhere in sight. Sarah had tried calling her several times on her cell, but the call wouldn't go through. Angel grabbed Sarah's hand in his and both their ice chests in his other. "Come on, let's go look for Valerie."

As they walked through the party, one of Dana's friends tried to stop him. "Hey, Angel, where's Dana?" Her eyebrows were arched, and she peered at Sarah. Angel kept walking, ignoring hear.

"Is Dana your girlfriend?" He could feel Sarah try to let go of his hand, but he only tightened the grip.

Angel pressed his lips for a second. "Nope."

Eric was right outside, looking a little irritated. Angel knew how Romero could get when he was drunk, and Eric had been on his own with him all night, so he understood his frustration.

"Dude, are you ready to go?" Eric asked.

Angel still held Sarah's hand. He looked at Eric apologetically. "Give me a sec. She needs to find her friend."

Sarah was calling Valerie on her cell again, but she wasn't answering. When they got to the car, she looked at him. "I can't leave Valerie."

"Okay." He pulled her closer to him out of the way of oncoming cars that still cruised past the party. She leaned against him, and he put his arm around her waist. He'd burned to touch her all night, and now all he wanted was to take care of her. He examined her face, smiling tenderly. "How you feeling?"

She smiled, finally looking in his eyes. "Better now."

It took all the willpower he could muster to not lean over and kiss her, but the last thing he wanted was for anything to happen tonight that she could dismiss tomorrow and blame on the wine.

He turned to see Eric adjusting Romero in the front seat. Romero was totally out. Angel motioned toward him. "By the way, meet my friend, Romero."

Sarah laughed. "Is that really his name?"

"Well, his last name. His first name is Ramon, but he doesn't like it."

Eric walked over and leaned on the car next to Angel and Sarah. He looked exhausted. Sarah rested her head on Angel's shoulder.

"Oh, hey," Angel said looking at Eric. "This is Sarah. Sarah, this is my friend, Eric."

Sarah held her head up just long enough to say hello. Angel knew Eric assumed she was just another girl he'd picked up. Sarah moved off of Angel and leaned against the car now, but he still held her hand. "Where could she be?" Sarah grimaced.

They all stood there watching the driveway of the house where the party had been. There were people still walking out and standing around the front of the house. A car pulled up, and someone got out of the back seat. It was Jesse Strickland. The car that had dropped him off drove right past them and up the street.

Sarah didn't see him at first, but when she did, she straightened out. Angel noticed and his muscles tensed. "Something wrong?"

"Can we leave?" Her eyes were still on Jesse.

Jesse walked in a hurry to the back yard. Eric and Angel exchanged glances.

"What about Valerie?" Angel asked.

"We'll come back for her," she said, "I just don't wanna be here right this minute."

Angel stared at her for a second. "Sure."

He let go of her hand to gather up the ice chests. Sarah tried Valerie again on her phone. For whatever reason, Jesse made Sarah nervous, and Angel didn't like it. He grabbed the ice chests and threw them in the trunk then walked Sarah around and into the car. He sat down next to her and reached for her hand immediately. Eric eyed him through the rearview mirror.

"Let's drop off this guy first," Eric said, motioning toward Romero. "Then if you want, you can drop me off and take my car. I'll pick it up in the morning."

Angel smiled. Suddenly he was relieved he'd only had two beers. He wasn't ready to say goodnight to Sarah yet. He could always count on Eric to understand.

* * *

Minutes passed while she sat in the passenger seat, heart pounding, waiting for Valerie to answer her phone.

"Hello?"

"Valerie?"

"Sarah, I've been so worried. Where are you?"

"I'm with Angel. We're dropping off his friend. Are you on your way home?"

"Home? It's still early. There's another party we're going to. Do you need me to come get you?" Valerie asked.

"No, I think I'm good for now."

"Oh, my God, are you and Angel gonna hang out?" Valerie gushed.

The thought of what Valerie meant by hang out made Sarah's heart beat even harder. She bit her lip. "I'm not sure," she said. "I'll call you and let you know where to meet me."

"Is he right there next to you?" Valerie whispered as if he might hear her.

Sarah giggled. "No, he's outside with his friend. I'm in the car."

"You have to make out with him, Sarah, so you can tell me all about it."

Sarah laughed nervously, her face suddenly warm. "Valerie!" she gasped, "I hardly know him."

"He's totally hot. What more do you need to know?"

Sarah's body heat went up. Valerie wasn't helping her already strained nerves. "I gotta go. He's on his way back," she lied.

"Okay, okay, bye."

Her cousin was so different from Sarah when it came to guys. Valerie was commitment phobic. She'd had one serious relationship, and she said it nearly suffocated her. She could easily just make out with someone without giving it a second thought.

Sarah didn't think any less of Valerie for enjoying her freedom. She just couldn't understand how Valerie could turn off the emotions just like that. To Sarah, even holding hands inevitably meant feelings were involved. It wasn't something she could do and not feel anything. Just the thought that Angel might kiss her tonight had her in knots.

She studied the guys standing outside, face-to-face. Eric stood a few inches shorter than Angel. His hair was a lot lighter and curlier too. He didn't have Angel's pretty boy good looks, but still had rugged good looks of his own, and he was so nice it made him attractive.

She'd watched them as they carefully helped Romero from the car, genuinely concerned that he got home safe. Albeit they did it with a lot of laughing and repartee, it was obvious they were very good friends.

Angel walked back toward the car. That smile—it was *unreal.* She shifted in her seat, trying not to look like a goofball, but her own smile was so big and hard to hold back. She'd been talking to him most of the night and had been doing pretty well. Except for spitting up her wine and her miserable attempt to be deep about loving the beach, she'd managed to keep the blundering to a minimum. Why was she having such a hard time breathing now?

She took a long deep breath as he opened the door and climbed in the car. His eyes were immediately on her, making her insides into mush.

"Are you hungry?"

She let out her breath and nodded.

"Good, 'cause I'm starving." He pulled out of the driveway.

They picked up some food at a drive-thru and headed to the beach, eating along the way. After driving up a winding road to the top of a cliff, he turned into a dead end and parked. The moon was bright, and the ocean went on as far as she could see. They were high above the ocean, and the view was breathtaking.

Sarah stared out the window in amazement. Her thoughts were muddled when her phone rang, and she went still. She had a feeling who it might be, and she didn't want to answer it. One look at the caller ID and her suspicions were confirmed: *Jesse*. Angel was eyeing her. "You gonna answer that?"

She shook her head.

Glancing at Angel, she noticed his eyebrows narrow, and she turned away biting her lip. Her phone rang one last time.

"Where are we?" She turned back to face him.

He still had the same expression on his face, but he didn't say anything. He opened the door. "Follow me." He got out of the car.

Sarah got out, and he came around and held his hand out. She put her hand in his, and they walked toward the dead end. There was a rock trail off to the side behind the homes that faced the ocean.

They headed to the edge of the trail where there was a wrought iron fence. She looked down as they walked along the side of the fence and could see the waves crashing into the rocks below. When they turned the corner, she saw the trail stretched across the cliff. There were benches and grassy sitting areas with flowering tropical plants and an endless trail of palm trees. Sarah took it all in with awe. She turned back to him.

"I love it," she whispered.

"This is my favorite place."

"I can see why." She stepped closer to the fence and gazed out into the ocean. The lights on a couple of ships and some small sailboats still out there shone brightly. Angel stood behind her, and he grasped the top of the iron rail, enclosing her body between his arms. His warm body against her back felt good, especially since it was getting cold. His face came over her shoulder next to her ear, and she felt him take a deep breath. She closed her eyes, and her body tingled all over. It was still unbelievable to Sarah that she was here, doing this, with *him*.

"You smell good," he murmured.

"Thank you."

They stood there for a few minutes in silence, his breath against her temple. Finally, he spoke. "Can I ask you something?

His tone made her nervous somehow. "Sure."

He pulled away from her shoulder slightly.

"Why were you in such a hurry to leave when you saw Jesse tonight?"

Sarah went stiff. God, she'd forgotten all about that. That was the last thing she wanted to be talking about right now. Jesse could be a pain in the ass when he was sober. Valerie had told her when he was drunk, he was even worse, and she had a feeling he'd been drinking tonight. She'd been afraid of another confrontation between him and Angel. "He can be a pest sometimes. That's all."

Angel put his hands over hers on the fence. "The other day, you said you'd *hung out* with him. What did that mean?"

Sarah squeezed her eyes shut for a second. *Shit.* She didn't want to tell him about that. Why hadn't she just said yes when he asked her if Jesse was a friend? She'd hardly expected to be talking to Angel again. And not like this.

"It was a long time ago." She thought she felt him suck in a breath, and he was quiet for a second.

"*What* was a long time ago?"

She braced herself, not knowing how he'd feel about her after she told him. But it was in the past, so what did it matter? She turned around, but he never let go of the fence, so she was still in his arms, so to speak. His eyes seemed darker somehow. He looked straight at her, waiting.

"Nothing really," she said. "I met him a few summers ago when I came out to visit my aunt, and we hung out one night."

"Was he your boyfriend?" Angel eyes were still fixed on hers.

She shook her head. "No."

"You still *hang out* with him?"

"Nope, he's still asking me out, but I'm not interested."

"Good," Angel said. "He's an asshole."

Sarah's eyebrow's shot up. "You know him?"

"Yeah." If distaste was an expression, he wore it on his lips unabashed. "We've gone to school together since we were kids, but I've never liked him. He's always been a whiny little bitch. Didn't think I could like him any less, until now."

Valerie had always gone on about how intense the Moreno brothers were. She'd told Sarah about how protective they were with their younger sister. Sarah felt his protectiveness earlier when he refused to leave her side at the party, but this was different. She could feel something: an intensity she'd never felt before from anyone. It made her a little nervous, made her stomach tighten up, but in a weird way, she liked it.

"I'm assuming then, since you're here with me, you don't have a boyfriend?"

Her heart at her throat, she shook her head slowly. "No, I don't."

She was dreaming. She had to be. Did he really just ask her if she had a boyfriend? Did Angel honestly care?

He dropped his hands from the fence and placed them around her waist. With her heart pounding against her chest now, she gulped, wondering if he could hear it.

"Can I kiss you?" he whispered.

She nodded, unable to speak. Then his lips were on hers. They were soft and warm. He explored her mouth slowly, softly. He tightened his hug around her waist with one arm and brought the other one up to her face. With a silky-smooth caress to her face, his hand started around and down her neck, pulling her closer to him.

His body was big and strong against hers His tongue moved faster, and he pressed against her, suckling her lips and tongue. She'd been kissed before, but never like this, never with so much passion.

It was too much. She felt him when he pressed against her thigh, and she panicked. She pulled away and heard him groan, burying his face in her hair.

Caressing his back one last time, she could still feel his heavy breathing as she moved her body away from his gently. She looked up just as he was opening his eyes.

"Can we go sit? My feet are hurting."

He took a couple of deep breaths before answering. "Sure," he glanced down at her shoes, "I forgot …. They're nice. I like 'em."

They walked over to a stone bench that was part of a huge rock planter with a palm tree in the middle. She sat down, and he motioned for her to move further back. She did, and he sat next to her and turned her around, so she was facing him.

"Lean back." He picked up her legs and pulled them on his lap, inches away from the tent in his pants. Wide-eyed, she stared for a second, and wondered what he had planned.

She watched him pull off her shoes and was about to protest, when his strong fingers began massaging her aching feet.

"Mmm, that feels *so* good." She let her head fall back. She wondered if he did this with all the other girls he went out with and if they'd all been treated to such a heart-stopping kiss. She lifted her head back up and saw his eyes swallow her up.

"Your feet are so small."

She looked down at her feet and wiggled her toes. Then she glanced down at his. They were huge. She started to giggle. "Well, compared to yours, they are."

His expression hadn't changed. "I love your smile."

Her smile disappeared in reaction to his compliment. "Thanks, I like yours too. As a matter of fact, that was one of the first things I noticed about you."

His eyebrows shot up curiously. "Really? Tonight?"

"Oh, no," she said. "Two summers ago, the first time I saw you."

Now he looked really interested. "You saw me two summers ago?"

"Yup, same summer I hung out with Jesse." *Damn why did she bring that up again?*

He stared at her, half frowning. "You went out with him and not me?" He teased.

"He asked—you didn't."

A look of disappointment flashed across his face. "I'm sorry, I don't remember seeing you."

Sarah smiled. "Don't worry. I can be pretty invisible."

Angel seemed almost annoyed. "You're anything but invisible." He paused for a moment, and then as if he just remembered something, "So, you said you're from Arizona. When'd you move out here?"

Sarah straightened up a little, suddenly feeling uneasy. She hadn't prepared herself to talk about her circumstances. Since she didn't plan on making any friends, she didn't think she'd be put in a position to explain something so personal to anyone, especially not Angel Moreno. "I haven't exactly moved here. It's just temporary."

"Really? 'Til when?"

"I'm only here for the semester, then I'll go back to finish up my senior year at my school in Flagstaff." She glanced at him and then away, hoping they could get on another subject. But he kept on.

"So, why are you here for this semester?"

She was never good at lying, so making something elaborate up was out of the question. If he ever asked her about it again, she'd probably forget and mix everything all up. Even a very short version of the truth was uncomfortable. She looked out into the ocean, not wanting to see his expression when she told him. "It's kind of a long story. "

"We've got time," he said.

Sarah was silent for a second. "My mom has some problems she needs to iron out, and I have to stay with my aunt now. My best friend's family offered to let me stay with them, so I could finish out my senior year at my own school, but my mom refused, so I'm here now. But once I turn eighteen this winter, she can't stop me from going back."

He looked at her, eyes full of questions, and she prayed none of them were about her mom. She really didn't feel like discussing that part of her life with him, with anyone.

"Does your aunt know you plan on leaving?"

"No, I haven't told her. I know she won't want me to, but Sydney and Sydney's parents are the closest thing I've ever had to family besides my mom. I have to go back. Sydney's waiting." She held her chin a bit higher.

Sarah noticed how intently Angel watched her when she spoke, as if he didn't want to miss a word.

"Besides, I've never really been close to my aunt. We only started visiting her about two years ago when she and my mom finally started speaking to each other again. Even then, it was only once or twice a year." She shook her head, looking away. "I'd rather be in Flagstaff. It's where I belong."

Angel's expression had changed. She couldn't put her finger on it, but he seemed genuinely concerned or maybe something else. *Damn it,* the last thing she wanted was pity, not from anyone, but especially not from him. That's why she was so determined to save money. Even when Sydney's family had offered to let her stay with them, they meant rent free, but she absolutely refused. If she was going to stay with them, she'd pay them.

"What about after high school? Will you be with your mom then?"

Sarah kept her chin up. "No, I'll work and go to school. Sydney's parents said I could stay with them as long as I need to, and as soon as I can afford my own place, I'll get it."

That look hadn't changed. It seemed even more intense now, and his lips were pressed tight. "Well, that's too bad."

Sarah's heart dropped. She knew it. He felt sorry for her. She pulled her feet back abruptly and sat up, startling Angel. She started putting on her shoes. "We may not all have a great start, you know, but it's where you end up that counts."

Angel looked at her confused. "What? What are you talking about?"

She finished putting on her shoes and stood up. He jumped up in front of her. "What's wrong? What did I say?" He searched her eyes.

Sarah glared at him. "My life is not that bad. Oh, sure, compared to yours maybe, but I don't need all—"

Angel put a finger on her mouth. "Stop, that's not what I meant."

She tried backing away, but he slipped his big hand in hers. She stopped, but stood firmly facing him, unwavering.

He looked at her thoughtfully and put his arm around her waist. "Listen to me. All I meant was it's too bad you'll be leaving. I'm really enjoying hanging with you, and now you're telling me it's only temporary? You're damn right I think it's too bad."

Sarah stared at him speechless and feeling a little stupid for over reacting. "Oh."

Angel smiled. "Wow, but you turned on me fast."

"I'm sorry," she whispered. "I just..."

His lips were on hers again. She allowed herself to indulge in a few more of his kisses and then forced herself to wrap it up before things got too heated again. It was getting late, and she still had to meet Valerie somewhere, so they could get home together.

They met Valerie in the parking lot of an In-and-Out near her aunt's. There were a lot of other kids there from school. Valerie and her friends were standing around her car. They all gawked when they saw that Angel was dropping Sarah off.

Sarah completely expected him to just drop her off as discreetly as possible and drive off. Instead, he got out of the car and walked her over to Valerie and her friends, holding her hand the whole way. When he said goodbye, he pulled her aside but still in plain view of everyone and gave her another mind-blowing kiss.

CHAPTER 4

Angel groaned as the music from his sister's radio blared in through his open bedroom door. He was having the best dream ever all about Sarah. It was so real: her beautiful eyes, her lips; he could even taste them. Who knew how far the dream may've gone. He frowned, listening to the music that interrupted his fantasies. His sister Sofia was only sixteen, but she'd recently discovered The Beatles and was blasting their music every chance she got. To top it off, the blow dryer was roaring.

His mood quickly shifted when he replayed last night's events in his head. He lay there thinking about everything that had happened. He chuckled to himself when he thought of how effortlessly he'd cracked Sarah up. Everything he was feeling now was so unexpected.

More than anything, he wanted to ask more about her mom, but it was obvious she didn't want to talk about her. Why would a mom dump her daughter on someone else, just like that? What kind of problems could she be *ironing out*? Something in Sarah's poignant eyes told him she'd been through a lot, and he felt for her.

Damn, this sucked. All week long, all he had wanted was a chance to talk to her, get to know her a little. But after last night, he wanted so much more, and soon she was leaving. He sat up and shook his head. He wouldn't worry about it now. Fact was her plans weren't carved in stone. Anything could happen between now and then. She could change her mind.

He glanced at the clock: 8:30. Deciding it was too early to call her, he showered and went downstairs. Eric was already there, sitting at the kitchen counter talking to Sofia.

His parents left early to open the restaurant, and Sofia had made breakfast. Eric looked up from his plate at Angel and smiled knowingly.

"Hey, how'd it go last night?"

"It was cool." Angel walked over to Sofia and kissed her on the forehead. He looked at Eric's plate of bacon and eggs then at Sofia.

"Any left for me, or did he eat it all?"

Sofia rolled her eyes. "There's enough for everyone."

Angel walked over to the refrigerator, glancing at the clock. It was just after nine—good enough. He pulled the orange juice out of the fridge and poured himself a glass. Walking by the table where he left the keys to Eric's car and his cell phone, he picked them both up and tossed the keys at Eric. "Thanks, man."

Eric caught the keys in midair, nodding his head. "Late night?" he asked with a smirk.

On his way out the back door, Angel motioned he'd be right back. Outside, he looked up Sarah's cell number on his phone. She'd programmed it in last night before he dropped her off. Just seeing her name, *Sarah Lynn*, did something to him. He sucked in his breath deep and pressed the call button. It rang a few times, then she answered.

"Hi, Angel." Her cheery tone made him smile. "I was on the other line. Let me hang up."

"No, that's okay. I can call back."

"No, it's Sydney. We've been on the phone for a while. I was getting ready to hang up anyway. Hold on, okay?"

"All right."

She clicked over to the other line. *It was only nine, and she'd already been on the phone for a while?* She wasn't kidding when she said she was close to her friend.

He thought about it and wondered if he'd feel the same way in her situation. Eric and Romero were his best friends, but he couldn't imagine himself so hung up on those two numb-nuts that he'd be dying to get back to them. Then again, girls were different in their relationships. Not only that, he thought, Sarah's situation was different altogether. He sat down on one of the patio chairs, and then he heard the line click.

"Angel?"

"Yeah."

"Sorry about that."

"That's okay. Chatting this early?"

"Yeah, Sydney can be an early bird. The phone woke me up, actually."

"Ah, she's like my sister. Her damn music woke me up this morning. Are you tired?" He hesitated then asked, "Any plans today?"

"Not now, but tonight I do."

Angel felt his face warm. "Oh?"

"I'm working," she said. "Babysitting for the neighbors down the street."

He exhaled slowly. "So when can I pick you up?"

"I can be ready in about an hour."

He'd never felt so damn eager to see anyone in his life. "All right then, I'll call you in an hour, and you can tell me how to get there."

Once off the phone, he walked back in the kitchen where Sofia and Eric were laughing. Angel was surprised he was still there. He remembered Eric saying he had to be up early. He walked over and grabbed a piece of bacon from the pan on the stove.

"Didn't you have to be somewhere this morning?" He leaned against the counter across from Eric.

Eric smiled. "You trying to get rid of me?"

"Nah, but I remember you tellin' Romero you couldn't stick around and hang out with those chicks 'cause you had to get up early."

Eric cleared his throat and wiped his mouth with a napkin. "Yeah, well, why do you think I'm here so early? I handled my business already and then came over to get my car."

"I need to change. I told Mom I'd be at the restaurant early." Sofia finished putting the dishes in the dishwasher and started out of the kitchen.

Angel winced. "How early, Sof? I gotta be somewhere soon."

"I can drop her off," Eric said.

Angel looked back at him. "You sure?"

"Yeah, I gotta go by there anyway. I'm gonna go work out at the gym. Maybe I'll pick up a burrito while I'm there."

"I won't be long!" Sofia yelled, running up the stairs.

Angel glanced at Eric's plate. "Dude, you just ate."

"Yeah, that's why I gotta work out." Eric patted his stomach.

Angel shook his head. He turned around and grabbed a plate out of the cabinet, emptying the rest of the eggs and bacon onto it.

"So, what happened last night? Did you score?" Eric cocked an eyebrow.

Angel had a mouthful of food and didn't respond immediately. After a couple more chews, he shook his head. He didn't usually kiss and tell, even with girls he didn't care about, and he knew Eric wasn't the type to go telling anyone. But he felt especially protective this time.

"What?" Eric chuckled. "You're kidding me? She shot you down?"

"No, she didn't shoot me down." Angel scoffed. "We just talked that's all."

Eric laughed some more. "Losing your touch, huh? I thought for sure I'd be hosing down the backseat of my car today the way you were looking at her."

"How was I looking at her?" Angel frowned.

"Like you wanted to swallow her up, that's how."

Angel feigned bewilderment, but he knew just what Eric meant because that's exactly how he had felt.

Eric kept on. "Come on dude, I can't believe all you did was talk."

Angel rolled his eyes, "Nah, man, it wasn't like what you're thinking. That's not what I was going for with her."

"What?" Eric shook his head. "Angel Moreno is into talking to chicks now? When did you turn into a total wuss?"

Angel shrugged and took another bite of his food. He avoided looking at Eric, suddenly not sure he wanted to talk about it. "I don't know, dude. She's just cool to hang with, I guess."

Eric nodded as if he got it. "So you're not into her? I thought she was pretty hot."

"I'm into her, you ass, just 'cause I didn't bone her the first night. Not all girls are like that, you know."

Eric grinned. "So you did get shot down."

Angel glared at him, sipping his juice.

"Well, you're not making any sense. Either you did or you didn't. What's the big deal?"

"It's *not* a big deal," Angel wasn't sure why, but he was getting frustrated. "I kissed her goodnight if you have to know. But we talked the rest of the time."

"So did you find out what was up with her and Jesse?"

Angel wished he'd slammed Jesse's head a little harder the other day. "She went out with him way back, and you know what a pussy Jesse is. He can't let it go."

"She actually went out with that idiot?" Eric spoke with a mouthful.

"Yeah, tell me about it. That's what I thought." Angel polished off the last of his breakfast and threw the plate in the sink. He glanced at the clock. "I gotta go finish getting ready."

"Where you going?"

"Got a date," Angel grinned, but avoided looking directly at Eric.

Eric seemed confused at first, then his eyes and mouth shot wide open as he put his hand over his mouth. "No!"

Before he could say anything else, Angel shot him a look. "Not a word," he warned. "Don't tell Romero anything either. I don't need to hear his crap on Monday."

Eric grinned from ear to ear. "Shut up," Angel said, walking out of the kitchen.

"I didn't say anything," Eric protested, chuckling.

"Yeah, well, you were thinking it." Angel could hear Eric laughing, even as he walked up the stairs, but he had to smile.

***

Sarah couldn't remember the last time she'd felt so alive. Standing under the shower with the warm water running over her body, she thought of Angel as she lathered herself and smiled.

The past year had been all but hell, and the past two months had been worse with Sydney having to drag her out of her funk every time. But now she felt jubilant. It scared her a little. She was still very aware of the fact that this was *Angel—the Angel* she'd heard so much about. But he said he was looking forward to getting to know her. He sounded so sincere, and his kisses, *God, those kisses...* Just thinking about them made her quiver all over.

Sydney's call woke her up just after seven, and they talked until Angel called. He knew she'd gone out last night for the first time since she'd been out here, and he was anxious to see how it went. Sarah told him everything, not wanting to leave anything out, especially about the kissing. Sydney hadn't been surprised at all that Angel was interested in Sarah and was happy she sounded so excited but warned her to take it slow.

She got out of the shower and dressed. She went back in the restroom to get her blow dryer and ran into Valerie, still in her sleep clothes, a long t-shirt and basketball shorts. "Where are you going so early?"

Sarah's cheeks reddened. "Angel is picking me up." She tried not to smile too big.

Valerie's jaw dropped and eyes popped wide open. "He is?"

Sarah nodded, smiling sheepishly. She grabbed the blow dryer and started back to her room with Valerie in tow. "Oh my God, you're so lucky! Was that who called so early this morning?"

Sarah stopped at her bed and looked through her purse. She didn't want to make a big deal out of it. The more she made out of this, the harder it would be if she turned out to be Angel's flavor of the week. A faint haze of pain sunk in, just thinking about it. But she knew it was a definite possibility.

"No, that was Sydney," she said. "Angel called while I was on the line with him."

Valerie rolled her eyes. Sarah knew what Valerie thought of Sydney. She'd never actually met him, but she didn't understand their friendship. "There's no way that guy is not in love with you," she'd said many times.

Sarah also knew Valerie resented the fact that she had preferred, literally begged, to stay in Flagstaff with him and his family, rather than come and live with Valerie and her aunt. Even now, she talked more to him and was closer to him than she'd ever been with Valerie.

Valerie plopped on Sarah's bed. "Are you gonna tell Angel about Sydney?"

"I already did." She left out the part about Angel referring to Sydney as a *she* this morning and the fact that she hadn't corrected him.

Valerie's eyebrows shot up in surprise. "Really? What did he say?"

Sarah made a face. "Valerie, we hung out one night. You honestly think he cares?"

"I'm telling you guys are territorial."

She shrugged. "Well, territorial or not, I'm not his girlfriend—"

"Yet," Valerie interrupted. "We'll see what he thinks of Sydney once you two get serious."

Sarah felt something tighten in her chest. She thought about how he'd gotten right to the subject of Jesse when they got to the beach—how stone-faced he'd turned when she told him she'd gone out with him. But with Sydney it was totally different. He'd have to understand.

"What makes you so sure we'll be getting serious? You, yourself, said he'd never had a girlfriend. Why would he want one now?"

It was almost a rhetorical question. She didn't really want to hear the answer. Valerie was ruining this for her. It was way too soon to start worrying about what Angel would think about her relationship with Sydney.

She'd given it some thought when she realized Angel had assumed Syd was a girl. But she pushed it to the back of her mind. She'd cross that bridge when she came to it. At the moment, she wasn't even sure she'd ever have to.

Valerie made herself comfortable against the headboard. "It's the way he was with you last night, Sarah. I've never seen him act like that before. He's never been one for public displays of affection. But last night, it was so obvious he wanted everyone to see you were with him."

Sarah tried to hide her exhilaration.

"I'm just saying," Valerie continued. "If you were like me, I wouldn't worry about it. Just tell him all about Sydney and if he walks, oh well, too bad for him, on to the next. But you're not like me. You're sweet, sensitive little Sarah. And I saw the way you looked at him last night too, missy. You're already falling for him. So unless you want troubles, you should start weaning Sydney off your everlasting devotion."

The butterflies in Sarah's stomach stirred, threatening to take off in a wild spin. Sarah walked back to her purse, eyeing Valerie. She put her makeup on silently. She hardly wore any, so it didn't take very long. She was about to respond to Valerie's observation, when her phone rang, making her jump. Valerie smiled eagerly.

"Is it him?"

Sarah looked at the caller ID and nodded. Valerie flew off the bed and ran over to Sarah's side, leaning in to try and hear him. Sarah looked at her and giggled. She flipped the phone open and answered.

Sarah gave him the directions with Valerie glued to her side the whole time. When she hung up, Valerie groaned.

"God, he even sounds hot. I swear you are so lucky!"

Sarah tried to play it cool, but the swarm in her stomach had spun out of control. She'd barely had enough time to absorb what had happened the night before, and now he was on his way to pick her up again. She smiled at Valerie and hurried to finish herself up.

She filled her aunt in on her plans and gathered her purse together. He drove a white Mustang. She could tell it was an older model, but it was still nice. She looked out the window and watched him get out of the car. He wore dark jeans and a gray crewneck shirt that hugged his chest perfectly.

"I'm leaving!" she yelled at no one in particular and walked out to meet him.

CHAPTER 5

He'd taken a few steps up the walk when he saw her come out the door. Immediately he was smiling silly. She was dressed casually, yet somehow she had the same incredible appeal as she had had last night when she was all done up—in some ways even more.

Her eyes seemed to sparkle as she walked down the steps of the porch. She met him in the middle of the walkway. He took her hand in his. He could definitely get used to her soft delicate hand in his. He wanted to kiss her, but he felt weird doing it right in front of her house. His reserve however wasn't strong enough to fight off the urge to hug her, so he did tightly. He squeezed her, feeling her hair against his face, breathing in everything about her.

Reluctantly, he finally pulled away and let her go. His hand was still fastened to hers. He looked up at the door. "Do I need to go in?"

Sarah's eyes widened, and she shook her head too quickly. "Oh, no, that's not necessary."

Angel wondered if there was something she was hiding, ashamed of. But he let it go and walked her back to his car.

Once on the road, he found it impossible to keep his hands off her. It was worse than the night before, maybe 'cause Eric's car was a stick shift. Angel's car wasn't, so his hand was free to roam, and roam it did. Every chance he got, he caressed her face, her leg, her fingers. Twice he brought her hand to his mouth and kissed it. *What the hell was wrong with him*? He had to get a hold of himself before he freaked her out. Although she didn't seem to mind, smiling as she caressed his hand.

He wanted to take her out and show her a good time. But that would have to wait for another time. Today he didn't want to be anywhere crowded. He had only one thing on his mind, well, besides holding her and kissing her. He wanted to talk to her, get to know more about her, more about this nonsense of her leaving. Most importantly, he hoped today they could come to some kind of understanding. He knew it was insane, but after last night, there was absolutely no way he'd be okay with her being free to see other guys, not as long as he was seeing her. And he planned on seeing her every chance he got. He knew it was a risk, but not riskier than not getting it out there on the table and then possibly seeing her with someone else. The very thought made him clench his teeth.

He'd packed sodas in Sarah's ice chest from the night before, and they stopped at a deli for sandwiches. They drove to Mount Soledad, the local state park. It had lots of cycling and hiking trails, but was known for its massive, man-made caves. It overlooked the ocean and had the most spectacular views. He was sure Sarah would love it.

Angel had been there many times with his brothers and the guys. He knew the place pretty well. He'd bring her back for cycling later. But today he had a much calmer visit planned.

Sarah looked out the window, admiring the amazing views. "My God, this place is better than the cliff last night. I didn't think that was possible."

She was right. No matter how many times he came up here, it was always as unbelievable as the first time. He took in the view himself then looked at Sarah. His body could feel the moment getting closer, the moment he would have her in his arms again. He held her hand the entire ride, and he squeezed it gently.

He picked one of the more private picnic areas. The park wasn't crowded at all. They pretty much had the area to themselves, except for the occasional cyclist riding by. Angel pulled the ice chest and a blanket out of the trunk of his car and took her by the hand. Sarah headed for the picnic table under a big wooden canopy. But Angel shook his head and pulled her toward a grassy area under a tree.

"Over here," he grinned.

Sarah's eyes widened a bit, but she smiled and followed behind him. They laid out the blanket and put down the ice chest. No sooner had they sat down, than Angel was kissing her, at first softly and sweetly. Then he pulled her back gently, laying her down on the blanket, and he propped himself up on his elbow next to her. He held her head on his hand, while his other roamed her body over her clothes.

His hand ran over her stomach and then down her outer thigh. He was completely aroused, and he knew she felt it.

He bit her lower lip softly then worked his way down her chin. She tasted so damn good. He moved her head up gently and dove into her neck, kissing, suckling, and biting softly.

"Angel," she whispered hoarsely.

He groaned as he continued to kiss and suckle her neck, wishing now they were somewhere more private.

"Angel." He could feel how hard she was breathing.

He sucked her neck one last time then glanced at it as he pulled away smiling, satisfied when he saw a small but noticeable dark pink spot just below her ear.

He looked at her and couldn't help kissing her one last time. When he was finally able to pull himself away from her, he lay there on his elbow staring at her wet pink lips and played with her hand. He was about to tell her how perfect it felt having her there next to him when she stunned him with an unexpected admission.

"I'm a virgin."

Angel stared at her blankly for a second, not sure how to respond. The idea of being her first rattled every nerve in his body, and his muscles tensed. When he didn't respond immediately, Sarah sat up and pulled away from him.

"Wait, hold on." He reached for her.

She pulled her hand away from his reach. "I'm only telling you, so you won't think I'm a tease if things don't go as far as you're expecting them."

He sat up, quickly pulling himself next to her again. But before he could respond, she added, "I'm just not ready for anything like that, especially with everything that's going on right now."

Damn it, he felt like a pushy prick, no better than Jesse. "That's fine, Sarah." He caressed her cheek. "I'm sorry I came on so strong. I'm not usually like this. I don't know what it is, but I can barely control myself around you."

She looked somewhat embarrassed and bit her bottom lip. "I feel the same way around you."

He put his arm around her and kissed her head. With her baby soft hair against his face and her alluring scent, he was afraid of getting carried away again. He pulled away, quickly looking at his watch. It was almost noon. "You hungry?"

"Starving, actually—I skipped breakfast."

Angel frowned. "You should've said something." He pulled the ice chest in front of him.

"You didn't give me a chance," she giggled.

He loved seeing her smile. "Ha, ha." The sarcasm prompted her to laugh even more.

They sat legs crossed, eating quietly for a few minutes. Though he didn't try too hard, he couldn't keep his eyes off her. He even enjoyed the way she ate, tearing the pieces of sandwich with her hands rather than biting right into it. She ate slow and gracefully. She was only half done with her sandwich when he shoved the last piece of his in his mouth. Angel's phone rang, and he patted his pockets then realized he'd left it in the car.

"I better get that. It might be my mom." He jumped to his feet and took off toward his car.

***

Sarah admired him from behind as he sprinted to his car. Once there, he leaned in the window and reached for his phone. She placed her sandwich down on its wrapper and slapped her hand on her forehead, leaving it there for a second. She shook her head. *I'm a virgin.* Good God, it's only their first date. They're at a park in broad daylight. Did she really think he was gonna jump her bones? Was there no end to her idiocy?

Angel walked back, still on the phone. He hung up before he got close enough for her to hear him. He sat down next to her again and picked up his sandwich.

"Sorry about that," He sat down across from her again. "I thought it might be my mom. Sometimes it gets really busy at the restaurant on the weekend, and they need me to come in and help out, even when I'm not scheduled to."

"What kind of restaurant do they have?" She already knew. Valerie had told her so much about the Morenos. But she was shooting for a safer subject. One she couldn't goof up.

He shook his head, wiping off his mouth. "A Mexican restaurant. It's just off La Jolla Boulevard. I'll take you there when we have more time."

He finished his sandwich and wrapped up the trash in the plastic bag it all came in. He looked at Sarah's sandwich. She'd only eaten half.

"I thought you were starving?

She looked down at her sandwich "I eat slowly." She lost her appetite after her stupid declaration, but she lied just so they could get off the subject. It'd worked, so far.

Angel propped himself back on his elbows and looked at her curiously. "So."

Sarah braced herself, shoving a small piece of sandwich in her mouth.

"You said your birthday is in the winter, what day exactly?"

Thank God. She washed down her food with a soda and looked at him. "January first. I'm a New Year's baby."

"Really?" Angel's eyebrows went up. "We're only a few weeks apart then. My birthday is December 20th."

"Really?" Without thinking, she let out an upset, "Oh, shit!"

She saw the confused look on Angel's face. "I'm sorry that just reminded me of something," she explained. "Today's Sydney's birthday. We talked so long this morning, and I never even said happy birthday. I feel terrible."

Angel shrugged. "So call her back." He pulled his cell phone off the clip of his pants and handed it to her. "Here, the reception up here is pretty good."

"No," she said, a little too hastily. "I can call when I get home." No way was she going to use his phone to call Sydney. She didn't want Sydney's number in any way programmed in Angel's phone.

"Go ahead." He held the phone in front of her "I don't mind, really. If she's upset at all that you forgot, she'll be happier you called back sooner than later."

Her. She. Sarah felt her stomach churn. She'd never been a liar in her life, and she'd reasoned earlier that this wasn't lying. She never actually *said* Syd was a girl, but now this was beginning to feel like one big hairy lie. She should tell him. She really should, but she couldn't. Not now. There would be a better time.

"You're right." She picked up her purse. "But I'll use my phone. The number is already programmed in there." She quickly pulled her phone out. She looked at him and gulped as she dialed the number. She was glad he was sitting across from her and not next to her. He might hear Sydney's voice. Even so, she backed up a little pretending to rid herself of crumbs as she listened to the ringing.

"Lynni?"

Hearing Sydney's voice only made her tenser. She pressed the phone closer to her ear, making absolutely sure

Angel wouldn't hear him. The smile on Angel's face made her sound even more remorseful when she spoke.

"Sydney," she frowned. "I'm so sorry I forgot to say happy birthday to you this morning."

She could hear Sydney chuckle. "Don't worry about it," he said. "I hadn't even remembered until I came in the kitchen and my mom had it all decked out with balloons and what not. We had quite a feast this morning."

"Oh." She was suddenly overwhelmed with emotion. Sydney's parents had always been that way, even with her. She remembered a couple of years back when her mom had gone to Vegas for New Year's, leaving her with the Maricopas. They'd celebrated New Year's Eve eating pizza, playing dominoes for money, and watching horror movies. Then on New Year's Day, Frances, Sydney's mom, surprised her by getting up early to make a huge feast of pancakes, bacon, sausages, eggs, and delicious homemade croissants. She'd even decorated with streamers and balloons all around the breakfast nook. *All* of it, *just* for Sarah. She'd never felt so special. She'd cried the whole time they sang Happy Birthday. Even now, she felt tears flood her eyes.

She looked up at Angel. He was watching her curiously. She realized he hadn't taken his eyes off her the whole time. She blinked hard, trying to regain her composure.

"Are you okay, Lynni?"

"Yeah, yeah." She cleared her throat, "I was just picturing it. It sounds wonderful, Syd. I wish I could be there with you to help you celebrate."

"You are here." Sydney said, softly.

"What?"

"I got the slideshow you sent. I started to watch it, but I kept getting choked up, so I had to turn it off. I'll try it again later."

She felt herself warm up and smiled. "Yeah, you have to. It's good." she said. She looked up again at Angel to see he was still looking at her; he hadn't flinched once. "Listen, I gotta go, but I'll call you later, and you can tell me how your day went, okay?"

"I love you, Lynni."

Her eyes still on Angel, she couldn't respond the way she wanted, and it clutched her heart. She'd told Sydney how much she loved him for years. It felt natural. She even told his parents she loved them. But she couldn't do it now, not in front of Angel. It was just a matter of time before he knew, and this would only make it harder to explain.

"Me too," she whispered. "We'll talk later, okay?"

After she'd hung up, Angel smiled at her warmly. "Wow. Such emotion, all that 'cause you forgot?"

Sarah stiffened. She should've never called Sydney in front of Angel.

"No." She wanted to kick herself. "Sydney's mom made a big birthday breakfast this morning, and it just brought back memories of when she did it for me a few years ago. That's all."

"Come here." He held out his hand, smiling. "I promise I'll try to control myself."

She lay down, facing him, propping herself on her elbow and smiled. He rolled off one of his elbows to face her and took a deep breath.

"Sarah, I hope this doesn't sound too crazy, but I like you a lot." He stopped to kiss her fingers. "It's *insane*. I just met you, but I feel like I could spend every minute with you if you'd let me."

Sarah stared, gulping hard. Her heart was swelling by the milliseconds. Was she dreaming? She didn't want to blink; she was afraid he'd disappear. He didn't wait for a response. Instead, he went on, staring right at her.

"Last night you said you didn't have a boyfriend. I know it's way too soon for that. You don't know anything about me. I know I have no right to ask you this, but," he paused, "you said you're only gonna be here a short while, so would it be too much to ask that until then we have an agreement?"

"Agreement?" Sarah had a feeling what he was getting at, but she was done making an ass of herself. She wanted absolute clarity.

He cleared his throat, and it was obvious he was uncomfortable. "I mean, would you be okay if we agreed to be exclusive while you're here?"

Sarah couldn't believe it. She stared ahead but not at him, shaking her head subconsciously, trying to take it all in. When she focused back on him, his expression had changed. "Is that a no?"

She shook her head even harder. "No."

Angel sat up quickly. "Are you seeing someone?" His voice was almost a whisper.

Before she could say or do anything stupid again, she sat up to face him and she spoke right in his face "I like you too. I can't even begin to tell you how much. Last night was the first night I've gone out since I've been here. It's been a long time since I laughed that hard."

Her expression turned more serious. Her next statement was a risk, but one she felt was necessary. "I don't have a problem with not seeing anyone else, Angel, but I know all about you and your brothers and your friends. I don't know if you'll be able keep up with your end of the bargain. I just don't want to get hurt."

Angel's eyes narrowed, and his lips pressed shut. He leaned forward and spoke with a bit of affliction. "You may think you know me, but you have no idea. So, I'll let the assumption slide this time. But if I say I'll be exclusive, I mean it."

As much as Sarah wanted to believe him, she was terrified. There'd been so many broken promises in her life, so many let downs. She couldn't bear another one. He must've seen the look on her face.

"Sarah, I don't lie." He was firm. "You can ask anyone who knows me. If there's one thing you can count on, it's my word."

The stab to her gut was wrenching. How could she sit here and be such a hypocrite when she herself wasn't exactly being forthcoming? She smiled faintly then decided right then and there she would allow herself to be happy—*very* happy—for the first time in too long. And then she was grinning from ear to ear. "Okay."

He stared at her blankly. Then, as if it suddenly hit him, his grin matched hers. He put his hand behind her neck, pulling her gently closer to him. He groaned as his lips met hers and then pulled her down again with him.

CHAPTER 6

Angel picked Sarah up early again on Sunday, and they had breakfast at a greasy spoon. They sat on the same side of the booth. Angel had given up trying to hold back. He kissed her and caressed her every chance he got.

Even when their food came, he couldn't keep his hands off her. Between bites, he nibbled on her ear and pecked her endlessly. Sarah seemed to object, whispering, "People are watching." It seemed to Angel with all the giggling she was doing, she was enjoying it more than she was admitting.

After breakfast, Angel asked if there was anywhere in particular she wanted to go, hoping she'd say somewhere he could enjoy her in private. But much to his chagrin, she said she'd never been to Old Town San Diego and knew it was less than half an hour's drive.

Angel frowned. "You don't wanna go there."

She pouted, making Angel smile. "Valerie said it's a must see."

He rolled his eyes, putting the last piece of sausage in his mouth. "She would. She's a girl, and it's nothing but shopping."

"No, I heard there's a lot of history to see there too," she said quickly. "And, she said the Mexican food there is great."

Angel smiled and kissed her nose. "All right, whatever you want, but if it's Mexican you want, I know somewhere better."

They spent the rest of the day in Old Town. They took a trolley that dropped them off at the most interesting points. The rest of the time they walked and talked and laughed. Her laugh was infectious, and he found himself smiling and laughing with her all day. It was amazing to Angel how comfortable he felt with her and so soon.

When they got to the main shopping area, Angel was on a mission. He was looking for something to get Sarah. He wanted something special she could remember their first date by.

They strolled into one of the shops. Angel took in all the junk on the counters. So far, everything he'd seen was either too cheap or too cheesy.

He walked over to where Sarah had stopped and was looking at little turtle figurines with heads that bobbled. Angel tapped the little head to make it wiggle.

"You like that?" He grimaced.

"It's cute."

"My sister has a bunch of those. Ever since her friends found out she liked them, they've started buying her more. So she collects them now," Angel chuckled. "I remember the time some idiot brought one to the restaurant for her. My brother Alex broke the head off."

Sarah looked at him weird. "Why'd he do that?"

Angel was still smiling. He picked out a couple of the turtles for his sister and turned back to Sarah. "She was only fifteen. Not only was she too young for a boyfriend, the guy was eighteen. He was nuts if he thought that was gonna fly."

He watched as Sarah crinkled her nose and got that little wrinkle between her eyes. He was beginning to love all her expressions. "Maybe he was just a friend."

Angel smiled. "No such thing."

"What do you mean?"

"I mean there's no such thing as guys and girls being friends." Angel moved along the aisle, still not seeing anything that grabbed him. He stopped when he noticed Sarah hadn't moved.

"What's wrong?"

"Nothing." She walked toward him. "You really believe that?

"Believe what?"

"That guys and girls can't be friends?"

Angel stopped looking through all the junk on the shelves and turned his attention to Sarah. "Yeah, don't you?"

"No. I think it *is* possible."

"Really?" He lifted an eyebrow. "You have a lot of guy friends, Sarah?"

Sarah cleared her throat and glanced back at the souvenirs on the shelf. "Not a lot. But I have some."

"Zat right?" He closed in on her and put his arms around her waist from behind. He spoke in her ear. "You wanna give me some names, so I can start kicking ass?"

He felt Sarah stiffen in his arms, and he smiled. "Relax I'm only playing."

He'd had this conversation before with other girls. They all seemed to think any guy that waved at them or forwarded them some stupid text was their friend. That's not what Angel was talking about at all. He knew it was debatable. But he had no intention of arguing with Sarah on their first date. He kissed the side of her face, and she seemed to lighten up.

Sarah didn't comment; instead, she reached for a pair of earrings. Angel looked at them over her shoulder as she examined them. They were very delicate looking, the kind that hung off the ear, not studs. The stone that adorned them was shiny and flat.

"Is that pearl?

"Looks like it."

"You like 'em?" he kissed her temple.

"Yeah, they're pretty." She held them up to the light, and Angel took them.

"Sold." He let go of her and started toward the register.

Sarah followed. "No, Angel, that's okay. I didn't mean—"

"They're yours now." He turned around and winked at her.

Angel helped her get them on when they were outside the small shop. She stared at him with that wrinkle between her eyes. "How do they look?"

"Perfect," he said and then kissed her again and again.

Angel had been to Old Town many times with his family. But he'd never really experienced it quite like he had today. He enjoyed every minute of it. It occurred to him that it didn't matter where they went or what they did as long as Sarah was with him. He would even enjoy sitting through a chick flick. He winced at what the guys would say when they knew.

He glanced down at Sarah leaning against him. Her head rested on his chest; his arm was around her as they sat in the back of the trolley. At that moment, he didn't care what anybody thought. After only a weekend with her, he knew he had it bad. There'd be no way of hiding it. It was a bit alarming. He'd never been in love, but this felt close. *Too close.*

Something gnawed at him. Even through all the laughter, it still bothered him, and any attempts to block it were in vain. *I'm only here for the semester.* He squeezed his eyes shut and held her tighter. He'd change her mind. He had to.

They exited the trolley and headed back to the parking lot and Angel's car. Even with all the snacking they'd done, Angel was getting hungry. As if on cue, Sarah squeezed his hand. "I'm starving," she said, looking up at him.

"Feel like Mexican?" he asked.

She smiled big and nodded.

✳✳✳

They parked on a small quaint-looking street, just off the main strip. The sign over the restaurant read *MORENO'S.* She felt her stomach tighten and wondered if his parents or brothers would be there. What was he thinking? This was too soon. She wasn't ready for it, but she didn't want to hurt his feelings.

He held her hand as they walked into the restaurant. It was much bigger than it looked from the outside. Angel had made it sound insignificant, but she knew better. Valerie had told her about it and said it was actually a very nice restaurant. Even with what Valerie had said, she still wasn't prepared for it.

It was anything but insignificant. She was immediately taken by the high ceilings and the huge round metal chandeliers that held what looked like small red candles all the way around. There were dramatic arches everywhere and the walls were textured to look old with brick showing through some parts, just like the historic houses they'd seen in Old Town.

The hostess at the front, a young pretty girl with big brown eyes and lashes that went on forever, was busy talking to one of the waiters when they walked in. Her uniform was snug fitting, and it accentuated her large bust. Her dark hair was pulled back in a braid, and Angel tugged it playfully, making the hair on the back of Sarah's neck stand. The girl glanced at Angel and smiled. Then her attention turned to Sarah, looking at her curiously.

Sarah tried to loosen her hold on Angel's hand, but he held it firmly. Jealously was new to Sarah, and she didn't like it at all. If this was all it took to make her see red, she wondered what she'd gotten herself into. She swallowed hard and tried not to frown.

"Who's here?" Angel asked the girl.

"Just Alex. Mom and Dad left about a half hour ago." She brought her attention back to Sarah. "Are you here to eat?

Angel nodded then turned to Sarah. "Sofie, this is Sarah. Sarah, this is my baby sister, Sofie."

His sister rolled her eyes and held her hand out to shake Sarah's. "Sofia." she corrected. "And I'm hardly a baby anymore, Angel. Nice to meet you, Sarah."

Relieved, Sarah exhaled. She shook Sofia's hand, smiling. "Nice to meet you too."

She was right, Sarah thought. His sister didn't look like a baby at all. In fact, if she had to guess, she would've thought Sofia was at least her age if not older. Sofia was taller than her with a heck of a lot more curves.

Angel ignored Sofia's comment and grabbed a menu. He led Sarah into one of the dining rooms. "I'll put in our order, no need to send anyone over."

The room was very big. Sarah took everything in, impressed. Brightly colored Mexican artwork tastefully covered the walls. Clay figurines like the ones they'd seen all over Old Town adorned the many shelves.

Through one of the arches, Sarah could see the other dining room and realized the music she heard when they walked in was actually a live trio of musicians singing. She stretched her neck to get a better look. There was a short man with an accordion, a taller one playing the cello, and the pudgiest of the three was the singer playing a guitar. They all wore cowboy hats and had thick mustaches. No wonder Angel hadn't wanted to go to Old Town. Why would he? He had it all here.

Angel took her to one of the more private booths near the back of the restaurant. "Look it over." He handed her the menu then kissed her. "I'll go get us something to drink."

Sarah's eyes bounced around from one dish to another on the menu. She was starving and everything sounded so good. She read everything that came with each plate and wondered if she'd get full. She was trying to decide between the green enchiladas and the wet burrito when she heard male voices coming toward her. Her eyes lifted from the menu and saw Angel and what appeared to be a taller, buffer, more mature looking version of Angel coming toward her. *Alex.* Her heart thudded a little faster.

"Well, this is a first," Alex said when he got close enough. He smiled mischievously, glancing at Angel then back at Sarah.

"Ignore him." Angel placed the chips and salsa in front of her, spilling a little of the salsa in the process.

Alex slipped into the seat directly in front of her, frowning down at the spilled salsa. "No wonder they don't let you wait tables around here." When his eyes met Sarah's, his frown dissolved. "Are those for real?"

Angel chuckled and introduced them. "Alex, this is Sarah. Sarah, this is my brother Alex—and he's not staying."

He placed his hand over hers on the table. "Very nice to meet you, Sarah."

Sarah gulped, holding the menu tight with her other hand. "Nice to meet you too."

Angel grabbed a napkin and wiped down the table where the salsa had spilled. "Have you decided, or do you need more time?" he asked Sarah.

Sarah could barely concentrate with Alex's hand still over hers. "Uh, are the green enchiladas good?"

Alex squeezed her hand and smiled. "Everything here is delicious."

Sarah sat up a bit, feeling her cheeks warm as Angel threw the crumpled napkin at Alex and laughed. "Knock it off. You're such an idiot."

Alex didn't take his eyes off Sarah, but he let go of her hand.

"Yeah." Angel looked back at Sarah. "They're real good, is that what you want?"

She nodded and handed him the menu. "Okay. Let me go put in the order. I'll be right back. And don't worry—he's outta here as soon as I get back."

"I think you're the one that's worried," Alex smirked.

Angel strolled away. "Whatever," he said without turning around. "And get your hands off her."

Alex put both his hands in the air, smiling. He sat back and crossed his arms, pretending to analyze her.

Sarah couldn't get over the resemblance between him and Angel, except Alex was thicker, fuller somehow. But not heavy, just buffer, and his neck was huge. He had those same amazing dimples as Angel. With him smiling like that, looking so perfect, it was hard to believe he had such a short fuse, as she'd heard.

His silliness made Sarah feel less nervous. "Well, I didn't know Angel had a girl. Did you know he had brothers?"

"Yeah, I did. I must say even though I've never seen you, I've heard an awful lot about you."

"Really?" he said. "Well, don't believe a word of it. Angel's just jealous."

Sarah laughed. "Actually, Angel hasn't said a thing about you. It's my cousin who's been doing all the talking." *Valerie was going to kill her.*

"Your cousin?"

"Yeah, I guess you can say she's one of your biggest fans." Sarah smiled.

Alex leaned closer to Sarah. "Okay, I gotta know now. What's your cousin's name?"

"Valerie Zuniga," she said. "She's a senior like me at La Jolla."

She watched as he concentrated. "Valerie Zuniga? What's she look like?"

"Tiny." Sarah giggled. "She's really petite. As tall as you are, she might have passed by you a hundred times, and you probably never saw her. Maybe that's why you don't remember her."

"Maybe. So your tiny cousin Valerie is a fan, huh? Does she have eyes like yours?"

Sarah felt herself blushing again. "No, actually she's my step cousin. My aunt married Valerie's dad. So, she looks nothing like me. She has shorter blond hair and brown eyes."

"Hmm. A blonde? Well, if I don't remember her, what can she possibly have to say about me?"

Oh no. Sarah hadn't expected the conversation to get this far. She couldn't possibly tell him Valerie worships him. What if he ever did meet her? She cleared her throat. "Oh, she's just told me about what a good football player you are and stuff."

"You're backpedaling, Sarah," he smirked. "You said you'd heard an awful lot. Now spill it."

Sarah's eyes opened wide. "Well, yeah but it's girl talk. I can't tell you that. She'd kill me."

He sat up even more interested. "Girl talk, huh? This is getting even better. You have to tell me now."

"No way!" She laughed nervously. *Where was Angel?*

Alex was playing with her now, and she could tell he loved it—loved seeing her squirm. "Okay, just one thing. You can't leave me hanging like this. You're the one that brought it up."

This was true, and now she wanted to kick herself for it. She sighed, feeling defeated. "All right, just one thing and then we drop it, okay?" She tried to sound firm.

"Yes ma'am." The corner of his lips went up, making the dimple on his cheek even deeper. How could he not guess what girls said about him?

"She's just told me many times about ... Well, you know ... how good-looking you are and how popular you were in school. Okay? I'm not going into any details either, so don't ask."

Alex chuckled. "Okay, fair enough, but now you're gonna have to bring her around some time, so I can get a chance to check her out."

"All right. Maybe one of these days." Somehow, she doubted Valerie would want to now. She changed the subject. "So I thought you were away at school."

He shook his head. "I'm in school, just not away. I go to UC San Diego. I wanted to stay close by, so I could still help out with the restaurant. I don't have school or practice on Sundays."

He glanced over her shoulder, and his smile stretched, revealing his deep big dimples again. He picked up her hand and kissed it. Sarah tensed up. "You're too late," he said. "We're getting married."

"Get the hell out of here," she heard Angel say from behind her.

She turned to see him walking back toward them. Their eyes met, and he puckered his lips at her, making her heart flutter. She'd been with him all weekend, and she still couldn't get enough of him.

By the time he'd reached the booth, Alex was already on his feet. "Yeah, you better leave," Angel said.

Alex messed Angel's hair. "You're lucky I have work to do." He smiled at Sarah. "It was a pleasure, Sarah."

Angel pushed him playfully. "Get to work, you bum."

Just as Alex began walking away, Sofia leaned in the dining room. "Your food's ready, Angel."

Alex seemed surprised. "You're still here Sof?"

"Yeah, there were people waiting, and Julio wasn't here yet."

"Who's taking you home?"

Sofia shrugged. "I thought you would."

"Sweetheart, I can't leave. I'm doing the payroll for this week." They both turned to Angel.

Angel's shoulders dropped, and he looked up at the ceiling. "I can take her," he conceded, "but I'm eating first."

He leaned over and kissed Sarah, before leaving again to get their food. They ate their dinner, and, as usual, Angel was incapable of keeping his hands and lips off her. After they finished, they sat there stuffed.

"God, that was good." Sarah stared at her empty plate.

Angel had eaten the biggest burrito on the menu. It looked big enough to feed at least two. He leaned his head on Sarah. "I think I ate too much."

"You think?" His plate appeared to be licked clean. She started giggling. "There's no way I could've finished even half of that."

Angel groaned. "It's not funny."

Sarah turned around and scanned the restaurant. "We better go," she said. "Your poor sister has been waiting all this time."

Angel stood up and started piling the plates up, but a busboy rushed over. "I got it, Angel."

"I can get this, Ernie," Angel said.

"No, no, I got it." Ernie insisted and quickly piled everything on top of Angel's plate.

"Thanks, man." Angel took Sarah by the hand. They walked by the door to the back office, and Angel yelled in. "We're outta here, Alex."

"All right," Alex yelled back. "You got Sofie, right?"

"Yeah, I'll drop her off."

"All right then," Alex said. "Byyye Sarah."

"Byyye Alex." She giggled. They heard Alex laugh.

Angel shook his head. "Don't encourage him."

CHAPTER 7

On the ride home from the restaurant, the two girls hit it off right away. They both loved running. Sofia was on the track team, and Sarah had been in track since the ninth grade. Sarah hoped Sofia wouldn't ask about her moving out here. She didn't. She was more interested in why she hadn't gone out for track at La Jolla.

"It's not too late, you know," Sofia said. "The meets aren't until next semester anyway. Have you done relays? 'Cause the girl that ran the relay with us last year was really good, but she graduated. So now we're trying to find someone to replace her, but no one so far has come even close to her speed."

Sarah knew she had the speed. She'd been the fourth place runner in both the 400m and 1600m relays back home and won plenty of times—a few times coming from behind. Her heart ached to think she wasn't there training with all of her old teammates. She hadn't even said goodbye to any of them, not wanting to answer any of the inevitable questions. Instead, she'd asked Sydney to keep it simple and just tell them she'd moved out of state over the summer. She'd figure out what to say when she got back. "I ran a few relays back home on the team."

"Oh, my God." Sofia sat up at the edge of her seat. "Are you fast?"

Angel turned to her. He'd been holding her hand the entire way. "Yeah, I'm pretty fast."

"Come out and meet the team, Sarah. See what you think. And, oh." Sofia glanced at Angel and then back at Sarah. "Coach Rudy is *fine*."

She mouthed the word fine again in case Sarah hadn't caught what she meant.

"He's a perv," Angel huffed.

"He is not! Those are just rumors."

That sparked Sarah's curiosity. "What rumors?"

"He's young and hot. Last year was his first year teaching ever." Sofia made a face. "So, a lot of the stupid girls are always flirting with him. Anyway, people started saying that maybe he'd dated some of the older ones outside school. Even if he did, he can't be more than twenty-three. That's not old."

Sarah's eyebrows shot up, and Angel gave Sofia a disgusted look. "I warned you about him."

"Yes, yes, Angel I know." Sofia turned back to Sarah and rolled her eyes. "I'm not allowed to be alone with him, can you believe it? Anyway, you should come out and run with us, Sarah. Coach Rudy will be so excited."

"But I'm not gonna be here next semester." Angel squeezed Sarah's hand, and their eyes met.

He turned his attention back on the road. She could see his jaw tense, and his expression turn hard. He turned into a long circular driveway.

The house was impressive, a lot bigger than her aunt's, and she'd always thought her aunt's house was big. Well, compared to the one bedroom apartment she and her mom had lived in, anything was big. But this was huge. She looked out the window as he reached the front entrance and stopped. It had an elegant double door entry. "Why?" Sofia almost whined.

"I'll have to tell you about it another time," Sarah said, looking back at her.

Sofia frowned and opened the back door. "Tell mom I'll be back later," Angel said.

Sofia got out and came around to Sarah's window. "Please tell me you weren't the fourth place runner 'cause that's what we really need."

The guilt was almost too much. "Yeah, I was."

"Uughh," Sofia was deflated. "Maybe you can at least come practice with us one of these days."

"Sure, I can do that. I should be training anyway. I plan on getting back on the team at my old school."

"Good." Sofia smiled. "I'll talk to my coach and let you know when."

"Sounds good."

Sofia thanked Angel for the ride and went inside. Still smiling, Sarah turned to look at Angel. His expression was so hard her smile disappeared immediately.

"We need to talk." He pulled out of the driveway.

***

They drove up to where he'd taken her the night of the party. Angel could feel the onset of a headache, and his stomach felt a little queasy. *What the hell was she doing to him?*

Except for when she'd asked him if he was okay and he had simply responded, "nope," the drive was a silent one. Still, he held her hand firmly in his. He parked facing the cliff where they had a perfect view of the setting sun. But Angel wasn't interested in that. He didn't even wait to get out of the car. As soon as he turned off the car, he leaned against his door and looked at her. The worried look on her face made his words softer than he originally intended them to be.

"I don't understand why you're in such a rush to get back to Arizona, Sarah." Without waiting for her response, he added. "I mean, is it really that bad here? I know you said your friend is waiting for you, but is your mom going to be there for you?"

He saw the hurt in her face, and his heart dropped. He immediately felt like an idiot. *Shit.* Who the hell did he think he was prying into her life like that? He had barely known her for a weekend, and her plans were made long before him. "I'm sorry, Sarah." He kissed her hand.

He saw the tears in her big eyes, and he felt like kicking his own ass. Her painful expression twisted his insides. Damn it. How could he be so stupid? For all he knew, her mom could be in a hospital somewhere. He leaned over and pulled her gently to him, kissing her head.

"God, Sarah, I'm so sorry," he said. "I had no right—"

She shook her head before he could finish. "It's okay," she said. "It's not your fault. There's no way you could know."

Know what? "So, tell me," he said, then quickly added, "Or don't. You don't have to if you don't want to."

He'd pushed her too much already. He wanted to be there for her, make her pain go away, but he had to stop being so damn pushy.

"It's not that I don't want to," she said. "It's just too embarrassing." Then added in a hushed whisper, "shameful."

"What?" He lifted her chin gently. "Sarah, there is nothing you can tell me that would make me feel any different about you." And he meant it. He had a feeling whatever it was, it couldn't be anything Sarah had done. He couldn't imagine Sarah doing anything shameful.

He pulled open the glove compartment and pulled out a napkin, handing it to her. She took it and cleaned herself up. "Can we get out?"

Angel pulled the keys out of the ignition and got out of the car. He walked around the car quickly, meeting her as she got out. He hugged her tightly, wanting her to feel just how sorry he was. "I'm really sorry."

"Don't be," she said. "You didn't do anything."

"I'm an ass."

"No, you're not," she laughed.

She closed the door, and they walked back to the exact spot they'd stood that first night. Sarah held onto the rail, and he stood behind her, his arms around her waist. As they looked out into the ocean, Angel felt her take a deep breath.

"My mom's in jail."

He stood perfectly still. The last thing he wanted was for Sarah to feel he was judging her. He was determined not to interrupt and let her say what she wanted, and only what she wanted.

She turned to face him, and he felt his heart sink when he saw the tears in her eyes again.

"My mom is a good person."

"Sweetheart, you don't have to convince me." He wiped away a tear that rolled down her cheek.

She threw her arms around him, and he held her tight. After holding her for a few minutes, she pulled back and looked him straight in the eye.

"Things weren't easy for us, Angel," she said. "It's always been just the two of us. We had no one else. My grandparents were non-existent, disowning my mom when she got pregnant with me. She was only seventeen when I was born, and I've never known my dad."

Angel hung on her every word. His heart broke as she bravely sucked it up, refusing to let herself fall apart.

"Then I started asking for things," her voice was full of disgust, "things she couldn't afford: expensive running shoes, and clothes, and an iPod. I was selfish. She kept up with everything I asked for, and I didn't ask how. Deep inside I knew we couldn't afford it all, but I didn't care." She paused to take a deep breath and wipe her nose.

"Then one day, she sat me down and cried. She told me she'd been bad. I still don't understand the whole thing, but she took money from her boss. She'd been doing it for years. Embezzlement is what they called it at the trial. Now she's doing three years, and it's entirely my fault."

She collapsed on his chest and cried softly. Angel held her tight, feeling an invisible hand squeeze his windpipe.

"It's not your fault," he whispered frantically in her ear as he kissed her again and again. He walked her over to the bench where they could sit and sat her on his lap.

She sat up straight, composing herself, and looked at him. "She's in a minimum security correctional facility in Flagstaff." She held up her fingers to emphasize the quote sarcastically.

Angel stared at her helplessly, taking her hand back in his and squeezing it.

"She doesn't want me to visit," she continued. "said she didn't want me to see her like that ever. But there's no way I can go three years without seeing her. I plan on visiting her, no matter what she says."

"Can she call you?"

Sarah nodded. "Yeah, she calls every week, and we write all the time, but it's not enough."

"Sarah." He tried to sound optimistic. "People rarely serve their full term, especially when the crime wasn't a violent one. She'll probably be out before the three years."

"That's what her attorney told her. But she just went in, so she's still looking at least a year and a half if she's lucky."

Angel cradled her, kissing her forehead. She leaned on his shoulder. "The thing is Angel, growing up we moved constantly. I don't know why, but most of the jobs she got would rarely last. Each time she got a new one, it was time to move. Sometimes she knew it was going to be a short stay ahead of time, and we wouldn't even get an apartment. We'd stay in a hotel for a few months at a time.

"Up until I was nine years old, we moved so much I'd been to more than a dozen different schools, sometimes moving twice in the same year. I'd given up making friends or even unpacking. It was almost a year after we'd moved to Flagstaff before I finally allowed myself to completely unpack."

"And that's where you met Sydney?" Angel felt her tense a little and straighten up again.

"Yeah," she said quickly. "But most importantly, we stayed there for eight years. It may not mean a lot to anyone else, but to me it was everything. I was finally home. And then just before I could finish school, this happens. Packing up all my things brought back all the painful memories of when I was a little girl. Thank God for Valerie. I don't know how I would've survived starting a new school all over again."

Her expression turned affectionate. "It's not that it's so bad here, Angel. It's just that it took so long for me to feel like I belonged somewhere. I just feel like I have to go back. I need to. It's my home."

Angel kissed her gently. "Sarah, you don't owe me any explanations. I had no right questioning you to begin with."

He was repulsed with himself. After everything she'd been through, she was sitting here trying to make him understand. She could go back to Arizona if she wanted to— she should. As much as he disliked the thought of her being so far, she deserved to be happy. Hell, he'd drive out there every weekend if he had to.

It was almost unbelievable to Sarah what an incredible mix of emotions this weekend had been. The roller coaster ride was over, and yet her stomach was still feeling the effects.

She'd kept Sydney updated all weekend on everything that was happening. When she told him about what had happened today, he was pissed at first, but she'd defended Angel ardently. He'd laughed, teasing that if he didn't know better, he'd say she was in love.

She got the feeling Sydney was happy that she had finally confided in someone else about her mom. She felt guilty now about the amount of crap she'd unloaded on him, and yet he'd always been there so ready to help her through it all. She hadn't told him yet that Angel assumed he was a girl. She didn't know why, but somehow she thought he might be insulted, betrayed that she was denying their friendship.

She glanced at the clock. It was 10:30 pm. She was almost out of the room, on her way to brush her teeth, when she heard her phone ring. Her face lit up when she saw it was Angel. She answered it with a smile.

"Hi, Angel."

"Hey." His voice was low. "Sorry I'm calling so late. I couldn't stop thinking about you. I just wanted to make sure you were okay. I still feel like an ass about today."

"No, you shouldn't." She clutched the phone. "Actually, I feel a lot better now that I told you."

"Good," he said. "'Cause I want you to know you can tell me anything."

Sarah's heart sank. She knew she should've told him about Sydney already, but truth was she was beginning to wonder if he really needed to know. Valerie had been right, she decided, about guys being territorial, and clearly Angel was no exception. She was certain now, especially after hearing his take on guys and girls being friends, that he wouldn't understand her relationship with Sydney.

She reasoned with herself that he probably would never get the chance to meet Syd anyway. She'd already decided to keep the subject of Syd to a minimum. Still, she couldn't help feeling deceitful.

She pushed Sydney to the back of her mind. There were other things she needed to get clear with him. "Listen, Angel." She sat down on her bed. "I'm glad you called. With all the talk about my mom today, I completely forgot to talk to you about tomorrow."

"What about tomorrow?"

"Well, I know we have an understanding now, but I don't want that to change things at school."

He was silent for a moment, but she heard the unmistakable change in his tone when he spoke again. "You don't want anyone at school to know you're seeing someone?"

"No." She was surprised that he would even think that. "I just don't want you to change anything you normally do, for me. I know how close you are with your friends. I'm sure we'll have plenty of time to spend together after school and on weekends. There's no need for me to cut in on your time with your friends at school."

She really hoped he'd understand. The last thing she wanted to do was suffocate him. After all, this was his school—his friends—she was the outsider.

The truth was she wasn't entirely sure she was going be able to handle this. It was well known the way the girls, especially Dana, acted around Angel. Just the thought of watching another girl throw herself all over him now made her cringe.

"Hey," he said. "I don't have a problem with everything staying the same as far as you hanging out with your friends and me with mine. But in case there's any doubt, I wasn't planning on keeping this understanding a secret."

Sarah felt her heartbeat speed up. For the first time, the reality of it was sinking in. This was really happening and with none other than Angel Moreno.

"Oh, I know that," she said. "That's not what I meant at all. I just don't want to smother you, Angel. I want you to still have your space."

"You have it all wrong, Sarah," he said "If anyone is gonna have to watch the smothering, it's gonna be me. In case you haven't noticed, I just can't get enough of you."

His words sent shivers up and down her spine. She felt the exact same way, yet Angel didn't seem scared. She, on the other hand, was terrified. This kind of happiness was uncommon in her world. She wasn't used to it and in some ways almost felt guilty about feeling so happy.

"You have to stop saying things like that."

"Why?" He sounded very serious. "I say what I feel, and I want you to do the same. Don't ever hold anything back."

"Okay." She loved the way he made her feel so uninhibited. "Can I tell you what I'm feeling right now?"

"Of course."

She bit her bottom lip. "I'd like to crawl right through the phone right now, and kiss you all over."

She heard him groan. "That's not fair. Okay, let's get one thing straight: things like that you can only say when I have you right in front of me. Damn, how am I supposed to fall asleep now?"

Sarah giggled. "Sweet dreams, Angel."

"Yeah, you know what I'll be dreaming of."

"I'm sorry," she said, still giggling. "I'll make it up to you. I promise."

He groaned again. "Sarah, baby, I know you mean well, but that's not helping my situation over here."

She forced herself to stop giggling, reminding herself to not make promises she couldn't keep. She'd already seen firsthand how hard, almost painful, it was for him to restrain himself. Not that she had any doubts he would, but it was cruel to tease him like that.

She stared at the phone for a while after they'd hung up and wondered how she, herself, would get any sleep tonight.

CHAPTER 8

True to his word, Angel didn't keep their relationship a secret. As soon as he saw her on Monday morning at her locker, he was on her. He slipped up behind her, wrapped his arms around her waist, and kissed her neck.

The rest of the day was pretty much the same. Anytime she was near, he was wrapped around her, unable to keep limbs or lips off of her.

She'd introduced him to a few of her girlfriends, and he'd also met one of her guy friends, Freddie, the guy that had his locker right below hers. But walking up while she'd been laughing with Freddie had Angel seeing red. He mentioned how his own locker was closer to her homeroom, but she didn't bite.

They were undeniably a couple. There were quite a few sneers and barefaced gawking from some of the girls Angel knew, but if Sarah had noticed, she hadn't said a word. He half expected her to be tense or apprehensive, given what she'd said to him at the beach about being afraid of getting hurt. But her brazen resolve throughout the day had surprised and impressed him, making him even more fascinated with her.

Although Angel's friends seemed surprised, they hadn't said much. Eric had just smiled knowingly but hadn't said a word. He knew better. Romero didn't remember much about Friday's party, so, he was at a total loss. After seeing Angel all over Sarah a few times though, he finally spoke up.

"Damn, that good, huh?" he'd said. "Let me know when you're done, so I can get me some."

Eric had choked back a laugh and waited for the fireworks. But Angel knew his friend could have no idea. So he let him off with a stern warning. "It's not like that, dude. So don't even think about it." And that was that.

By the end of the day, it was out there for everyone to see. And Angel was quite pleased.

***

Sarah took Sofia up on her offer to come out and run with the track team that week. Instead of running by herself after school that Wednesday, she met Sofia in the locker room and walked out with her to where the team was practicing.

Angel gave her the same warning he'd given Sofia about the coach. "Do *not* get caught alone with the pervert."

Sarah was surprised at how young the coach really was. If he hadn't been wearing the shirt that said coach, she would've easily mistaken him for one of the bigger guys in school.

He had a baby face, and while she didn't agree with Sofia about him being fine, she could understand why the girls would be attracted to him. He did have that muscular body you'd expect on a young coach. Sarah didn't notice anything perverted about him, only that his wit was appealing and the girls did a lot of giggling around him—something he seemed to take pleasure in. Given how protective Angel was about his sister, it didn't surprise Sarah that he'd be so apprehensive about the coach.

Practice went well. The team seemed impressed, and Sarah felt good about the workout. She and Sofia were on their way back to the locker room when the coach caught up to her. "So, was the team good enough for you?" he teased.

Sarah felt flattered. She was still winded from her last run and took a moment to catch her breath.

"Say yes, say yes." Sofia held her hands to her mouth as if she were praying.

"I can't."

She saw the disappointment in the coach's face. "Why?"

"I won't be here next semester. I'm going back to Arizona."

The coach scratched his eyebrow and made a face. "Damn, that's too bad. We could really use you in the relay. You're here all this semester though, right?"

Sarah nodded and was startled when she felt strong arms around her waist. Angel kissed her temple and held her against him. "What's going on?"

Eric and Romero were on either side of Sofia, staring at the coach. The coach smiled. "We'll see you here after school every day." He reached his hand out. "Welcome to the team."

Sarah reached out and shook his hand. He excused himself and walked away. Angel whispered in her ear. "He just had to touch you."

Sarah laughed. "You're so silly."

She turned around, but he kept his arms around her. The expression on Angel's face was a stern one. "You're not serious, are you?"

"I told you I don't trust the guy, Sarah. You shouldn't either."

Sarah couldn't help smiling. She'd never met someone so vehement. But his expression softened quickly. He kissed her, and they turned and followed Sofia and the guys who were already headed to the locker room.

"He seems nice enough," Sarah said

Angel squeezed her hand and groaned. "Can you trust me on this? I've heard too many stories."

"Okay, okay." Sarah leaned into him.

Sarah was beginning to understand what Valerie meant about Angel and his brothers being so intense. But she liked it. Her whole life it had been just her and her mother. There had been too many times when having a man there to protect them would've come in handy. So having Angel fret over her safety didn't bother her. On the contrary, she embraced it.

***

After a few weeks, they'd pretty much slipped into a comfortable routine. Sarah would practice with the team after school while Angel was at football practice. They'd meet afterwards and go grab something to eat then park at what had become their spot, over the cliffs where'd he'd taken her on their first night together. They'd spend about an hour there and then go home.

Everything was going well, except for a couple of incidents with Dana. She'd made it a point to pull Angel aside as often as she got the chance. Sarah had seen some of it and though she hadn't said anything yet, Angel worried it might become a problem.

Fridays were different. It was game day. Instead of meeting up after practice, Sarah would go straight home with Valerie and get ready for the game.

This week was an away game, so the stands would be less crowded, and Angel would have a perfect view of Sarah.

He was having a good game. They were up by fourteen at the half, but when they came back out after halftime, the cheerleaders had changed their tops into jerseys—real jerseys from the players on the team. They tied them in a knot in the front just under their chests to make them fit more snugly. To Angel's dismay, Dana wore his. He'd forgotten about the jersey she borrowed last year. He glanced up at the stands and saw Sarah sitting with Valerie and a few other girls. If Sarah got upset about this, he was going be so pissed at Dana.

They'd agreed to meet at the after party back by their school. Sarah left the game with Valerie and had arrived there before him, so when he got there, he wasn't sure what to expect. He walked into the party with Romero and Eric, looking around for her. He spotted Valerie first, and then he saw Sarah. There were a few guys talking to them, and he tensed up. He walked straight to her and took her hand immediately. Pulling her back away from everyone, he kissed her. To his delight, she wasn't mad. She kissed him readily.

"You had a great game." She smiled.

He stared at her, holding her tighter. "You're beautiful, Sarah."

"Thank you." She tilted her head sideways. "You really want to be here?"

Was she for real? He could almost feel the hair on the back of his head stand as he looked around and found Eric. He walked over and tugged Eric's shirt.

"I'm outta here."

Eric smirked. "Already?"

"Bye." Angel grinned.

They'd barely made it to Angel's car, and he was already kissing her neck. Every time they'd made out, things got heavier and heavier. The last time they made out, she'd let him under her bra. He made the most of it, leaving quite a few red spots all over her breasts, confident no one would see them and she wouldn't get in trouble. He was dying to know how far she'd let him go tonight. He could hardly contain himself running his hands up and down her back.

When they got to their special place, they pushed their seats back all the way, and his lips were immediately on hers. His hands explored every inch of her. But anything below the waist he touched only over her clothes and even that nearly pushed him over the edge. He kissed her hard, suckling her tongue and lips. She moaned softly, making him even more insane. Unbuttoning her blouse, he took her breast in his mouth.

His hand made its way slowly down her body, caressing her stomach then down between her legs.

Angel's heart hammered away wildly as he passionately kissed her and brought his hand up slowly, just above her waist and in her pants. When he felt her hot flesh against his hand, he almost lost it. He pulled his mouth away from hers to catch his breath, burying his face in her neck.

"You're driving me crazy," he groaned as he inhaled her arousing scent.

Slowly he slid his hand further down in her pants. She spread her legs, making him stop cold. "Oh, babe," he gasped, as he began moving his hand again even further.

His fingers caressed her for a few seconds, but not being able to stand it, he moved his hand even lower. She arched her back, and he had to stop.

He pulled himself off her just a few inches, knowing that if he kept going he'd be done. "God, I want you so much, Sarah." He could barely catch his breath.

"I want you too, Angel, but I'm just not ready for that yet."

"I know." He struggled to sound calm. "We won't go there, I promise."

Gently, he let his fingers work their magic until he could feel her trembling and heard her moan. He kissed her, sinking his tongue deep in her mouth. Her squirming and soft pants were almost more than he could take. He kept on until she was trembling all over until she could take no more until … it happened.

She moaned louder, pushing his hand away. He felt her heart pounding, and he kissed her just off the side of her mouth, allowing her to catch her breath. His own heart threatened to pound right through his chest.

"Oh, Angel."

His name had never sounded so good to him. Kissing her one last time, he lay back in his seat. He was so close to exploding himself that he knew if he kept touching her, he would. He put his hand over his chest and took a deep breath.

"Man," he said, breathlessly. "Now I know why so many old geezers have heart attacks during sex. My heart's going crazy, and I didn't even finish."

Sarah turned on her side to face him. "I wanna return the favor—"

"Sarah, don't," he said quickly. "That's not why I said it. I was just tripping out on my heartbeat. I know you're not ready, and I respect that. But if we talk about what might happen someday, I'm gonna mess my pants. I'm serious."

She smiled at him playfully. "Well, we wouldn't want that." She put her hand over the hard bulge in his pants. "I may not be ready for some things, but there are ways I can return the favor without going there, and I want to."

His eyes grew wide, and his entire body stiffened, as she reached for the top button on his jeans. He let his head fall back and closed his eyes, feeling her pull his zipper down. *Control yourself.* He'd been handed this favor before, and had always managed to hang in there for a while. But this was totally different. This was *Sarah.* He was afraid he'd be a goner as soon as he felt her hand on it.

"Sarah," he whispered hoarsely.

"Hmm?"

He felt her hand slide in his underwear and nearly lost it right there. "I'm not gonna last long, babe." He was almost in a panic. "The tissue is in the glove compartment."

She reached for the tissue with her free hand while she worked him with the other. In the next second, he was done. He squeezed his eyes, the intensity was more than he'd ever felt. It seemed to go on forever; all the while her soft hand still caressed him. He pleaded with her to stop. He couldn't take anymore.

When he finally opened his eyes, he saw her sit up and smile at him. She was beautiful, her dark hair was tousled, and her green eyes glimmered. God have mercy. He'd died and gone to heaven.

CHAPTER 9

Sarah cradled the phone on her shoulder as she made her bed. This time she'd been the one who woke Sydney early in the morning.

After the night she'd had, she'd hardly been able to sleep. So many things invaded her mind, some more glaring than others. She had to talk to someone about it. It was times like these she missed her mom more than ever. She would've been able to tell her even this. That's how close she was to her. Thank goodness she had Syd.

Angel and his mom were driving out to Los Angeles that night to have dinner with his oldest brother, Sal. He wanted Sarah to come, but she couldn't. She was booked both nights this weekend babysitting. They weren't leaving until late in the afternoon, and of course Angel still wanted to see her today, so he was picking her up in an hour.

Sarah hadn't mentioned anything about Dana wearing his jersey last night. She'd been so busy watching Angel play she might not have even noticed if Valerie hadn't pointed it out. But she refused to let Dana ruin the night for her, and even Valerie had insisted she not let Dana get to her.

"He's totally into you," she'd said. "He couldn't give a rat's ass about her, and she knows it. She is so desperate it's pathetic. Don't go arguing with him because of her. It's what she wants."

Sarah knew Dana would've been showing up at the party, and she wasn't sure if she'd still be wearing Angel's jersey. She hadn't wanted to stick around and give her the pleasure of making them uncomfortable. So she was glad when Angel was so willing to make an early exit.

What had happened in his car hadn't been totally on impulse. She'd watched Dana parade around in Angel's jersey seductively during the game. She even saw Angel eye Dana as she did a dance, caressing the jersey. A small part of her wanted to show Angel she had just as much to offer. It was something she'd been giving some thought to for weeks. With Angel being so ardent, she knew it was just a matter of time.

Though she'd never actually done anything like that before, she'd read about it plenty of times. And Valerie had filled her in as well. Surprisingly, it wasn't so bad, and it was over a lot faster than she had expected. Now, the morning after, she had mixed feelings. But she wasn't sure if she regretted it, yet.

Today would be different. She and Angel had to talk. She'd put up with Dana's antics for weeks now and wasn't sure how much longer she could deal with her crap. The only plans they had were to hang out for a few hours, and she was going to take advantage of it. She was nervous though. The last thing she wanted was to seem insecure. But she was. Every time she'd seen Dana around Angel, it had burned her up, but she'd let it go. She hadn't thought she had the right to demand anything from Angel—yet.

Things were different now. They were exclusive after all, and the jersey thing had pushed it.

She'd been on the phone with Sydney for a while now. He seemed to think she should just ask Angel straight out what was up with him and Dana. From everything she'd told Sydney so far about Angel, even Sydney knew there was no way Angel would've kept quiet if the tables were turned. Sydney had even jokingly started referring to Angel as her badass husband. Then unexpectedly, Sydney asked. "Hey, Lynni, what's Angel think about us being so tight?"

She stopped and closed her eyes. She didn't want to lie but she had no choice. She wasn't about to hurt his feelings. "You know ..." She hoped to sound convincing. "He really hasn't said much about it. I guess 'cause I really haven't gone too much into it." That was true wasn't it? Technically she hadn't lied.

"Hmm," Sydney said. "Maybe it's better that way."

There you had it. As usual, she and Sydney were on the same page. She smiled triumphantly. Her reasoning on not clarifying things about Syd to Angel held a little more validation now. Then as if someone had pushed the slow button on her, making her thoughts warp, he continued.

"I mean, be honest of course. You don't wanna start things off by keeping things from him. Just don't tell him more than he needs to know. Last thing you want is for him to think you're rubbing our friendship in."

And just like that, she was back to feeling deceitful. This shouldn't be so complicated. She plopped down on her bed. Up until last night, she hadn't really thought about the seriousness of the relationship and the real effect Sydney might have on it.

She looked up to see Valerie standing by her door in her sleep clothes as usual for this time of the morning, holding a plate loaded with food and a glass of milk. She had a big silly smile on her face. "Is that Angel?" she mouthed.

Sarah shook her head and mouthed back. "Sydney."

Valerie frowned and walked over and set her food down on Sarah's desk. She sat down, facing Sarah.

Sarah cut her conversation with Sydney short, telling him she needed to finish getting ready. She'd been done getting ready for a while now, but she could tell Valerie wanted to talk. She saw Valerie shake her head disapprovingly as she hung up. She hadn't even flipped her phone shut when Valerie started in on her. "You know, you're gonna blow it with Angel because of this guy," she said. "I mean have you not noticed how possessive Angel acts around you? Don't get me wrong. I think it's cute. He's not rude or anything. But it's so obvious he wants everyone to know you're off limits. Something tells me he doesn't know just how much you talk to Syd."

The knot that had formed in Sarah's stomach during her conversation with Sydney was still there, and it was getting bigger.

She swung around sideways on the bed and brought her feet up, so that she could lean on her knees. She exhaled loudly. "I know."

"Thank you," Valerie said. "Finally, you're listening." She put a spoonful of eggs and food in her mouth and took a swig of milk, holding up a finger for Sarah to give her a second. Apparently she wasn't done.

Sarah looked at Valerie's plate. There was enough food for two people. It'd always amazed her how much Valerie could eat, being that she was so tiny. She smiled, thinking Valerie could probably give Angel a run for his money in an eating contest.

"Look, Sarah, I get it. Okay? Sydney's been your best friend since you two were kids, and his family is the only family you had growing up. He's like a brother to you, and you're very close, blah, blah, blah. But this whole needing to talk to each other every single day is a bit much, don't you think?"

Sarah grimaced. "That's so unfair though. If it was a girl that was like a sister to me and we talked every day, it would be just fine, wouldn't it?"

Valerie shook her head as she downed more of her milk. "But that's the thing, Sarah. Fair or not, he's not a girl, and I can guarantee you if Angel knew how much you two talk, he'd be pissed." She paused to eat another spoonful and then spoke with a mouthful. "You never did tell me what he thought of your best friend being a guy."

Sarah winced and hugged her knees tighter. "He thinks Syd is a girl."

Valerie's eyes popped wide open. She took a quick drink of her milk, hurrying to wash her food down.

"Sarah Lynn!" Her tone was reminiscent of Sarah's childhood, when she'd been caught being bad. "Please tell me you're kidding."

Sarah put her hands on her face and groaned. "I'm not."

She brought her arms down, crossing them over her knees, leaning her head against them. She looked at Valerie who was still staring at her shaking her head, and shrugged. "He assumed Sydney was a girl when I told him about my best friend, and I just let him go with that. It didn't seem so bad at first, but then when we were in Old Town that first weekend, he told me he didn't believe guys and girls could be friends."

"He did?"

Sarah nodded. "Yeah, and he was pretty adamant about it."

"Not surprising. I'd expect nothing less from a Moreno," Valerie said. "So, what are you gonna do when he finds out Sydney's a guy?"

Sarah put her legs back down on the side of the bed and sat up straight. She put her hands under her thighs.

"That's just the thing." She chewed her lip. "How's he gonna find out?"

"Are you insane? You plan on never seeing Sydney again?" Valerie stopped and seemed to ponder what she had just said. "Actually, that wouldn't be such a bad idea. But I'm sure that's not part of your plan, is it?"

Sarah looked at her, still chewing her lower lip. There was no way she could just dismiss Sydney as if he were just an old boyfriend. He was so much more to her. He was family. Angel was just going to have to understand that. But Valerie did have a point. She could cut down on the phone calls.

"No, of course I plan on seeing Syd again," she said. "I'll just have to be honest with Angel, just not yet."

Valerie raised an eyebrow. "When?"

"Well, I'm not planning to sit him down and talk to him about this. I don't wanna make *that* big a thing out of it. We haven't discussed Sydney lately. The next time the subject arises, and he refers to Syd as a she, I'll just correct him."

Valerie looked at her unimpressed. "That easy. huh?"

Sarah held her chin up. "Sure, why not?"

Valerie shook her head. "Well, cuz," she said. "I wish you luck. Just remember the longer you wait, the worse it's gonna be. Just don't be too disappointed if it doesn't go over that well when you just *correct him.*"

Sarah frowned, but before she could respond, her phone rang. It was Angel. Valerie jumped up and ran over to listen in as usual.

"Hello?"

"Hey, I gotta go to the restaurant. We're a little short on staff this morning. I'm not sure what time I'll be able to pick you up, but I really want you to come down for the brunch. Would you be okay if I sent Eric to pick you up?"

Valerie motioned that she could give Sarah a ride. "Valerie can give me a ride, Angel. But are you sure I'm not gonna be in your way?"

"No, not at all," he said. "Yeah, bring her. Tell her brunch is on the house."

Valerie clapped her fingers together, smiling big. Sarah looked over at her almost empty plate on the desk and wanted to laugh.

"Okay, what time should we be there?"

"Be here as early as possible. That way as soon as I'm done, we can take off."

Valerie made a coddling face and puckered her lips. Sarah nudged her playfully. "Okay, as soon as she's ready, we'll leave."

No sooner had she hung up than Valerie ran to the desk to get her plate. She was nearly out the door, when she stopped sharply. "Oh, hey, did you ask him about stupid Dana?"

Sarah shook her head. "No, I might today."

"I almost forgot why I came in here to begin with." She made a sour face. "Last night after you guys left, she showed up still wearing his jersey. Within a couple of hours, she was crying drunk. Her bonehead friends hovered all around her, consoling her, making a ridiculous scene. I even heard her asking Eric how Angel could hurt her so bad. I'm telling you she's pathetic. She really acts like they had something. It's such a joke. Like I said before, Sarah, don't argue with him because of her. But you might want to ask him to get his jersey back."

Sarah felt an uncomfortable fog settle over her. Valerie was adamant that there was never anything real between Dana and Angel. But she wasn't so sure anymore. She'd seen the way he acted when Dana talked to him at school. It was too nice for her to stomach. She knew he wasn't rude, but she wished he'd just ignore her. Instead, he listened attentively. Now she was crying over him at a party in front of everyone?

She was absolutely bringing it up today.

CHAPTER 10

Valerie squealed in delight when Sarah told her about meeting Alex. But Sarah had left a few things out. On the way to the restaurant, Sarah thought it was only fair she fill Valerie in on everything she'd told Alex. To her surprise, Valerie wasn't fazed.

"God, Sarah," she laughed. "As if he doesn't have a big enough head already."

Sarah thought of the outrageous way he'd flirted with her. Yeah, he was a ham, but not necessarily conceited. "I didn't get the impression he had a big head."

Valerie rolled her eyes. "Sarah, I told you they're all sweethearts. I'm sure he's a real nice guy, but trust me he knows he's hot."

Sarah smiled. She had to admit there was no way he couldn't know. "But you'd go out with him if he asked you, right?"

"Are you kidding?" Valerie said. "He's the ideal guy for me. He's so hot, older, and more experienced than most of the lame guys from school. The last thing I'd have to worry about with him would be any pressure to commit."

Sarah's jaw dropped. "You mean you wouldn't want a relationship, even with him? I thought he was the man of your dreams?"

Valerie turned to look at her. "Oh, he is, and I'd be all over him if I ever got the chance. But I learned my lesson with Reggie, Sarah. As much as I liked him, after a while it just got to be too much. I couldn't stand it. If I hadn't broken up with him, I would've cheated on him for sure."

Sarah was floored. "Really?"

Valerie nodded as she pulled into a parking spot across from the restaurant. She turned the car off and pulled down her visor to check her face in the mirror.

"Yeah." She powdered her face. "I know it sounds terrible, but Monica and the girls had already gone to T.J. a couple of times, and it killed me that I couldn't go because of Reggie. When you go to T.J., you're gonna hook up. No question about it. I'd already told them that the next time they went, I was going with them for sure."

She flipped the visor down and looked at Sarah who was staring at her still in disbelief. "So I broke up with Reggie before we went, and sure enough, I hooked up with this hot guy from LA. I had such a blast. I knew the committed relationship thing just wasn't for me. Maybe someday, but not now, I'm just having too much fun."

Sarah still couldn't believe it. Valerie had told her the whole Reggie story before, leaving out the part about T.J. But Reggie was no Alex. Still, if that's the way Valerie felt, who was she to tell her otherwise?

"You're something else," Sarah said as she opened the car door.

"But I'm honest," Valerie said.

"Yeah," Sarah couldn't argue there. "That you are."

As they crossed the street, Sarah's thoughts shifted back to Angel and Dana. She took a deep breath and frowned. She wasn't looking forward to having that conversation with him, but she knew she had to address it before things got worse.

When they walked in, Sarah felt faint when she realized Angel's parents were there. She hadn't counted on meeting them so soon.

As soon as Angel saw them, he'd walked over and planted a kiss on Sarah that made her legs weak. He introduced both her and Valerie to his parents.

His mother, Isabel, was an average height, slender woman in her mid-forties. Sarah could see Angel and his siblings had gotten some of their most attractive features from her. She had big eyes and the thick lashes. Her lips were big and pouty, and when she smiled, she had the same dimples Angel and Alex had. Sofia had them also, just not as pronounced.

She was very nice and spoke with a slight accent. Angel thought she went a little overboard, trying to make Sarah and Valerie comfortable, offering them more of everything a few too many times. But Sarah and Valerie thought she was very nice.

His dad, Salvador, was also in his mid-forties and very tall with broad shoulders. He was built very well for a man his age. He didn't talk nearly as much as Angel's mother did, saying only that he was glad to meet them, and then quickly excusing himself to get back to work. But Sarah had been able to see, just by the way he spoke to Angel and Sofia, that he was a no nonsense kind of man.

At the same time, she heard tenderness in his voice when he spoke to Isabel and Sofia, referring to both as *my love* or *sweetheart*. She'd felt the same familiar hint of envy she'd felt all too many times when she'd been around Sydney and his parents.

The restaurant was busy, and Angel had hung with Sarah and Valerie off and on while they ate. At the moment, he'd been called back into the office by his dad.

Valerie was on her second round at the buffet, and Sarah sat at the table lost in thought. All through breakfast, she kept thinking of what Valerie had told her that morning about Dana and could feel herself getting anxious. She sat there playing with her food when she was startled. "Is that Valerie?"

Sarah jumped, almost spilling her drink, and looked up.

"I'm sorry. I didn't mean to sneak up on you." Alex put his hand on her shoulder.

Sarah smiled feeling silly. "That's okay."

She moved her drink a little further away from her plate. When she glanced back at Alex, he was busy sizing up

Valerie. Sarah followed his eyes over to Valerie who was still piling food on her plate.

"Well," he smiled, "I'm partial to brunettes, but a cute little blonde every now and then could do a body good."

Sarah rolled her eyes. *Every now and then?* Valerie wasn't kidding when she'd said he was her ideal guy. There'd be no talks of commitments between these two. At least there'd be no hard feelings if anything happened.

"That's really romantic," Sarah said.

Alex smiled at Sarah. She was sitting all the way in the booth, so Angel could sit next to her whenever he stopped by their table. Alex slid in next to her. "You think so?"

Sarah sat up a little straighter and kept her eyes on her food. "I didn't think you were here today."

"I just got here," he said "You missed me?"

Sarah felt her cheeks warm. *Damn him.* Why did he like to make her squirm? "No, Valerie asked about you, actually."

Valerie walked toward them with a big giddy smile.

"Did she now?" Alex raised an eyebrow.

Valerie put her plate down on the table and sat down facing Alex. Sarah immediately did the introductions.

"Alex, this is my cousin, Valerie." Then smiling silly she said, "and I think you know who Alex is, right, Valerie?"

She'd meant to embarrass Valerie playfully, but Valerie took it in stride.

"Of course, I do." She reached her hand out to shake his. "I'd have to have been buried for the last few years if I didn't."

Alex smiled. "Really? I remember you now."

Valerie rolled her eyes slightly.

"I saw that." he said.

"I wasn't trying to hide it." Valerie laughed.

"You don't think I remember you?"

"Nope." She dug in to her food.

"You wanna bet?"

Valerie shook her head. "You'll lose."

"Does that mean you're scared?"

"Of betting that you don't remember ever seeing me before? Of course not. But what are we betting for?"

Alex thought about it for a second then smiled big. "You have plans for tonight?"

Sarah choked back a laugh. As if he'd have to win a bet to get a date with Valerie. "I might," Valerie said.

Sarah nearly spit up her food, and Alex turned to look at her. She put the napkin to her mouth, coughing.

"Are you okay, sweetheart?" Alex asked.

She put a hand up, feeling stupid. "I'm fine." She managed to say. "Just went down the wrong pipe."

She saw Valerie glaring at her but quickly changed her expression back to a smile when Alex turned back to her.

"You might?" he said. "What does that mean?"

Valerie shrugged. "All depends on if anything better comes up."

She took a spoonful of food and chewed while smiling sinfully at Alex.

"Okay," Alex smirked. "If I win the bet, you cancel whatever plans you have, and I take you out."

"You're on."

Sarah was amazed at the ease these two were talking. She remembered barely being able to breathe the first few times she spoke with Angel, let alone flirt. She watched and listened to Valerie, completely impressed.

Alex sat forward with that wicked smile of his. "What time do I pick you up?"

Valerie and Sarah both laughed. "You haven't won yet," Valerie reminded him.

Alex turned to look at Sarah, then back at Valerie. "Oh, yeah, that. Sure, I've seen you before. You're Reggie Luna's ex."

Valerie's expression went blank. She looked at him then at Sarah.

"I never mentioned Reggie." Sarah said quickly.

"No," Alex said. "We played on the same team last year. You broke his heart."

Valerie's eyes opened wide. Sarah smiled, glad it was Valerie he was making squirm now and not her. Valerie tried to regain her composure. "Did I?" She looked at Alex curiously.

"Sure did." His expression was smug. "So, why'd you dump him?"

Alex's eyes were fixed on Valerie. Sarah could see Valerie's face turn bright pink. Angel approached their table just behind Valerie, and she decided to come to Valerie's rescue.

"Angel, how much longer do you have to work?"

Angel shook his head. "That's it. I'm done." He reached the table. "Now that this lazy slug finally got here, I can leave."

"Work?" Alex said. "I'm busy."

Angel glanced at him then at Valerie. Sarah smiled. "I've pretty much been invisible for the past fifteen minutes or so."

"Well, at least he's not hitting on you anymore."

"Who said that?" Alex leaned on Sarah.

Angel pulled him off her. "Are you done?"

Sarah put her hand on her stomach and made a face. "Stuffed."

"Really?" Valerie asked. "We haven't even had dessert yet."

"Stay and finish," Alex said. "I'll keep you company. This guy just can't wait to get Sarah away from me."

Angel smiled and pulled Alex by the back of his shirt. "Let her out."

"Are you okay with me going?" Sarah asked Valerie.

"Not really," Alex said, getting up. "But if he's gonna be an ass about—Oh, you were talking to Valerie."

Sarah laughed and Angel shoved him, barely moving him.

"Yeah, go ahead," Valerie said. "I'll see you at home later."

CHAPTER 11

Sarah and Angel headed to the beach. Not the cliffs where they usually went. Sarah wanted to walk on the beach. It wasn't too crowded for a Saturday. They walked for quite a while and were already on their way back to the car, when Angel brought up his Spanish class woes.

"You don't know Spanish?" She was completely surprised.

"Well, I thought I was okay at it," he said. "But according to the scores I've been getting on my quizzes, I suck."

Sarah couldn't help laughing despite the agitation she was feeling about the impending conversation. "I can help you."

Angel turned to her curiously. "You know Spanish?"

"Claro que si." *Of course.*

Angel smiled at her impressed. "Good, because I have a quiz Tuesday, and progress reports go out on Wednesday. If I don't get higher than a D on my quiz, I'm sitting out the game on Friday."

Sarah smiled. "I'll be your private tutor."

They got to the car and Angel leaned on it, pulling her against him. "Mmm, sounds good."

Sarah knew she needed to ask him now or she'd have to wait until tomorrow, and she wanted it over with. She took a deep breath. "Speaking of your game, Angel. Can I ask you something?"

Angel's hands moved all over her back. "Of course."

"Why would Dana be wearing your jersey at the game?" She thought she saw a flicker of panic in his eyes for a second, and then it was gone. He exhaled, glancing away then back at her.

"I don't know, Sarah," he said. "I've hung out with her in the past, but she's always made more out of it than it really was."

Sarah felt something inside her ignite. "Was she your girlfriend?" She was trying so hard not to sound jealous. But she was, *completely*. She'd heard all the stories from Valerie about him and Dana, but hearing it from him set her on fire.

"No," he s said with conviction. "I told you I've never had a girlfriend."

"Have you slept with her?" *What the hell*? She hadn't intended on going there, but the words just flew out and they kept coming.

She saw his eyes widen for a second then go back to normal. He rubbed her back gently. "Does it really matter, Sarah?"

Her heart jumped to her throat. She wanted to scream. What had she expected? Why had she let herself fall for him? This was just one girl. How many other girls was she going to have to deal with?

"So she was never your girlfriend. You just slept with her? Is that what you're planning on doing with me?"

His eyes narrowed, and his expression hardened. "Sarah, as far as I'm concerned, you *are* my girlfriend. Only reason I hadn't said it was because I wasn't sure you took our agreement that way."

Sarah wouldn't listen. All she could think of was the fact that he'd slept with Dana, and it made her sick. "Were you *exclusive* with her?" Her voice dripped with sarcasm.

"No, I wasn't."

The lump in her throat was beginning to suffocate her. *Don't you dare cry*. She tried pulling away from him, but he tightened his grip around her.

"So why does she have your jersey, Angel?" She gulped hard. The words just kept coming, and they wouldn't stop.

"Did you give it to her after you slept with her? How many other girls have your jersey?"

"No one else does." His voice was too calm. "She borrowed it last year and never gave it back."

He tried giving her a peck, but she turned away. "What do you wanna hear, Sarah?"

That only heightened her anger. Was he going to humor her now? She squirmed, trying to get away from him, but her struggle was futile. She was no match for his strong arms. She stopped and looked him in square in the eye. "I want the truth about you and Dana."

"There was no me and her," he insisted. "Even if there had been something, why would I lie?"

"Because maybe you still have feelings for her?"

"What?" His laughter irritated her. "No, babe, the only feelings I have are for you, and they're big time. She's got absolutely *nothing* on you."

Sarah stared at him, desperately wanting to believe him. But if she hurt this much now only a few weeks into this relationship, how would she deal with anything worse? Being around Angel was doing something to her senses. She could hardly believe how wild her emotions had become. It scared her.

Shit! shit! shit! How stupid was he to think Dana's behavior hadn't bothered Sarah? Her deliberate attempts to spite Sarah had been undeniable for weeks. The wounded expression on Sarah's face said it all.

Sarah shook her head. "I'm sorry. I should've known better, Angel."

Angel glared at her. "What the hell does that mean?"

"I mean this is who you are. This is what your world has always been like. Who am I to think I can fit in somehow?

Things like this are going to keep happening, and I don't think I can handle it. I should've never agreed to—"

"Don't even say it." He took her hand and put it to his chest. His heart beat so hard he could feel the pulse raging in his throat. "You're scaring me. I can't believe you don't see how crazy I am about you."

She shook her head. "It's too hard, Angel. I thought I could do this, but I can't. Please try to put yourself in my place. Would you be able to deal with other guys constantly on me? I don't know what I was thinking coming into this. I let myself get caught up in all the passion."

Passion? Is that all this was to her? And what was that other absurdity she'd spat at him? *Him* deal with other guys on *her? Like hell.* He stared at her hard, all the while squeezing her hand, and spoke through his teeth.

"What exactly is *this* to you?"

She turned away for what seemed much too long then finally turned back to him. Her eyes glistened, but she didn't cry.

"My feelings for you are what have me so terrified," she said. "If I didn't care so much, I wouldn't be backing out now before it's too late."

He stared at her in disbelief. *Backing out?* He felt the panic sear through his body. He searched her eyes for more, but there was nothing.

"I'm sorry," she whispered.

His heart still hammered away, but he was strangely relieved. "Stop saying that, Sarah. You have nothing to be sorry about. This is my fault, and I intend on fixing it. But I won't let you back out now, sweetheart. I can't. It may not be too late for you, but there's no turning back for me."

He leaned over and kissed her forehead, then her cheeks, and all around her mouth. "Angel," she whispered.

He continued to kiss her mouth, her chin. She said her feelings for him terrified her. So he wasn't alone in this.

That's all he needed to work with. He'd set everything straight on Monday.

"Angel."

He didn't want to talk anymore, just hold her and kiss her.

"Angel." She pulled away. "How are you gonna fix this? So you get rid of Dana, what about all the others?"

He struggled to mask his exasperation. "There are no others, Sarah. Sure I've hung out with others, but ironically thanks to Dana not as many as I know you're thinking. Dana's been the only thorn in my ass that I haven't been able to get rid of. Until now, I really had no reason to put any effort into it. I let her do and say whatever she pleased. I didn't care."

He kissed her then held her face in his hands. "Trust me, baby, if Dana is gonna cost me being with you, she's gone. Just like that. I'll make sure of it."

A smile slowly lifted the corners of her lips. "Are you gonna have her whacked?"

Angel smiled, relieved at the change in her mood. "I had something a little less violent in mind. But if you want…"

Sarah wrapped her arms around him and leaned her head on his chest. "Just take care of it."

✳✳✳

The next day was far less emotional, though thoughts of yesterday's exchange made things a little tense when he first picked her up. As the hours passed, Sarah seemed a lot better and gave in to her feelings again. They even spent a lustful hour parked in their spot until she had to leave for work.

The night before, she was asleep when Valerie got home, and this morning between talking to Sydney, and Angel picking her up so early, she hadn't had a chance to talk to her.

Valerie was just out of the shower, and Sarah was finally going to hear about her date with Alex.

She was about to walk out to look for her when Valerie walked in, smiling from ear to ear. Sarah smiled just as big.

"So?"

Valerie did a little dance and closed Sarah's door. She motioned Sarah toward the bed and sat down next to her.

"I gotta ask you something, Sarah," she whispered. "Is Angel big? 'Cause Alex is huge. I mean *huge*."

Sarah's jaw dropped. "You slept with him?"

Valerie expression was blank. "Of course not."

Sarah exhaled, relieved.

"I'm on my period," Valerie said. "How embarrassing would that be?"

Sarah's expression made Valerie laugh. "Sarah, how long have I been dreaming of this guy? It's not like I'm a virgin, you know. I slept with Reggie."

"You did?"

"I was with him for like six months. There's only so much you can do before you just can't stand it anymore."

Sarah could feel her face flush, thinking about the things she and Angel had already done. Valerie eyed her. "Have you even seen Angel's—"

"Shh!" Mortified, Sarah jumped up, walked to the door, and peeked out.

The lights were all out. She tiptoed back as if her footsteps might wake someone. Valerie watched and laughed. "What are you doing?"

Sarah held her finger to her mouth again. She sat down on her bed across from Valerie and leaned over. "Yes, I've seen it, and yes, it's big. But since everything about Alex is bigger, I'm not surprised he's huge."

"I haven't seen that many." Valerie made a face. "But his puts the few I have to shame. I'm almost afraid it's gonna hurt."

Sarah stared at her, still unable to believe what she was hearing. "You're really gonna do it?"

"Of course," Valerie said. "Think about it, Sarah. I'm not dumb. I know it's just a matter of a couple of dates before he moves on to the next girl, and I'm okay with that. But I've been lusting over this guy for years. If I blow what may be my only chance to know what it's like to be with him, do you know how much I'm gonna regret it, looking back years from now?"

Sarah continued to stare at her. She still couldn't get over how different she and Valerie thought. "Aren't you afraid of getting pregnant?"

"Nope, I got on the pill when I started going with Reggie," she said. "And I never got off. I figured better safe than sorry."

Sarah didn't blink for a few seconds. The curiosity about what Valerie had actually done with Alex was killing her. But the fear of Valerie asking her about her and Angel's intimacy kept her from asking. As it turned out, she didn't have to. Valerie made herself comfortable on Sarah's bed and began telling her. "He is absolutely the best kisser ever."

Sarah smiled, thinking of Angel's amazing kisses. She'd never had a conversation like this with a girl, and she liked it. Even though she could talk to Sydney about anything, there were certain things she knew she never would, especially about Angel. It just felt wrong. She had told him about them making out and stuff but left out the details.

Valerie continued. "And oh my God, he's an animal. From the moment we started kissing, he barely gave me a second to breathe. You'd think with someone like him, who I'm sure can get it anytime he wants, he wouldn't be so hungry for it."

"Where were you?" Sarah asked.

"Oh, get this." Valerie smiled. "Earlier, before we even left the restaurant I brought up football, you know asking him how different college was compared to high school. So he gets all into it, telling me about it and said his friend has a lot of it on video and maybe someday he can show me it. So later in the evening, he took me to get sushi, and then we walked on the beach. That's when he first kissed me—"

"Did you have to stand on something?" Sarah giggled.

Valerie tried to look mad, but her smile gave her away. "If you must know, he was sitting on the brick wall that separates the beach from the walkway when he pulled me to him and said he *had* to kiss me."

Sarah grinned.

"Anyway!" Valerie said. "After he kissed me, he wouldn't stop and started talking about how we should go to his friend's house to watch the video of him playing. So I said okay. Why not, right? Turns out his friend, who's not in town, has a bachelor pad not too far from where we were. He left Alex a key. Tell me he didn't have that one planned."

Sarah was still trying to picture tiny little Valerie with brawny Alex. He had to be at least 6'4, and looked every bit the linebacker that he was. Valerie was maybe 5'3 and was as petite as they came. "So did you watch the tapes?"

"We started to." Valerie chewed her nail. "But we hadn't been on the sofa very long before he was all over me. I swear if I hadn't been on my period, I so would've gone for it."

Sarah's eyes were as big as saucers again. "Did you tell him you were on your period?"

"No way!" Valerie gasped. "I told him I didn't feel comfortable considering that I'd just met him, which was stupid 'cause next thing you know, I'm on my knees, gagging on his massiveness."

Sarah covered her face and laughed. "Spare me the visual, please!" She took her hand away from her face. "So, did he ask to see you again?"

"Well, he didn't last night. But he asked for my number and called this morning, saying he wanted to see me again."

"You went out with him again already?" Valerie nodded, smiling. "Valerie, maybe he really is into you. You two really seemed to click yesterday."

"We went right back to his friend's place, Sarah. The only thing he wants to get into is this." She pointed at her crotch. "And he will as soon as the curse is gone."

Sarah looked at her disappointed. Valerie didn't seem disappointed at all. She crinkled her nose. "Is that my phone?"

She jumped off the bed and ran to her room. She was gone for a few minutes, and Sarah walked to her room to say goodnight. When she got there, Valerie was on her bed talking on the phone with a big smile on her face. "Alex," she mouthed, smiling.

Sarah did the Valerie, and ran to listen in, leaning against Valerie's ear.

"So cancel those plans," he said. "I'll pick you up at seven."

"All right, I guess."

"You guess?"

Valerie laughed. "I'm kidding, Alex. Yes, that sounds good."

There was a long silence on the other end, then finally he sighed. "You're real funny, Z."

"You're just too easy."

"Yeah, well, you're not," he said. "I gotta go. I'm up at five tomorrow, but don't forget."

"I'll try."

"You know what—"

"You see!" She smiled. "Of course, I won't forget. Better?"

"Much better," he said. "Good night."

Sarah watched Valerie flip her phone shut. "You are so bad. He was really getting mad."

"Nah," Valerie said. "He knows I like playing with him. He just goes along with it, acting the part."

"Why'd he call you Z?"

"For Zuniga," Valerie said. "It's a football thing I guess. He says he calls just about all his pals at school by their last names. But I've noticed he only does it when I really push his buttons."

Sarah cocked an eyebrow. "I don't know Valerie. He saw you all weekend, and he's calling already for another date?" She got off the bed. "And what plans are you canceling?"

"Oh, when he asked if I was busy on Wednesday. I told him I had plans. I'm telling you it's probably just throwing him for a loop that he hasn't gotten in my pants yet. As soon as he does, I can guarantee you he's gone."

"So why give it up then?"

Valerie looked at her sympathetically as she got up in front of the mirrored closet door. "Silly little, Sarah," she said. "You really think he's gonna hang around forever, just to get some of this?"

Sarah frowned, but before she could say anything, Valerie continued, "Besides I told you. I'm not looking for a relationship. I'm perfectly happy with the chance to be with *the* Alex Moreno just a few times. This is all I've ever wanted."

Sarah wasn't so sure about that. She didn't care what Valerie said; she knew what she heard. Alex sounded pissed. But if Valerie insisted, what could she say? Valerie did know Alex a lot better than she did.

The phone rang again, and they both jumped then exchanged glances. Valerie looked at the caller ID.

"It's him again!" She sat down on the bed, and Sarah assumed the position right next to her ear.

"Hello?"

"Z, one question."

"What?"

"What *were* your plans Wednesday night?"

Valerie turned and looked at Sarah wide-eyed and covered her mouth. "Um, nothing really," she said. "I was just gonna go out with my girlfriends. Why?"

There was silence again on the other end. "Just wondering," he said. "All right, I'll let you go to sleep now. See you Wednesday."

Valerie smiled and said goodnight. She looked at Sarah, who was giving her a knowing look. "Before you say anything," she held her hand up, "I've already told you guys are territorial, especially ones with such big egos. That's all it is. It means nothing."

She looked so smug and sounded so sure, but Sarah felt uneasy. She would've never believed it, but she was beginning to worry about Valerie playing games with Alex.

CHAPTER 12

By Monday, everything was back to normal with Sarah and Angel. They'd never spent their morning or lunch breaks together. So when Angel saw Dana by her locker just before lunch, he figured it was as good a time as any to take care of this once and for all.

Two friends were with her. Her eyes brightened when she saw him approach. She quickly dismissed her friends. "I'll talk to you guys later."

"Hey." She smiled big at Angel, tossing her hair back. "What's up?"

"Do you have a minute?"

"For you? Of course."

"I know what you were doing Friday, Dana. It's gotta stop."

Her smile dissolved, and she glanced into her locker. "I don't know what you mean."

"Sure you do." He spoke calmly.

She stared straight ahead. "You gave me that jersey, don't you remember?"

"No, I lent it to you, and you never gave it back."

She shifted her weight and finally met his eyes. Angel saw right through her attempt to appear injured. "You want it back? Is that what this is about?"

"Yeah, I do. And I want you to stop doing everything else you've been doing, Dana. It's getting old."

"You never complained before."

"Well, things are different now." Angel could see the rage in her eyes. Knowing how much she loved making scenes, he was glad they were the only ones left in the hall.

"Did *she* tell you to do this?" He heard the venom in her words loud and clear.

Angel wasn't about to give her the pleasure. "To be honest, she's never mentioned you."

Dana laughed, attempting to sound sarcastic but fell short. She slammed the locker shut, and it echoed loudly in the empty hallway. She scowled at him, lips almost quivering. "You think *your* jersey is the only one I have?"

"No, I'm sure you have plenty."

"Go to hell, Angel!" She began to stalk away. After only a few steps, she stopped and turned around. "And don't flatter yourself. You don't have to worry about me speaking to you ever again."

"Thank you."

With that, she spun around and walked away in a hurry. All things considered, it went a lot better than he had hoped for. He walked out to the cafeteria, feeling an enormous weight taken off his shoulders. He couldn't help smiling. His problems with Dana were over.

✳✳✳

Practice was unexpectedly called off early that afternoon because one of the players was seriously injured, requiring paramedics to be called in. Angel had looked up at the bleachers and saw Sarah completely absorbed in her running. She hadn't noticed the team was off the field.

He could wait for her to finish. He hadn't hung out with the guys after practice in a while. Now he had a few minutes.

Angel had just stepped out of the gym with Eric and Romero when he saw Dana rush toward him, looking very determined. "Can I talk to you?"

He kept walking. "Go ahead."

"I mean alone." She glanced at Eric and Romero. They both turned to Angel, who shrugged.

"We'll be over here, man." Eric pointed. They didn't walk too far, sitting on a table nearby in front of where the girls on the flag team were practicing.

"How dare you dismiss me just like that!" She crossed her arms and stood in front of him, forcing him to stop. "As if I'd never meant anything to you."

He bit his tongue, not wanting to be cruel, but he had Sarah to think about. "Shit happens, Dana. I'm seeing someone now. I can't be dealing with you." He waved his hand up and down in front of her. "With this."

"Did you know she slept with Jesse Strickland?"

Angel laughed, though he didn't feel the least bit of humor. "Is that what he said?"

"That's what everyone is saying. I'm surprised you haven't heard."

"I don't listen to bullshit." She'd managed to stun him, but he'd die before he'd let on. He knew it was all a bunch of crap, but the idea alone of a rumor like that about Sarah sickened him.

"I don't mean to hurt you, Angel. I just thought you should know."

The inflated attempt to sound sympathetic was infuriating. Angel was never one to be disrespectful, especially to girls, but he could feel the blood curdling in his veins. Sarah had been close to dumping his ass—too damn close—and for this? He was done being nice.

He glared at her. "Don't worry. You could never hurt me, Dana. I'd have to care about you for that."

She shrugged. "And I suppose she knows about us?"

Angel chuckled. "There was never an us, Dana, and you know it. You made up all that crap, not me." The tears welled up in her eyes. He rolled his eyes and backed away. "God, don't start this shit."

He turned and began to walk toward Eric and Romero.

"You made love to me, you bastard!" She yelled. "Don't you remember that?"

His stomach dropped. *Fuck*! He spun around and charged toward her. He saw her eyes open wide in alarm, but she stood her ground firmly. He walked right up to her face and spoke through his teeth just loud enough for her to hear, but his words were strong and cutting. "Get this through your head. We never made love. We had sex, cold meaningless sex like you've had with many others. It meant nothing to me. *You* mean nothing to me. Stay out of my fucking life. I mean it, Dana."

With her mouth half-open, she stared at him. Her eyes grew wide, then she turned and hurried away with her face buried in her hands. Her friends stood by the gym door, waiting to console her, and he heard her sob as they turned the corner.

He took a deep breath and walked back slowly toward the guys, ignoring the whispers and staring faces of all who had been standing around.

Romero was shaking his head. "Dude, I hope you told that bitch off."

Angel nodded, still feeling a little shaky. He hadn't intended on being so harsh, but the words had just spewed out. He stood there, still reeling from what Dana had said about Sarah. He didn't want the guys to notice that Dana had gotten to him, but he couldn't even force a smile.

Eric seemed concerned. "Are you okay, man?"

Angel nodded again and glanced back in Sarah's direction. He turned back at Eric. "You think I should tell Sarah about this?"

"Hell no!" Romero said.

"Nah, I would," Eric said.

"You would?" Angel asked.

Romero shook his head, eyes closed. "Fuck Dana! Why you gonna get Sarah all upset 'cause of her?"

Eric made a gesture, looking around. "She's gonna hear about it eventually. I guarantee it. Dana was loud, dude. They'll probably add to it too. I'm just saying, if it were me,

I'd come clean. It's not like you did anything wrong. Just leave the part out about her yelling that she slept with you. Sarah's cool, dude. She'll get it. Just don't make that big a deal out of it."

Angel eyed them both. There was no way either of them could know Sarah had almost broken things off because of Dana.

Feeling as if he'd swallowed a brick, he turned to see Sarah walking toward him. She smiled and blew him a kiss. He managed to smile, but, damn, he dreaded having another conversation about Dana with her.

✳✳✳

No one was home, when Sarah and Angel got to his house. Angel walked Sarah to the den and put his book bag down on the coffee table.

"I'm thirsty." He walked toward the kitchen. "You want something to drink?"

"Yeah, I'll take water or a diet soda if you have it."

Angel walked to the kitchen and grabbed a couple of waters out of the refrigerator. When he walked back into the living room, Sarah was on her knees on the sofa looking at the pictures that sat on the shelf behind it. She picked one up to get a closer look. Angel saw her eyes brighten and knew immediately which one it was. He put the waters down on the coffee table.

"Oh my God, is this you?"

"Give me that." He reached for it.

Sarah pulled away. "You're so cute!" She giggled.

He tackled her on the couch, but she hid it behind her. He held her down, trying to take the picture from her. She squirmed and laughed hysterically. "What a cutie you were with your little mullet."

"It's not a mullet." His arms were under her now, searching for the picture. She could barely breath; she was laughing so hard.

"Okay, okay!" she shrieked. "You can have it."

Angel took it from her and put it back on the table face down. He leaned over her and kissed her. They made out for a while but straightened out quickly when they heard something outside. It turned out to be nothing, and Angel lay right back against her.

"What time do your parents get home?"

"Different times." He continued to peck her. "Depends how busy they are."

"So they could get home any minute?"

"Um hum." He began to kiss her neck.

"Then get off me," she giggled, squirming and arching her back at the touch of his tongue on her neck. She pushed her hands against his chest. "Angel, I'm serious. If your parents walk in, I'd die."

He kissed her long and deep one last time then sat up and straightened his pants. "I can't stand for a while."

Sarah smiled, looking at the tent in his pants. She sat up and rubbed his shoulder. "You'll be okay."

"Oh yeah, just give me a few minutes." He grabbed the remote and turned the television on. The first thing they saw was a heavy older woman being interviewed about her twenty cats on the news. "Okay, I'm good now."

Sarah gasped. Then immediately burst into laughter. "That is so mean."

He changed the channel, flipping around for a while and finally left it on an episode of a reality show about building motorcycles. He pretended to be into it. "I talked with Dana today."

Sarah pulled her arm off his shoulder, but he grabbed a hold of her hand. She'd told him that morning she didn't need to hear the details about his talk with Dana so long as he took care of it. "I'm only bringing it up 'cause you're probably gonna hear about it."

She stared at him.

"I'd already talked to her earlier in the day and thought that would be it," he said. "But I should've known better when she hadn't said too much."

He could see Sarah searching his eyes. "She made a scene after practice."

"A scene?"

"Yeah, a scene." He hugged her and pushed her back gently on the sofa. "Sarah, it's nothing. I wouldn't have even brought it up, but I didn't want you to hear about it from someone else."

"What did she say?"

Angel tried kissing her, but she pulled away. "Sarah, let's not do this again, babe. Seriously, the only thing that matters is that I straightened things out, and she won't be acting stupid anymore."

"Are you sure?"

"No question about it." He kissed her and hoped he was right.

She stared at him for a few moments. "Okay."

Thankful it hadn't turned into another dreaded discussion about his feelings for Dana, Angel groaned and buried his face in her neck. He pressed himself against her, and his hands made their way down her body. He started putting his hand up her blouse when they heard someone at the door.

Sarah jumped, pushing Angel off her. It was Alex. Sarah pulled her notebook out of her book bag, and Angel put a sofa pillow on his lap.

Alex grinned. "Did I interrupt your *studying*?"

Angel ignored him but smiled and drank his water.

Sarah sat straight faced with her chin up. "As a matter of fact, we *are* studying. Angel has a very important quiz tomorrow."

Alex had already grabbed the remote from the table and was flipping through the channels. "Well, you're not doin' it here." He looked back at Angel. "The guys are gonna be here any minute. We're watching the game."

Angel was confused at first then it dawned on him—Monday night football. He glanced at the TV. "Don't tell me Chargers are playing?"

Sarah shot him a stern look. "You have to study, Angel. The quiz is tomorrow. No buts about it."

Alex tsked. "Sucks to be you." He motioned for Angel to get off the sofa. "Go in the kitchen. I told those guys they better not show up empty handed, and I'm ordering pizza. I'm gonna need this table."

Angel and Sarah moved into the kitchen. They settled down on the counter in the center island. Sarah turned out to be a tough tutor, not wanting to waver from the task at hand. Angel didn't make it easy with all his continual kissing and groping. She pulled away, giggling from his ear nibbling.

"Okay Angel, pay attention. This is easy stuff. '*Donde estan*' means 'where are.' They looked up and saw Romero come in the kitchen. He pulled his fingers across his lips to show his lips were zipped.

Sarah continued. "You already know all these words." She pointed at a list of words in the book. "So '*Donde estan mis zapatos?*' means 'where are my shoes?' and '*Donde estan mis llaves?*' means 'where are my keys?' Now you try it."

Before Angel could start, Sarah's cell phone rang. "I'll just send it to voicemail."

"Nah, get it." Angel welcomed the break. "I'm gonna grab some pizza anyway."

She answered and stood up, walking toward the patio door. The guys in the other room cheered loudly, and she covered her free ear to try to hear better. She motioned to Angel that she was stepping outside. Angel nodded, barely paying attention.

"Did they score?" he asked, turning his attention toward the den.

"Sure did!" Romero said, walking toward him. He'd run back out when the guys started cheering.

They both walked over to the counter where the pizza was. "Hey, try this one," Romero said. *"Donde estan mis bolas?"* Where are my balls?

Angel laughed, grabbing a slice and leaned against the counter.

Romero shook his head, his face disgusted. He took a quick look out the window to make sure Sarah wasn't listening. "Dude, you're that whipped you're missing the Charger game?"

Angel smiled, chewing his pizza. "I have to study, man. If I don't do well on this quiz tomorrow, I sit out Friday's game."

Romero shook his head still unconvinced. "Well you're missing a hell of a game." He grabbed another slice before heading back into the den.

Angel frowned and finished up his slice of pizza. He glanced out the window and saw Sarah still on her phone, laughing. She saw him and stuck her tongue out. He smiled and walked away, taking advantage of the time to watch a little of the game.

He was just outside the kitchen when he heard the patio door open. He walked back in and saw Sarah standing at the door facing out. He caught the tail end of her conversation.

"Of course not," she said. "Don't be silly. I'm thrilled for you. This is huge. You know me. If I was there, I'd be jumping all over you, celebrating."

Angel's eyebrow went up.

"Yes. Yes. I swear. Okay, talk to you later."

She hung up and turned around. She looked a little surprised that Angel was standing there. "That was Sydney."

Angel's expression softened, and he nodded, walking around the island to get another slice of pizza. "What's going on with her?" he asked without turning around.

***

Sarah bit her lip, wincing, thankful that his back was turned at that moment. She knew she had said the next time he referred to Sydney as a female she'd correct him, but somehow now didn't quite seem like the right time or place.

Something told her Angel's studying would be shot, and she didn't want to be responsible for him not playing on Friday.

By now, Angel had turned around and was facing her. Careful to not further the already growing lie she had to think about her wording. "Sydney accepted an early music scholarship to Columbia University in New York."

Angel's eyes narrowed a little. "And she didn't think you'd be happy?"

He walked over to join her. She'd already sat down where they'd been studying.

"Well." She cleared her throat. "I was quiet for a second when I heard Columbia 'cause Syd had always said UCLA was the ultimate goal. So Syd thought maybe I was upset because Columbia was so far. But I'm actually getting used to the distance between us. Besides with technology being what it is now, it's almost like we're not even apart. We talk so much on the phone." As soon as she said that last part, she was wishing she could take it back. She kept forgetting Angel would eventually know the truth and little details like that would only make it harder for him to understand.

"Yeah," Angel nodded. "Then there's email. No matter how far away, I'm sure you two will keep in touch."

Sarah was getting nervous about the whole wording thing. She didn't know how much longer she could keep doing it before Syd's name being repeated so much began to sound weird. She tried changing the subject.

She nodded her head in agreement. "I'm starving."

Alex and Eric walked in. Angel stood up and walked over to the pizza. "Is it over?" Angel asked.

"No, it's halftime." Eric said

Angel put two slices on a paper plate then grabbed another for himself. Alex and Eric were already eating their pizza, leaning against the counter. Sarah was thankful for the interruption, but her relief quickly turned into dismay.

Angel set the plate down in front of her then grabbed a soda out of the fridge.

"So, Sydney's a musician, huh?" He handed her the can of soda.

She took it and nodded, refusing to refuel the conversation. He came around and sat back down next to her. "What does she play?"

She took a long drink of her soda and looked at Alex and Eric. They were both eyeing her. "Saxophone."

"Really?" Angel seemed surprised.

"That's a turn on." Alex said, just as Romero walked in.

"What's a turn on?" Romero asked. He took a slice of pizza and stood next to Alex.

"Her friend plays the saxophone." Alex said.

Romero's eyebrows shot up. "A girl?"

She was about to shake her head, but didn't get the chance. "Of course, ass." Alex shoved Romero. "Like I'd say that about a dude."

Angel and Eric laughed. Sarah wanted to groan. The testosterone in the room was suffocating.

"Really?" Romero said. "A chick that really knows how to blow, huh?"

The guys all laughed. Sarah sunk in her seat. This was a nightmare. Now they were all in on her lie. She felt Angel rub her back. He mistook her look of despair for annoyance. "Easy," he said. "That's her best friend."

Romero peered at her. "Oh yeah? Well, introduce."

"She likes playing the saxophone, Romero, not the piccolo Pete." Alex grinned.

Eric almost spit out his food, and even Sarah had to laugh.

"She's in Arizona," Angel said, getting up for more pizza. He looked through three empty boxes before finding one with any in it. "We've gone through three pizzas already?"

Alex looked at him wide-eyed. "You guys are fat. Those were extra-large too. There's only four of us."

"I had some too," Sarah said, holding her hand up.

Alex looked at her plate unimpressed. "Sweetheart, I had two slices before the pizza even made it to the kitchen."

Romero walked over and leaned on the sink in front of her. "Arizona, huh? Well, have her come down for a visit."

"Dude, get the hell out of here!" Alex said.

"What?" Romero protested.

"No, I'm serious. Get out of here," Alex smirked.

Angel laughed sitting back down next to Sarah. "Yeah, get out of here. I gotta study."

Romero leaned over closer to Angel and looked at him very seriously. *"Donde estan mis bolas?"*

This time it was Sarah that almost spit up her food. Angel rolled his eyes.

Eric had already walked back to the den. "It's back on!" he yelled.

Alex and Romero each grabbed a slice to go. They weren't even out the door when Angel was all over her again. She sat there kind of limp. "What's wrong?" he asked. "You feeling tired?"

"No." Just underhanded and deceitful.

He pecked her a few more times. "Maybe Sydney can come and visit sometime. We can all go out. Don't worry. I'll handle Romero."

Sarah hoped he didn't hear her thunderous gulp and forced a smile. "Yeah, maybe." *Not in a million years.*

This was totally out of hand. She had to think of a way to fix this. Fast.

CHAPTER 13

Angel scored an eighty on his Spanish quiz and was happy to be in the game that week. It was an important one too. They were playing their rivals, and both teams were in the running for the playoffs.

Sarah sat in the stands with Sofia, Valerie, and Valerie's friend Monica. Angel's parents had flown out earlier that evening to Florida for Alex's game the next day. Sofia was Angel's responsibility until they got back. Rather than leaving her alone at the restaurant tonight, Angel got the go ahead to close up early and have her tag along with them.

Sarah didn't mind having her along for the night. She liked Sofia, and ever since Sarah started practicing with the track team, they'd gotten a lot closer. Sarah felt bad though. The relay team never even came close to the times Sarah put on the board when she stood in for the fourth place runner during practice. The coach was always going on and on about how heartbroken he was that she wouldn't be sticking around for next semester. She'd started to keep some of the comments to herself because Angel would get so annoyed by them.

The entire week had gone without incident, and now the game seemed to as well. There were a few guys from another school who sat near the girls. One of them was hitting on Sofia, making Sarah a little nervous. She'd looked out onto the field several times, but as far as she could tell, Angel hadn't noticed anything.

When the game was over, Sarah stood against Angel's Mustang in the parking lot. Valerie and the girls, including

Sofia, talked to the guys they'd met at the game over by Valerie's car parked just a few spaces over.

Angel had given Sarah the keys to his car in case she and Sofia wanted to sit in it while they waited for him after the game. Sarah had the door open and the radio on. She motioned to Sofia to come over, and she did right away. "What?"

"You're making me nervous," Sarah whispered, trying not to sound like a nag.

"Why?"

"You don't think Angel is gonna be mad if he sees you hanging out with all these guys?"

"That's Alex," Sofia smiled. "Angel's not so bad. He won't be thrilled, but he wouldn't do anything, unless the guys are being disrespectful, and they're not. They're really nice."

Within seconds, Sarah regretted having called Sofia over to her. The guy who seemed most interested in Sofia followed her, while everyone else followed him. Now they were all standing around Angel's car, five guys and four girls. None of them were nearly as intimidating as Angel and his friends, with two of them being short and chunky, and another looking like he was too young to be with them. Sarah knew Angel still wouldn't be happy about it.

The one interested in Sofia was the tallest, best looking of the bunch. Sarah looked up and saw a group of guys walking toward them. It was dark, and they were still relatively far, but Sarah could tell it was Angel, Eric, and Romero just by the way they walked.

When they got close enough, Sarah made eye contact with Angel. He glanced at her then at the group of people standing around his car. Sarah was the only one standing away from everyone. He raised an eyebrow, but smirked.

She knew he couldn't possibly think she'd be dumb enough to stand around his car flirting, but was still nervous for Sofia. She was off toward the front end of his car, talking to the guy who had been hitting on her all night.

Romero made the first comment. "What is this a fucking party?"

Sarah saw Eric speed up when he saw Sofia talking to that guy. "What are you doing over there, Sof?"

Angel hadn't noticed Sofia until Eric said it and turned to them with a frown. The other guys stepped away immediately to let them get by.

Angel walked straight to Sarah and kissed her. "What's going on?" His voice was hushed. "Who are these crumbs?"

Sarah turned toward the group. "I don't know them. They're just some guys the girls were talking to at the game."

"The girls?"

She smiled and hugged him hard. "Yes, the girls."

"Who's that with Sofie?"

"I dunno." She shrugged. "But they all seem nice enough. She said you wouldn't mind."

Angel frowned, looking over at the boy who was making Sofia smile. "Yeah, well, her ass better get in the car before I do mind."

Sarah didn't have to hear it twice. She turned in Sofia's direction. She was going to tell her they were leaving, but Eric was already there. She couldn't hear what Eric said, but whatever it was, it made the guy she was talking to angry.

"Who are you?" the guy asked with an attitude.

"Who the fuck are *you*?" Eric barked back.

Sofia jumped in between them, and in a second, Angel and Romero were there at first holding Eric back then having to be held back themselves when they saw the other guys headed toward Eric.

The girls tried holding them back. Monica helped Sofia with Eric, who was the most adamant, although, Romero was, as usual, the hardest to hold back. The poor guy tried to stand tough, but still looked terrified. The guy's friends managed to get him away before he got hurt.

Sarah struggled with Angel, pleading with him, "Stop it, Angel. He was just talking to her for God's sake."

When the guys were finally far enough away, Sofia let go of Eric. Looking very disgusted, Sofia stalked away to Angel's car. She climbed in the back seat and slammed the door.

Angel's head spun around, and he was about to say something to Sofia.

"Let's go," Sarah said.

"She slammed my door." He looked at Sarah in exasperation.

"Let's just go, please."

Angel and Sarah walked back to the car. Romero and Eric followed.

Once in the car, Angel turned and glared at Sofia. "What's the matter with you?"

"What's the matter with *you*?" Sofia shot back.

Sarah sunk in the passenger seat. Eric stuck his head in Sarah's window. "Who was that, Sof?"

"Nobody." She crossed her arms in front of her.

Romero stuck his head in Angel's window. "What happened?"

Sofia's exhaled loudly, sounding more like a groan.

"What's that about?" Angel asked.

"How many brothers do I have anyway?"

Angel was about to say something when Sofia put her hand over her face and shuddered. "Sofie?"

"Is she crying?" Eric stuck his head in further.

"She's crying?" Romero asked.

"All right!" Sarah sat up. "That's it. All of you out." She pushed Eric's head out the window and shoved Angel to get him out of the car. His head clunked as it hit Romero's.

"Ow!" Romero yelped.

"Well, move your ass!" Angel said.

Angel got out, and they all walked away grudgingly. Valerie and Monica were still there, and they joined them.

Sarah turned around to face Sofia. "Are you okay?"

Sofia shook her head, her hand still over her face. Sarah reached over and rubbed her knee. Sofia's big chest rose high as she inhaled and fell as she exhaled slowly. "They mean well," Sarah offered.

"I know," Sofia sighed. "But just once I wish I could be like any other girl and hang out with guys, without all of them turning into cavemen."

Sarah chuckled. "They're just not used to it. They still see you as their little Sofie. They'll get used to it eventually."

Sofia rolled her eyes and wiped her face. Sarah handed her a tissue. Sofia blew her nose and sat up. "You know what the stupidest thing is?"

"What?"

"They have nothing to worry about anyway."

Sarah wasn't so sure about that. She'd seen the way the boy looked at Sofia. "What do you mean?"

"I'm saving myself for one guy, and I'm beginning to think he knows it."

Sarah's eyes opened wide. "Really? Who?"

Sofia held the tissue to her nose, looking at Sarah apprehensively. She looked out the window to make sure the guys were far enough to not hear. "You promise you won't tell Angel?"

Sarah nodded but gulped, not sure she wanted to know anymore. Sofia shut her eyes tight then stared at Sarah again. She whispered something, but Sarah didn't catch it the first time. Sarah peeked out the window to make sure they were still far enough. She saw Eric glance their way then back at Angel. She leaned closer to Sofia.

"What?" Sarah whispered.

"Eric."

Sarah stared at her speechlessly. They both glanced out the window. Angel and Eric were on their way back toward the car. "Please don't say anything," Sofia pleaded.

"I won't."

What made her think Eric knew she was saving herself for him? Sarah wanted to ask a lot of things, but the guys were too close. It'd have to wait until the next time they got a moment alone.

They went to the beach and made a bonfire. Sarah watched and observed the whole night, careful that Angel didn't catch on. She couldn't believe she'd never noticed before. Well, she had, but she'd never made anything out of it. It'd always seemed so innocent. It still did, only after what Sofia had said tonight, some things seemed a little questionable.

Eric lingered around Sofia the whole night. They even went for a walk just the two of them, and Angel hadn't thought anything of it. She wouldn't have, either, before tonight. She always thought Eric was just being a sweetheart. Eric knew Angel was busy with Sarah, so he was just keeping an eye on Sofia. Right?

Sarah thought about how Eric always offered to give her rides to and from the restaurant and how many times she'd spoken to Angel on the phone and he'd mentioned that Eric was there hanging out early in the morning or late in the evening but always when Sofia was home. Still, she thought of how Eric seemed so loyal to Angel and his brothers. She just couldn't picture him actually doing anything with Sofia.

Between watching Sofia and Eric and being disgusted with Valerie's outrageous behavior, Sarah had been pretty quiet the whole night. She watched Valerie, who'd had way too much to drink, let Romero peck her softly on the lips. She'd been flirting with him since they got there.

"What's wrong?" Angel asked.

Sarah's eyes met his, and she shook her head. But he knew better. "You haven't said much tonight—something bothering you?"

Sarah sighed and motioned toward Valerie and Romero. Angel glanced up at them. Romero was sitting on an ice chest, and Valerie was on his lap, giggling. He turned back to Sarah and shrugged.

Angel and his brothers obviously didn't talk too much about their romantic affairs. Angel knew they'd gone out but didn't realize Valerie had finally gotten what she wanted. Just this past Tuesday she'd "bedded" Alex Moreno. And now here she was, shamelessly carrying on with Romero.

Sarah frowned. "What's Alex gonna say?"

"Sarah, babe, I hope you don't think Alex is really into Valerie. I mean, she's cool and everything, but it really doesn't matter with Alex. He's never been into the relationship thing." He chuckled. "I'm sure he's making full use of his hotel room tonight."

He must've seen the disgusted look on Sarah's face because his smile immediately dissolved. "Of course, I think it's appalling."

Sarah rolled her eyes. "I know he's not into the relationship thing, but you don't think he's gonna be upset at all that she's doing this with one of his friends?"

"Nah." Angel shook his head. "Alex isn't like that. He could care less. I mean, don't tell Valerie that. I don't want to hurt her feelings or anything. But I'm sure Alex had his fun and is already on to the next. That's just the way he is." Sarah stared at him. "That's him, Sarah, not me."

"That's not what I was thinking. I'm just hoping you're right. I'd hate for his feelings to be hurt."

"Trust me, babe," Angel smiled. "I know my brother. He's gonna be just fine with it."

Sarah remembered hearing Alex on the phone with Valerie, and how he called back just to ask what her plans *had* been that Wednesday. Something told her Angel might be wrong about this.

CHAPTER 14

Saturday mornings were always busy at the restaurant. Angel's parents wouldn't be back until that evening, so Sarah offered to come in and help. Angel picked her up an hour before they opened. Sarah smiled when she saw Sofia in the car also. She was anxious to speak with her alone.

No sooner were they in the restaurant than Sofia pulled Sarah by the arm. "I'll take Sarah to the back, so she can try on one of the shirts."

Angel frowned. "That's okay, Sofie. Sarah, you don't have to wear a uniform, babe."

Sarah lifted her chin. "But I like the shirts." She turned to Sofia. "I'll take a medium."

Angel smiled, and she blew him a kiss. When they got to the back room, Sofia closed the door behind them and grinned wickedly.

"Oh my God, I've been dying to talk to someone about this, and you're the only person I can."

Sarah wasn't sure she wanted to be the only one that knew. From the very beginning, Angel didn't even have to say it. It was so obvious how protective he and his brothers were about Sofia. She thought of Alex breaking the head off the turtle figurine and smiled feebly.

Sofia opened a drawer and grabbed a polo with the restaurant's logo on it and an apron. She handed them to Sarah. She continued eagerly, apparently unaware of Sarah's sudden lack of enthusiasm. "I told him!"

Sarah gulped. "Told him what?"

Sofia glanced at the door then whispered, "That I'm saving myself for him."

"What?" Sarah's heart raced. She couldn't believe what she was hearing.

Sofia put her hands over her mouth and giggled. Sarah couldn't help laughing too. She felt silly, but Sofia's attitude about the whole thing was startling. *Was she crazy?*

Sarah clutched the polo and the apron in both hands in front of her face. Her eyes were wide open. "What did he say?"

Sofia's face lit up even more. "He kissed me."

Sarah blinked, unable to find words. Sofia didn't seem to notice Sarah's anxiety. She mistook Sarah's previous nervous laughter for excitement and went on.

"I've never been kissed before. But he was amazing. He knew exactly what he was doing. I never wanted it to stop. I was so glad your cousin was there to keep Romero busy. He probably would've ruined everything. I can hardly wait for it to happen again."

Again?

"Oh but there's so much more I wanna tell you." Sofia gushed.

"More?"

"Yeah, there's more than just kissing."

Sarah wasn't sure, but she could swear it was getting hot in that room.

"I mean he's so much more to me than just a crush. I'm really falling for him, Sarah. It killed me that I knew he was thinking the worst about me and that guy after the game, so I was glad when he suggested we go for a walk. That's when I told him."

Sarah stared at Sofia. "So, what's going to happen now?" There was no way her brothers would allow it.

Sofia looked defiant. "I don't know. All I know is I want to be with him, and no one is going to stop me."

This was only getting worse. There'd be hell to pay if Eric was honestly considering going forward with this.

"You have to be careful, Sofia. You don't want him to get hurt." She thought of Alex's temper. That would be a world of hurt.

"He wants to wait until I'm seventeen to tell Angel. But that's not until next year."

That sounded reasonable to Sarah, but she could tell by the expression on Sofia's face that wasn't going to happen.

There was a knock at the door, and Sarah jumped.

"She's still getting dressed, Angel."

"All right, we're getting ready to open in a few minutes."

"Okay." Sarah finished adjusting her apron. "We'll be right out."

She almost lost her balance when Sofia hugged her. "I'm so glad I have someone to talk to about this."

At first, Angel had protested her helping, but, of course, Sarah insisted. Now he watched as she waited on a table, smiling and talking to the customers as if it were second nature.

Angel went back and forth from the hostess desk to the back office where he was trying to finish up writing a help wanted ad he was going to upload to the local newspaper online that week. His parents were looking to hire a few more cooks and a couple more people to wait tables.

He thought about asking Sarah if she wanted the job waiting tables, but something told him she might be insulted. Plus she had her weekends full already babysitting. She was so damn devoted to the families she worked for. He knew she wouldn't want to let them down.

The phone on the desk rang, disrupting Angel's thoughts.

"Angel?"

He was surprised to hear Valerie's voice. "Hey, Val, what's up?"

"Sorry I'm calling on this line, but Sarah's not answering her phone."

"It's all right," he said. "She's waiting tables. She doesn't have her phone on her. I'll get her for you."

"Wait." She sounded nervous. "Maybe you should tell her 'cause she's probably gonna freak."

Angel sat up slowly. "What is it?"

"Sydney was in a car accident this morning."

Angel gripped the receiver a little tighter. "Is she okay?"

There was silence on the other end for a second, and then Valerie cleared her throat. "*Her,* uh, parents were calling from the hospital, but they don't know anything yet. I have all the information: the hospital and the number and stuff. They gave me their cell phone number in case she doesn't have it, so she can call them directly."

Angel took all the information down and hung up. He picked up the phone again and started dialing Sydney's parents' cell. He thought it'd be better if he knew something before he laid the news on Sarah.

He let it ring twice then changed his mind. It was already his fault they hadn't been able to get a hold of her earlier. He knew she'd want to know as soon as possible. He hung up and walked out into the restaurant. Sarah was walking toward him with a tray in her hand. She smiled proudly. He walked straight to her and took the tray away, setting it down on the bar counter.

He looked over his shoulder. "Sof, take over Sarah's tables."

He put his attention back on Sarah and took her by the hand into the office.

"What's going on?" Sarah asked.

Angel sat her down on the chair in front of the desk and closed the door. Sarah began to look worried. "What's wrong," she said. "Is this about the coffee I spilled? 'Cause it didn't get on—"

He knelt in front of her and spoke calmly. "It's about Sydney."

Sarah's eyes opened wide. He could see her searching his eyes. "Angel, I was gonna—"

"She was in a car accident this morning, baby."

Her expression went slowly from confusion to panic. "What? Oh my God!" She jumped from her seat. Angel moved out of her way and watched her rush over to her purse. She pulled out her cell phone. Her hands shook as she fumbled with her phone.

He walked over to her and put his hands on her shoulders. "Relax okay? I have Syd's parents' cell phone number so you can call them directly."

Her eyes shot up from her phone. They were already welled up with tears. "You talked to them?"

"No." He walked toward her. "They called Valerie at your aunt's when they couldn't get a hold of you, and she called here when she couldn't get a hold of you either."

Sarah inhaled deeply, her face crumbling. "Did she know anything?"

Angel shook his head. "No." He turned around and walked over to the desk picking up the paper with all the information. He walked back and handed it to her. Her breathing was all over the place. "Sarah, calm down."

She took the paper from him and started dialing. Angel watched as she waited for someone to answer. He braced himself, hoping for the best.

"Frances?" She was almost in tears. "Yeah, it's me. How's Sydney?"

She clutched the paper Angel had handed to her at her chest and listened. She stared at Angel. "Oh, thank God," she said. "I was so scared."

Angel exhaled relieved. "No, no, I'm glad you called." she said. "So, what happened? Why was an ambulance called?

She was on the phone for a few more minutes, and Angel sat down on the desk chair, leaning all the way back. He watched as Sarah hung up and looked at him. He held his arms out for her to come to him. She walked over and sat on his lap. He wrapped his arms around her. "So, she's okay?"

Sarah nodded. "The ambulance was called because Sydney complained of pain in the stomach. They wanted to make sure there was no internal bleeding."

"Was there?"

Sarah shook her head and took a deep breath. "No."

Angel leaned his forehead against hers. "How are *you* doing?"

She smiled weakly and shrugged. "I was just imagining the worst."

"Sarah." He kissed her head. "Tomorrow, when my parents are back, we can drive out there, so you can see her."

She pulled away from him and sat up. "That's like a five-hour drive, Angel."

"That's okay," he caressed her cheek and smiled. "We can leave early."

She stared at him blankly and then shook her head. "I already told the Salcido's I'd watch their kids tomorrow afternoon. I can't cancel on them now. I'll be fine once I talk to Sydney."

"You sure?"

"Yeah." She smiled. "But thanks, that's very sweet of you."

She stood. "I better go help Sofia. She's probably swamped." She slipped her cell phone in her pocket.

Angel frowned. "You don't have to go back to waiting tables, Sarah. What if Sydney calls you?"

Sarah smiled and patted her pocket. "I have my phone." She walked toward the door, stopped, then rushed back to kiss Angel. "You're such a sweetheart. Thank you." She smiled and walked away again.

Less than an hour later, Angel watched Sarah from the hostess desk. Her face lit up when she answered her cell. Her eyes filled with tears as she talked, and he knew it had to be Sydney. There was no doubt how special Sydney was to Sarah. Angel smiled, feeling a small pang in his heart. The chances of her changing her mind about staying were dismal at best.

* * *

Sunday morning Sarah called Sydney early to see how he was feeling. She'd just gotten off the phone with him when Valerie walked into the room. "So Angel still doesn't know Sydney's a guy?" She sat down on Sarah's bed.

Sarah winced and shook her head.

"You should tell him already, Sarah," Valerie said. "Alex says he's never seen Angel like this. He's really fallen for you. If he's that into you, I'm sure he'll understand or try to anyway."

Sarah thought about how she'd almost spilled it yesterday when he first pulled her into the office and said he needed to talk to her about Sydney. Her first thought was he'd found out somehow, and she was ready to plead if she had to for his understanding. Then he told her about Sydney's accident, and she'd lost it.

"I know, I know," Sarah said. "I just keep waiting for the perfect moment, but there never is one. And the more time passes, the harder it gets."

She saw the disapproval in Valerie's face. Then thought about what nerve Valerie had. "What's going on with you and Alex?"

Valerie frowned. "I haven't heard from him since Wednesday. I think his curiosity with me was over once he got what he wanted." She shrugged. "It's better if we don't go out anymore though. In between all the making out, we'd started doing a lot of talking, and surprisingly, I was beginning to feel a connection with him that was more than just physical. I'm sure he'll call again when he's ready for more. But if we keep going out, I might start falling for him for real. I'd just be setting myself up for heartache."

Sarah looked at her sympathetically. "Well, you never know. Maybe he felt the connection too."

Valerie chuckled. "I know what he was feeling all right."

"You think he'll say anything about you hanging out with Romero?"

Valerie's face soured. "I doubt it. First of all, I don't think I'll be hearing from him anytime soon, unless he gets horny, and even then I really don't think he cares. Besides, I didn't do anything with Romero. He kissed me once, but it felt wrong, so I stopped before we went any further."

"Good," Sarah said. "'Cause I don't care what you say. I saw the two of you the very first day at the restaurant, and there was a definite connection."

Valerie half smiled. "Well, apparently he's been too busy this weekend—probably making more *connections*—to call me."

"Angel's picking me up in a bit. We're going back to the restaurant for brunch again." Sarah gave her a crooked smile. "You wanna come?"

"No way!" Valerie gasped. "How desperate would that look? Me, showing up without being invited. No thanks."

Valerie stood up and walked to the door, stopping when she reached it and turning around. "So Sydney's okay?"

"Yeah." Sarah nodded "Just a couple of bruises, but otherwise he's fine."

"Did he wreck his car?"

"No. Luckily, he was in his dad's truck. It's a full size truck, so it might have been worse if he had been in his car. Sydney said it was mainly the passenger side door that was smashed."

Valerie raised her eyebrows. "Well I'm glad he's okay." She turned around and walked out.

Sarah strolled over to her dresser. She picked up the string bracelet Sofia had given her. All the girls on the track team wore them for good luck, and even though Sarah wasn't officially on the team, Sofia still wanted her to have one. Sarah thought it was sweet and smiled as she put it on.

Angel picked her up, and she was back at the restaurant again. Alex and the guys were already there. They were sitting at a table in the corner. Sarah and Angel sat with them. Romero and Eric were engaged in one of their inane football disputes.

"I don't care what you say. They should've never got rid of Drew Brees," Eric said. "The guy threw five touchdown passes in one game!"

Romero shook his head. "Yeah, but against who?"

"Doesn't matter, five touchdown passes, *five!*"

"Doesn't count when it's against the Raiders," Romero said. "Shit, I could score five times against them."

Alex laughed. "That'd be a first for you."

"I've scored, ass." He turned to Sarah. "Speaking of me scoring, where's Valerie?"

Sarah went stiff. She glanced at Alex; his face was unreadable. "Home."

"You should've brought her," Romero said.

When Sarah looked at Alex again, he was staring at Romero but didn't say a word.

Eric laughed. "Scored? She shot you down on Friday, and she was drunk. If she takes one look at your mug sober, she's gonna freak that she even let you kiss her."

Alex's eyebrows shot up. "You kissed her?"

"She liked it," Romero said, more to Eric than Alex.

"So you went out with her?" Alex asked.

Romero turned to look at Alex. "Nah, we hung out after the game. All of us did at the beach."

"But you kissed her?"

Sarah squirmed, wanting to disappear. Alex had that same tone he'd had on the phone with Valerie. The same unmistakable tone Angel would get when he was getting heated.

Romero made a face. "Yeah, so what? I can't help it if the chicks dig me."

Alex rolled his eyes and looked at Eric. "And she shot him down?"

"Yeah." Eric laughed.

Sarah nodded vigorously and then stopped when she saw Romero was looking at her. The look on his face was almost comical. "She told you that?"

"Well, no. I mean … I can't tell you what she said. It's girl talk." She stood up quickly. "I'm starving."

"You got shot down." Alex smiled.

Sarah could see it was a forced smile. Angel stood up with Sarah and followed her to the buffet table. When they got back, Romero and Eric were arguing again about the Chargers and Alex was gone. Something told Sarah Valerie would be getting that call she'd been waiting for.

CHAPTER 15

Coach Rudy set up a friendly relay with another school in the middle of the week. Sarah was torn because the football team had made the playoffs and they were starting that same day. The game was during the day and away. Sofia and the coach really wanted her at the meet. Angel told her not to worry; it was supposed to be a pretty easy win. They were playing the wild card team.

It had been a while since she'd last competed, and she was nervous. The football team was due to be back just after school around the time the relay would be going on. The boys were in the middle of their relay when Sarah saw the bus with the football team pull in. They were loud and being rowdy, so she knew they'd won. She smiled even though her stomach was doing flips. She hadn't realized how nervous she was about Angel watching her race, until now.

There were a few more relays before hers, and she knew Angel would be out of the locker room and in the bleachers in plenty of time. She concentrated on stretching, bending her leg up behind her and holding her foot with her hand against the back of her thigh. Sofia stood next to her doing the same thing.

Valerie was in the bleachers with a few of her friends. She'd been excited to hear about Sarah running and was there to cheer her on.

The race before hers was about to start when she saw Angel and few other guys from the team heading to the bleachers. They were wearing their jerseys and were obviously still in a good mood about their win.

"Let's go La Jolla!" Romero yelled at the track team.

As they got closer, Sarah turned to Angel and their eyes met. He was freshly showered, and his hair was still wet. He gave her his breathtaking smile, and she melted.

They all sat in the bleachers behind Valerie and her friends. The race ended with the other school winning, but it was very close.

"We're up," Sofia said.

Sarah's stomach tensed up even more as she walked to her place on the track. She glanced back at Angel. He was standing on the bleacher bench now, looking right at her. He gave her a thumbs up and flashed that smile again.

She'd done this so many times before. Why the hell was she so damn nervous now?

The runners took off, and Sarah frowned when she saw what a bad start her team got. The baton reached Sofia about two lengths after the other team's second place runner had already taken off.

"Turn it up, Sof!" Eric yelled.

Sarah glanced at Eric who was standing next to Angel now on the bench then back at Sofia, who was just reaching the third place runner. The other team had an even bigger lead now. She'd been in this situation before and hoped she'd have the same outcome this time.

She got in position. Her opponent took off, and she waited for her team member to catch up. The second the baton was in her hand, she took off and felt the familiar adrenaline rush.

The other runner was a few lengths in front of her and running hard. Sarah concentrated, gaining speed slowly as she made the turn. She felt it coming, and she smiled. On the straightaway, she did what she'd always done best and gunned it. She gained on her opponent fast and could hear the bleachers going wild.

They were almost at the end of the stretch and were neck and neck. She could hear the girl grunting to stay with her.

But a few feet before the finish, Sarah took the lead and won. By the time she'd stopped, it sunk in. She still had it.

She was still holding her knees and catching her breath when Sofia came running after her screaming. "That was awesome, Sarah!"

Coach Rudy hurried toward her with a huge smile on his face. Sarah stood up straight, and Sofia hugged her. She heaved but smiled. The coach handed her a bottle of water. "Damn, I need you on my team. That was outstanding."

Sarah took a big drink of the water. It was ice cold and delicious. "Thank you."

"C'mere," he said and hugged her hard. "Sarah, I knew you had it, but not all that. You're a natural."

The three of them walked back toward the rest of the team. He kept his arm around her shoulders and continued to praise her performance.

He brought in the team for a short speech, congratulating the standouts. The team cheered the loudest when he mentioned Sarah. By that time, the guys and Valerie and her friends were standing close enough to hear, so they cheered as well.

The coach smiled but shook his head in despair. "Sarah, sweetheart. I gotta find a way to keep you here. You're breaking my heart."

Sarah hated being put on the spot like that, and she blushed. He put his arm around her and laughed. "She's blushing. Will you look at that? Fast and adorable."

Sarah felt her face burning. She didn't even want to look at Angel. She could only imagine what he would say.

"All right, bring it in."

They all put their hands in a circle for the usual cheer and the meeting finished. She walked toward the guys.

Eric and Romero high-fived her as soon as she reached them. "Girl, you were smokin'!" Romero said.

Sarah smiled and finally looked at Angel. To her relief, he didn't look as mad as she'd thought he'd be. He walked up to her and leaned his forehead to hers. "You were amazing."

"Thank you."

"I'm so proud of you right now. You don't even know." That really made her feel good, and she kissed him.

"This is your moment. I won't ruin it." He kissed her again. "But if I ever see that pervert's hands on you again, I'm gonna kick his ass."

Sarah had to laugh. For a moment there, she actually thought he was going to let it go.

***

The football team didn't make it to the championships, losing in the second game of the playoffs to a team they'd beat during the regular season. It was a heartbreaking loss, but Sarah had her own special way of consoling Angel.

It had been just over two months since she'd started going out with Angel, and already she felt as if she'd known him forever. Still, every kiss they shared felt as exciting and as passionate as that first night, if not more so.

Sarah loved the way Angel touched her with such urgency—the way he never even tried to hide his need to feel her, taste her. They'd done things lately that were getting awfully close to the real deal.

Because of the circumstances in which Sarah had been born and all that her mom had gone through, the birds and the bees talk had come early for Sarah. She was only eleven when her mom sat her down and told her everything. And ever since, she'd been hammering the importance of birth control and protection from disease into Sarah's head. She used herself as an example, reminding Sarah how one moment of weakness could bring enormous life changing consequences.

Her mom called that night, and after gushing about Angel for the umpteenth time, her mom wasted no time getting right into the subject. "Sex is a huge responsibility," she said. "You have to be prepared not only physically but emotionally."

Sarah became defensive immediately when her mom asked if Angel had been pressuring her in any way. "Of course not!" She snapped. "He's not like that, Mom."

"Listen to me, Sarah." She paused. "Trust me. I know how fast things can happen. And I can already tell you've really fallen for Angel. If I had it my way, I'd tell you to abstain from having sex and everything would be just fine. But I'm not naïve. I've already talked to your Aunt Norma about this. She's taking you to get on birth control."

Sarah was speechless. She knew how important it was to her mom that what happened to her didn't happen to Sarah, but she wasn't expecting this.

"Did you hear what I said?"

"Yeah, I heard."

"You're going tomorrow."

The next day, Sarah skipped track after school. She told Angel her aunt was picking her up because they were going out for her uncle's birthday. It was partly true. Her aunt did pick her up and did accompany her to the clinic. And they did go to dinner after, which would come in handy if Angel asked her about the dinner. She wouldn't have to fumble around trying to come up with more lies.

Sarah hadn't realized how many forms of birth control were available until she got to the clinic. She decided the pill was the best choice for her. She had a pelvic exam and they gave her a prescription for the pill, along with reading material on safe sex and sexually transmitted diseases.

She felt rotten about lying to Angel, but at least this lie was for a good reason. After thinking about it so much the night before, she decided it was a good thing. She wanted to surprise him. Besides, she had a feeling he'd find it in his heart to forgive her once he knew the truth.

*

Almost three weeks later, Sarah stood in front of the mirror. Somehow she thought she'd look or feel different. But after examining herself, everything seemed the same. And she didn't feel any more mature than before like she'd imagined.

She got in bed but couldn't sleep—too much on her mind. So much had changed in just a matter of months. Just a few months ago, the only thing she could think about was her mom and getting back home. Now here she was, utterly consumed with the fact that she was so close to losing her virginity to Angel. She smiled, inhaling deeply. The thought alone was enough to awaken the butterflies in her stomach.

She hadn't told anyone about getting on the pill yet. Her aunt told her it was her business and she wouldn't be telling anyone, not even Valerie. She was glad. She wanted Angel to be the first to know. She hadn't even told Sydney.

Sydney. She winced just thinking about him. She still hadn't told Angel the truth. Valerie had been right again. The longer she was with him the harder it got. At this point, Angel's unwillingness to share anything about her with anyone was irrefutable. As far as he was concerned, he was her best friend now.

Still, she thought if she had only told him sooner. Things had gone from bad to worse. She was more worried now about how he would feel, knowing that she'd deceived him all this time, than what he'd think about Syd being a guy.

After Sydney's accident, she'd gone out of her way to avoid the subject of him altogether. She even made a point of putting her cell phone on vibrate whenever she was with Angel, afraid even a phone call would solicit conversation about *her*.

She might have gone a little overboard killing off Syd though because just the other day Angel had asked, "So, what's up with Sydney? You still talk to her?"

She'd just shrugged and said, "Yeah, sometimes."

Since that first night Angel had kissed her, they hadn't gone a day without seeing each other. The more time she spent with him, the more she couldn't imagine leaving him.

But how could she do that to Sydney? They'd made a pact. He'd already questioned her a few days ago about whether she really thought she could go back to Arizona and leave Angel behind. She assured him she could and would. But in her heart, she knew if she didn't feel so obligated to Sydney and his family, she'd stay without question.

The following day he called her to tell her he needed to talk to her in person. That worried her because Sydney knew her better than anyone. He would see right through her.

The calls with Sydney were cut shorter, but she still talked to him daily. Tonight however had been a long call. Their conversation had been a strange one. They debated on whether or not she should go back to Arizona. Sydney insisted she should stay. Sarah knew what a selfless sweetheart Sydney was and that he would put aside his own happiness for hers.

All those years he spent in her miserable life keeping her company when he could've been out having fun with others. His parents had money that allowed him to do the things other kids did. He could've gone to camp in the summers, skiing for the holidays in Colorado, or anywhere he wanted over spring break. But no, all those years he chose her. He stayed and kept her company.

She felt an overwhelming shame. How could she even think of dismissing their plans just because she had a boyfriend now? She swallowed hard. She wouldn't be seeing Sydney until Christmas. She had time to work on her poker face.

*

It was two days before Thanksgiving, and the entire Moreno family was scrambling. The weekend after the holiday was always their busiest. Angel never understood it. He knew people's fridges must be overflowing with leftovers. Why would anyone go out and eat?

His mom's theory was that people were burnt out from cooking, eating leftovers, and entertaining out of town guests. So, they went out. Whatever the reason, Thanksgiving week was anything but relaxing for the Morenos.

Although the restaurant was closed on Thanksgiving and only open half the day on Friday, they always stocked up in preparation for the busy weekend. Now Angel's dad was having a fit because he'd just been informed some of the deliveries might be delayed due to the weather up north.

"Up north? What the hell does the weather up north have to do with me? We're in San Diego County!" His voice boomed all the way up stairs.

Angel couldn't tell if he was on the phone or if he was just talking to himself, as he often did when he was mad.

He finished putting on his shoes and pulled a hooded sweatshirt over his head. He rushed into the restroom, brushed his teeth and ran a comb through his hair.

"Hey, Sofie," he yelled toward her bedroom as he walked down the stairs. "You got five minutes. I'm gonna go warm up the car."

His dad still cursed in the kitchen. The smell of his mom's biscuits lingered. She made the absolute best biscuits, completely from scratch. He walked into the kitchen to grab a few. "Hey, Pop, bad morning?"

"I'm gonna need you to keep your plans open this weekend." His dad frowned. "Alex made the schedules for this weekend and gave too many people the weekend off.

We're gonna be really busy. If anyone calls in, we'll be short."

Angel grabbed three biscuits, biting one. "Sure, you got it."

His dad sat down on one of the barstools. Angel could tell he was winded. "You okay, Pop?"

His pop nodded. "Hey," Angel said. "You gotta take it easy. Why do you do this every year? Just relax. You get yourself all worked up, and it always turns out fine."

His dad's expression was dreary. "Alex won't be here this year. He's got a game out of state."

"Yeah, so?" Angel shrugged. "I'll be here and so will Sofie and Sal. Don't worry about it. You're gonna make yourself sick."

Angel put his hand on Pop's shoulder. Pop patted it and smiled. "I'm getting too old for this shit."

Angel laughed. "Nah, something tells me you'll be around kickin' ass for a long time still." He took a drink of his dad's coffee and almost gagged.

"Damn!" He grimaced. "Too much sugar in that, Pop. I'm telling mom."

His dad waved him off, frowning.

*

All day Angel got a strange vibe from Sarah, but he couldn't put his finger on what it was. It wasn't a bad vibe, just different. She was more bubbly than normal. Although lately she'd become quite the aggressor, he'd always been the one unable to contain himself around her, sometimes, interrupting her mid-sentence, because he couldn't look at her lips very long without kissing them. Today, however, she'd done that to him several times.

After school when they got in his car, she leaned over and kissed him long and with such passion and eagerness it nearly put him over the edge right there.

When she was done, she licked her lips. "Wow. What's with you today? Not that I'm complaining."

"I have a surprise," she smiled.

His mind raced, searching for clues in her beautiful eyes. Had she decided to stay? He hadn't asked her about it ever since the day he had made her cry. He'd hardly allowed himself to think about her leaving, much less hope that she'd stay. But it'd been a while since she stabbed him in the heart by mentioning anything about going back, and she'd all but stopped talking about her friend Sydney.

His heart thumped against his throat. "What?"

"Not here," she said, "let's go to our place."

He peered at her for a second then turned on the car. It took everything in him to not drive recklessly, but he did go over the limit most of the way anyway.

As soon as he parked, he turned the car off and leaned against his door to face her. She still had that giddy smile which made him smile with her. "What is it?" He tried hiding his impatience.

She took her seatbelt off and turned to face him. "Okay, remember the day I left early to go have dinner for my uncle's birthday?"

Angel nodded "Yeah?"

"I lied."

Angel's eyes narrowed a bit. "Okay? Why?"

She bit her bottom lip. "I went to a clinic."

He stared at her clueless.

"I got on the pill."

Angel still didn't get it.

"Birth control!" she blurted out.

Angel's eyes widened. He felt like an idiot. His lips slowly curled up into a smile. "So, does that mean…"

"Yes." She leaned over to kiss him. "I'm ready."

Angel couldn't get the stupid smile off his face. Just the thought had him rock hard. He wanted to take her right there.

But he had to control himself. He wanted her first time—
their first time together—to be special.

He grazed his lips across hers, feeling a tenderness
inside him that almost scared him. He held her face in his
hands. He could hardly believe that soon she would be his—
completely.

His hands were all over her again. He wasn't sure what
would've been better, to hear her say she was staying or this.

How was she able to keep something this big from him
for so long? That must've been three or four weeks ago.
"How long have you been on the pill?"

"Almost three weeks." He remembered the day she told
him about her uncle's birthday dinner. She'd looked him
right in the face, and he hadn't caught even an ounce of
insincerity. Even when he'd talked to her that evening and
asked how the dinner had gone, she'd told him all about it
without a flinch. He smirked.

"What?" she asked.

"You're good. I had no clue."

Sarah laughed. "I could tell. Even after I told you, you
looked lost."

He kissed her again then met her eyes, raising an
eyebrow. "Since when did you get so good at keeping things
from me?"

She stiffened, and he thought he saw her expression
change. Then she smiled "I just wanted to surprise you."

"Well, you did a hell of job. So, why now?"

Her coy expression made him hotter. "I thought maybe
we could take advantage of the long weekend."

He stared at her soft pink lips, his own mouth slightly
parted. The words still danced in his head. *She wanted it all
weekend?* Not just any weekend, a four-day weekend. His
mind spun into overdrive. The things he'd do to her. All the
ways he'd take her. Then his thoughts came to a screeching
halt—the restaurant. Although he loved the way she was

thinking, Sarah's timing couldn't have been worse. He tightened his lips and thought.

"What's wrong?"

"This weekend is gonna be a busy one for us at the restaurant."

"That's okay. We can wait until next week then."

Was she insane? "No way. Trust me. I'll think of something."

With the wheels spinning out of control in his head, he was already getting an idea.

***

It was only seven in the evening, a little early for Sarah to be home already. But it was a school night, and she had a paper she absolutely had to turn in before the end of the week. Since this was Thanksgiving week, the end of the week would be sneaking up real fast.

She thought she heard Valerie get home and stopped to listen. She hadn't expected her home until much later. She was out with Alex and usually got home pretty late, even if it was a school night.

It turned out Sarah had been right about Alex. He had been pissed about Valerie having hung out with Romero—very pissed. At first telling her off, then calling her back when he'd calmed down, saying he'd never been jealous in his life and hadn't known how to handle it.

With that said, Valerie had allowed herself to continue to go out with him, even at the risk of getting hurt. They'd been going out at least twice a week since. From what Valerie had told her, Alex was a lot like Angel when it came to being possessive. Only there was one big difference. There had been absolutely no mention of being exclusive.

Angel hadn't been able to believe that Alex was so mad at first but had no choice but to believe it when Alex had let

Romero know in no uncertain terms that Valerie was off limits.

Sarah got up to see if it was Valerie she'd heard, partly out of curiosity, and partly because she was sick of working on her paper.

When she walked in the room, she saw Valerie sitting on her bed going through her phone. She looked up, and Sarah could see she'd been crying. Her eyes were all puffy, and her nose was bright red. One side of her mouth went up in a sad attempt to smile, then she shook her head and wiped a tear that rolled down her cheek.

"Hey, what's wrong?" Sarah walked over and sat next to her.

Valerie leaned over and put her head on Sarah's shoulder. "I'm done with Alex."

"Why? What happened?" Sarah rubbed Valerie's back.

Valerie wiped her face with the tissue she had in her hand. "I just can't deal with it anymore. I was stupid to think that just 'cause he'd admitted to being jealous and that he'd never been so before, it might mean something. Here I'm the one always preaching about guys being territorial. Well, hello! That's all it was. He doesn't give a shit about me."

Sarah patted Valerie's knee, not knowing what to say. "Did something happen tonight?"

Valerie nodded. "Well not anything that hasn't happened before though. I hadn't told you because I feel stupid. But every time I'm with him, his phone is constantly ringing, and he always sends it to voicemail. I never really say anything except maybe give him the look 'cause I know it's all girls. He always just laughs and says 'What? I have lots of friends.' Oh, but God forbid my phone ring and I not answer it. He always wants to know why and if it's a guy." She stopped to blow her nose.

"Anyway," she continued, "his phone rang tonight like five freakin' times in less than fifteen minutes. So, I told him to just answer it already. At first, he didn't want to, but he knew I was getting pissed, so he did, and sure enough, it was a girl. You should've seen the big smile on his face and the way he talked to her. It just made me sick. He hung up when he saw the look on my face, and I told him to bring me home. You know what he says?"

Sarah shook her head.

"You're the one that told me to answer it!" Valerie used the stupidest guy voice she could make.

Sarah had to fight the urge to smile and felt guilty when she saw Valerie wipe another tear away. "So you told him you're not gonna see him anymore?"

"Yeah, I told him I couldn't deal with him anymore. He said I was being silly, but when I asked if he'd be okay with me sleeping with someone else, he shut up real quick. Then he turned it around, accusing me of having someone else I want to sleep with and saying that's why I was breaking things off."

"No way," Sarah said. "What did you tell him?"

"To go to hell and I asked him how it could be that there was anything for me to break off when he was obviously still seeing other girls. He didn't say anything. All the way home, though, he kept trying to convince me that I was overreacting and that he did care about me, only right now, with school and his football schedule, he can't commit to anything. He said he still wanted to see me, but I refused. I'm done with him. It hurts too much." Her eyes welled up again.

"I did tell him though before I got here that there were no hard feelings in case I ran into him, being that you and Angel are together and all. I don't want things to be awkward." She leaned against Sarah again.

Sarah rubbed her back again, feeling terrible and partly responsible. She was the one that kept telling Valerie that there was a definite connection. But she really thought there was. She saw it in Alex's eyes when they were together. Angel had tried to warn her Alex was a heartbreaker. She should've listened and warned Valerie, instead of egging her on.

CHAPTER 16

Thanksgiving felt different this year. From the moment Angel woke up, he was all nerves. Sarah would be spending the day with his family, then he'd take her back to her aunt's for dinner there.

It'd worked out perfect because his family's Thanksgivings were always more of a brunch with everything meticulously laid out by one in the afternoon at the latest, buffet style in the kitchen.

He was worried about Sarah. He knew this would be her first Thanksgiving without her mom. The only time she'd mentioned the holiday at all was a few days ago and only to ask him to please not be hurt that she wasn't inviting him to dinner at her aunt's. She wasn't looking forward to being with a bunch of family members she'd never met, and she thought having him there might make her even more nervous.

He did want to be there to protect her from any unpleasantness, but he respected her wishes and agreed.

Angel had big plans for this evening. Depending only on if she was up to it, he wanted tonight to be *the* night. Tonight would be a night Sarah would never forget.

While most boys his age were still dreaming about getting laid, Angel already had a good share of experience. From the time he was fifteen, the girls had made it just too easy for him. But Angel had always been extremely careful, even passing politely the first several times girls had literally offered themselves to him. Thanks to his older brother Sal's lecturing, he'd been deathly afraid of disease and knocking someone up.

Eventually though, it'd become too much of a temptation, and he'd given in. But in the beginning, Sal's words would ring in his head, rattling him every time just as he was about to do the deed. "Think with your head, not your dick. ALWAYS use a condom, no means no, and don't go sleeping with everything that moves unless you want to end up with something you can't get rid of, like a disease or a baby. Remember condoms aren't 100% effective." And the most endearing of all: "don't be stupid."

That was the main reason why he'd end up with Dana so often after parties and dances. The idea of switching partners so often made him nervous, but nothing compared to the nerves he was feeling now. Ever since Sarah had told him she was ready, he'd felt on the edge. Even with the experience he had, he knew this would be a first for him too. This was *Sarah*. Just being around her made him feel things he couldn't even begin to describe. And now he was going to be making love to her. Not once had he slept with someone he cared about. And saying he cared about Sarah was an understatement.

He eyed the front door of her aunt's house, turning off the engine. The keys weren't even out of the ignition when he saw her rush down the front stairs and toward the car.

Angel had told her not worry about dressing up. Thanksgivings at his house were anything but formal. Even in jeans and a sweater, she looked amazing.

The moment she stepped in the car and he touched her hand, he felt a tenderness that swelled his heart. There was something more beautiful about her than usual, and he loved the way her delicate scent always filled his car. She leaned toward him and brushed her lips against his, pausing to gaze in his eyes for a moment, then smiled.

He always felt like an untamed animal around Sarah, but lately it was different. She was all he ever thought about now, and any time away from her felt too long. Angel closed his eyes and kissed her. Then the words came out without warning. "I love you, Sarah."

His eyes flew open, and he pulled back to see her expression. Sarah's eyes were as wide as his felt. They were both stunned. But he knew he meant it. "Really?"

"Yeah, really." He took a deep breath and leaned his forehead against hers. As absurd as it sounded, he thought he felt it from the moment he kissed her that first night. But now he was certain. There were no two ways around it. He'd fallen for her hard.

He searched her eyes for what she might be thinking. Then she smiled really big and hugged him hard. "That means so much to me."

Not exactly the words he'd hoped to hear, but he held her tight anyway. Saying it felt right, and that's all that mattered.

*

Brunch at his house went well with other members of his family meeting Sarah for the first time, including his oldest brother Sal. She was such a natural, and everyone seemed to like her immediately. He'd hardly been able to keep his eyes off her the whole time. He took her home as soon as they were done eating, so she could get her dinner at home over as soon as possible.

When he got back from dropping her off, Eric was in the kitchen, sitting at the bar with a plateful of food, and Sofia was warming something up in the microwave.

"Thought you were spending the day with your dad?" Angel asked as he walked to the fridge.

Eric spoke with a mouthful of food. "Already ate with him."

Angel looked down at Eric's abundant plate. "You're kidding right?"

Eric didn't flinch. "Nope. He's watching some boring ass golf highlights DVD, so I thought I'd come over and see what you guys were up to."

As if he couldn't imagine. But Angel didn't mind. He felt bad for Eric. Since it was only him and his dad and neither cooked, he rarely got a home-cooked meal. That's why he was over so much in the Moreno kitchen. As far as Angel was concerned, both Eric and Romero were like family.

Sofia pulled a plate with sliced apple pie on it from the microwave. She added a big spoonful of vanilla ice cream to the top.

"Looks good, Sofie," Angel eyed the pie as he pulled an energy drink out of the fridge.

"Not for you." She took the plate and set it in front of Eric.

Eric grinned at Angel. "Thank you, Sof."

"You're a fat ass. You really gonna eat all that?" Angel leaned against the sink.

"Shit, I'm gonna go get me some more of your mom's kick-ass mashed potatoes," Eric said, putting another spoonful in his mouth.

"I made those." Sofia beamed.

"Sarah liked them too." Angel smiled at Sofia. "You're getting better every year, Sofie."

Sal walked in the kitchen. "Getting better at what?"

"Everything," Eric said.

The comment threw Angel, and he thought he saw Eric and Sofia exchange a glance. Both Sal and Angel stared at him. Eric finished chewing and cleared his throat. "I mean, I heard Sarah say Sofie is getting pretty fast in track." He looked at Sal. "But Angel was talking about her cooking."

Sal turned to Sofia with a big smile. "That's my baby sis."

Sofia started putting dishes in the dishwasher. "Not a baby, Sal."

Sal turned his attention to Angel. "So, I guess everyone is growing up around here. You brought a girl home to mom and pop, Angel? Really?"

"He's got it bad," Eric grinned.

Unamused, Angel shot him a look. "What's the big deal?"

He took a swig of his drink and hoped someone would change the subject. But he had a bad feeling. He saw it in Sal's face. He walked in the kitchen with a purpose. Sal pulled a chair from the breakfast table and straddled it.

"So how long?" Sal asked.

Sofia answered for him, "Three months and a few weeks."

That surprised Angel. He wasn't even sure how long it'd been. He knew it'd been a few months. "How do you know?"

Her expression teased him. "Sarah and I talk about a lot of things." She glanced at Eric and then back at Angel. "She just mentioned it the other day."

"Wow." Sal said. "So tell me about it. What made you decide you wanted to be a one-woman man?"

Knowing Sal wouldn't let up until he knew everything, Angel decided to just give him a brief rundown of the whole thing.

Very brief.

Sal looked settled in for a full detailed account, but that wasn't going to happen. Angel did his best to sound bored.

"I met her in school. She was the new girl this year, didn't really know anyone." Angel shrugged for good measure. "I thought she was cool, so we hung out, introduced her to the guys and Sofie, and I've been hanging with her since. No big deal."

He wondered if anyone was buying it. Everyone had seen him tonight. Hell, he'd never made an effort to hide his affection for Sarah before. But tonight was different. Telling her he loved her had done something to him. He couldn't figure it out. All he knew was that every time he kissed her, touched her, or even looked into her eyes, it ignited something in him.

Sal looked satisfied. "She seemed nice enough."

"She is really nice," Sofia agreed. "I like her a lot."

Eric groaned. "Oh, I ate too much. Sofie, why'd you feed me so much?"

Glad they were off the subject, Angel took advantage. "Good, that's what you get. So, we working out tomorrow?"

Eric sat back in his chair with his hands on his stomach. The pained look on his face made Angel laugh.

Without missing a beat, Sofia put a cup of fizzing water in front of Eric. "Here, drink this."

Angel and Sal looked at Sofia. "What? That's what dad drinks when he eats too much."

Eric did as he was told and downed half the concoction, stopping with a face of pure revulsion. "What was that?"

"Seltzer water," Sofia said. "Drink it all."

It amused Angel how Sofia was really turning into a mother hen lately. He enjoyed her irritation when he called her his baby sister, but he was damned if he'd ever stop calling her that.

His phone rang, and when he saw it was Sarah, it immediately worried him. She hadn't been at her aunt's very long. He flipped it open. "Hey, what's up?"

"I'm ready." She sounded fine.

"How'd it go?"

"Everything went good. I was still full from your place, so I just had dessert. Come get me. I'll tell you all about it."

Just thinking of seeing her again made him smile. "Okay, I'll be there in a few."

"Angel," she whispered.

"Yeah?"

"I said I'm *ready*."

It took a moment for it to register. But when it did, he felt his heart speed up and a stir in his pants. Damn, she drove him crazy. "I'm on my way."

Angel didn't realize until he hung up, but Sal had been watching him the whole time.

"You bringing her back here?"

Angel flashed him a fat smile. "Nope."

"Yeah, well, just remember. Don't be stupid."

With a wink, Angel grabbed his keys and was off.

✳✳✳

Aunt Norma had made it sound as if there would be a lot of her mom's relatives there. If Sarah had known how things were going to work out, she would have had Angel over.

She hadn't been able to stop thinking about his saying he loved her the whole day. She'd wanted so badly to tell him she loved him too, but how could she? How could she sit there and tell him she loved him when she would be leaving him soon and he knew perfectly well it was by choice? She just couldn't do it. As much as hearing him say he loved her had been music to her ears, she almost wished he hadn't. It only made the guilt that much harder to bear.

"So, what happened?" They drove out of her aunt's driveway. Angel put his hand on her lap, and she wrapped both her hands around it.

She took a deep breath, "First of all, all that worrying was for nothing. Most of the relatives who showed up were from my uncle's side, and the few that did show up from my mom's side were very distant relatives. Apparently, all their closer family members still live in Arizona. No one really seemed interested."

"My aunt had to literally remind them that she had a sister. The adults ate in the dining room while," she lifted her fingers to quote, "we kids ate in the kitchen. It was actually kind of boring."

She left out the part about her step-uncle's nephews flirting outrageously with her. It had amazed her that both were the same age as Angel, and yet compared to him, they were such immature goofballs.

Angel smiled. "Well, that's good. I was kind of worried when you called so early. I thought maybe something happened."

She leaned against him. "No, I just couldn't wait to be with you again."

He squeezed her hand.

At first when they drove up the alley to the back entrance of the restaurant, Sarah wasn't even sure where they were. She glanced around a little confused.

When they got inside, she smiled. What could he have in mind? Surely, he didn't plan on making use of one of the booths, did he? They walked down a short hallway and through the small cluttered office. They went through another door that led to what looked like a break room.

She knew about it but had never actually been in there. There was a counter with a microwave, a toaster, a refrigerator against the wall with cabinets above it, a table in the middle of the room, and a small sofa next to the table, facing a T.V. that was in the corner.

Then she saw *it* at the end of the room—a bed. It was a small twin bed with a dark bedspread, nothing fancy, but it would do. She felt her heart speed up a little.

Angel strolled over to the fridge, opened it up, and pulled out a jug of wine.

Sarah grinned. "Hey, my precious!"

"I thought maybe you'd want to unwind a little first."

Were her nerves that transparent? He poured her a cup then went back to the fridge and grabbed a beer for himself. She chewed her lip when he tugged her by the hand toward the bed. She sat down, feeling the swarm in her stomach go wild. Taking a big sip of her wine, she watched him go back toward the counter. He opened a cabinet above it, and took a small white plastic bag out. Then he came back and sat next to her.

He smiled and took a deep breath. "I want you to know, that even though you're going to be leaving, I still want us to be together."

Warm tears blurred her vision. She'd thought about that so many times but dared not ask. It was way too much to ask of him. After all, it was her choice to go back. How could she possibly have the nerve to suggest it?

Angel pulled a small box out of the bag and handed it to her. Before she could open it, he put his hand over hers.

"Sarah this isn't gonna be easy, but I'm willing to do whatever it takes. I don't care if I have to drive out there every weekend. Just 'cause we're so far doesn't mean I plan on being a part-time boyfriend. Do you understand what I'm saying? I want everything exactly like it is now. I won't share you."

Sarah closed her eyes for a moment, feeling a myriad of emotions—guilt being the strongest of all. She forced a smile and nodded. "Of course."

He kissed her and took his hand off hers so she'd open the box. She did and pulled out a silver charm bracelet. "It's beautiful." She examined the different charms. "Did you pick these out?"

He nodded. "Every one of them."

She went through each one. First was a small starfish, then several different seashells, a sailboat. The running shoe and then the bottle of wine made her smile.

"The lady looked at me kind of funny when I asked if she had a charm that was a jug of wine."

Sarah laughed. "You must not have been at a very classy place then."

"Yeah, that must've been it."

The heart charm was engraved *Sarah*. "Turn it around," he said.

She did and read the engraving. *Forever Yours ~ Angel.*

She put her hand over her mouth as the tears rolled down her cheeks. They gazed into each other's eyes for a moment, then he kissed her. She inhaled deeply and then brought her attention back to the bracelet. There was one more that looked like a chicken or a duck. She turned to him confused.

"Quack!"

She burst into laughter "Oh, Angel, it's perfect." She threw her arms around his neck.

He kissed her and pulled back a little to look at her face, wiping her tears with thumbs and smiled. "Let me see."

He took the bracelet from her and placed it around her small wrist, fastening it. She held her hand up in the air. "I love it."

"I love you." He gazed into her eyes.

I love you too. The words almost flew out her mouth, but she held them back and smiled. It was torture, but she just couldn't do it.

He took the cup out of her other hand and placed it on the floor then pulled her to him. His eyes were on her lips, and he lowered his head and kissed her, immediately going after her tongue. She offered it eagerly, wanting him to feel how much she loved him—to make up for not being able to say it. He kept kissing her while he moved further back on the pillow and then lay down partially over her.

His breathing became stronger, and he sucked her tongue a little harder. His mouth moved down, kissing her cheek then her chin and pushed her head up gently. "I love you so much," he whispered as he licked and suckled her neck softly, making her body tingle. She caressed his strong biceps as he unbuttoned her blouse.

When he was done undressing her, he undressed himself and put on protection. Then he crawled in next to her.

"Sarah," he whispered. "The first couple of times are gonna be fast. I just can't control myself with you."

Sarah gulped. First couple of times?

"I'll make it up to you though. I promise."

Sarah gave herself to him willingly. Even through all her nerves, she hoped he could feel how much she loved him. He had to know that. He meant the world to her, and there was never a doubt that she wanted her first experience to be here—with *him*.

CHAPTER 17

Overwhelmed with such staggering emotions, Angel lay there still in her. He kissed her temple and then her forehead. He'd felt so many unfamiliar emotions since he'd met Sarah, yet none compared to what he was feeling now.

All those times he'd laughed and thought of guys with girlfriends as fools. How any guy could be satisfied with just one girl had been unimaginable to him. Now here he was, looking at Sarah, knowing without a doubt he'd never be satisfied with anyone else but her.

From that very first day when he'd looked into her haunting eyes, she'd captured something in him. He'd stupidly thought getting to know her would be enough. He'd been taken in by her wounded eyes, her infectious laugh, and her stubborn determination, and without warning, he'd been brought to his knees.

He kissed her temple breathlessly. "You're mine, Sarah."

She nodded, tracing her fingers down his back.

There was no way he could let her out of his life now. The thought smothered him, gripping his every sense. He kissed her softly and tenderly as he rolled over and off her. He sat on the side of the bed for a moment, feeling dazed. He stood up and walked toward the door, still naked.

"Where are you going?"

He turned and smiled. "To clean up, I'll be right back."

He walked out of the room and across the hall to the restroom. When he got back, Sarah was sitting up on the bed, holding her pants in her hands. He slid back in bed with her. "You won't need those any time soon."

He took the pants, bunched them up, and threw them on the sofa across the room. He handed her a towel. "Are you hurting?"

The silly look of concentration on her face made him smile. She shook her head. "No, but I might be too sore to try again right away."

Angel got back out of bed and lifted the bedspread up from the top. Sarah moved and crawled under it. He slipped in next to her under the bedspread and pulled her next to him, slipping his arms around her warm naked body. "God, I'm gonna miss being with you every day."

She tensed up.

"What's wrong?"

Sarah shook her head. "Nothing, I just don't like to think about it."

Angel didn't say anything but couldn't help wondering why she was so determined to go back if she didn't even want to think about it. Then he remembered—Sydney. He kissed her nose. "Maybe once Sydney leaves for school, you can consider moving back here."

The look on her face puzzled him. He'd seen that look before, and it'd made him uncomfortable, but he didn't know what it meant.

"What's the matter?"

She looked at him for a second, the disconcerting expression still on her face. "Sydney," she said. "Well, it's not all ... how you think." She hesitated.

His eyes narrowed, not understanding. Then he saw her expression change slightly. "I'm just saying it's not all Sydney, Angel. I don't know for sure what's gonna happen with my mom. She may be out by then."

The last thing Angel wanted was to talk about her mom. As selfish as it felt, he didn't want anything to ruin the night—not *this* night. He kissed her softly. "Let's not worry about that now, okay?"

He ran his hands all over her naked body and closed his eyes, inhaling deeply. Having her this close with absolutely nothing in between them drove him nuts. He was ready again.

He kissed her harder this time, wanting to swallow her. As much as he wanted to make love to her again and again, he knew she was sore, and he wasn't about to hurt her. That's not how he wanted her to remember their first time.

But he made good on his promise to make it up to her. After catching his breath, he worked his way all the way down her. Feeling her tremble as he kissed the inside of her thighs made him smile. Oh, she wouldn't be forgetting this night. He'd make sure of that.

✳✳✳

Valerie drove Sarah to the mall. They were all going out to celebrate Angel's birthday later that evening. Sarah was picking up her gift to him, and Valerie wanted to buy a new outfit. Alex was going to be there, so, of course, she was hoping to make him drool.

Sarah was nervous about her gift. The bracelet Angel had given her was so special. She wanted her gift to be just as special. Angel wasn't one for flashy jewelry, but she felt this called for something special. She'd picked out a simple silver chain and had it engraved. *Forever Yours ~ Sarah.*

Sarah *was* his in every way now. She wanted something that would remind him of that every day, especially when she went back to Arizona. It had been over two weeks since she'd given herself to him for the first time. Ever since then, they'd done it every chance they got. It got more enjoyable every time. Just thinking about it made her warm.

Both she and Valerie examined the chain when the clerk handed it to Sarah over the counter.

"Hey, that's real nice," Valerie said.

Sarah crinkled her nose. "You think so? It's not too cheesy?"

"No, not at all." Valerie traced the engraving. "Oh, he'll love that."

Valerie walked out to answer her phone, and Sarah finished paying for the chain. By the time she was out of the shop, she caught the tail end of Valerie's conversation and knew she was talking to Alex. She turned to face Sarah.

"What's that smile about?" Sarah teased.

They walked slowly through the mall.

Valerie shrugged. "He's funny, but I don't know. I hate getting my hopes up."

"What did he want?"

"To know if I'm going tonight."

Sarah was surprised. She knew Alex was still calling Valerie, but she didn't expect him to still be trying to see her. "Is *he*?"

"Yeah, he said he was hoping he'd see me there. He wants to talk to me."

"Well, that's good. Right? "Sarah frowned, thinking of how she'd egged Valerie on before and how it had come back to bite her. She was doing it again.

"Not really. I told him I've been talking to Reggie again. I didn't lie. He really has been calling and texting me lately. Alex asked if I was going back to Reggie, and I told him I wasn't sure. *That* was a lie." Valerie's face soured. "I don't want a boyfriend, especially not feeling the way I do about Alex. I think he's just being a Moreno. The whole Reggie thing struck a nerve I'm sure."

"You still have feelings for him?" Sarah couldn't figure Valerie out. She thought she got over guys so easily. But Alex had made her cry pretty bad.

Valerie's expression said it all, and Sarah felt for her. "I was doing fine until he started calling again. If I see him tonight, I know it's gonna be even worse."

Sarah stopped herself before saying something too hopeful. She wasn't going there again. "Well, no sense in worrying about it now. Just play it by ear."

They finished up their shopping and were headed home in the car. Valerie stopped talking about Alex, and Sarah didn't want to bring it up again. She was flipping through a Cosmo when she got a text from Sofia that almost stopped her heart.

OMG, Romero walked in on me and Eric! Can you talk?

Sarah bolted upright and hit the send button. Sofia answered on the first ring.

"What happened?"

"I went over to pick up a DVD I wanted to borrow," she giggled. "Hold on."

Sarah waited, stunned. For the life of her, she could not figure out how Sofia could find anything about this whole situation humorous. From the first time Sofia had mentioned Eric kissing her, she could hardly contain herself. Ever since, much to Sarah's horror, she'd filled her in on every stolen moment she and Eric had. Each one got heavier than the last. Her heart was racing, and Sofia was giggling!

She heard a door close then Sofia's voice again. "Okay, I came outside. Angel just got home. Anyway, Eric was home alone but had just gotten out of the shower. He only had a towel on, and we started making out." She lowered her voice. "Sarah, his towel came off, and I saw everything!"

Sarah was going to need smelling salts soon. She fanned herself with the magazine.

Valerie glanced at her. "You want the air on?"

Sarah shook her head. "Then what?"

"I turned away. He felt really bad, kept apologizing and asking if I was okay. I was. It just really took me by surprise. But it was exciting." She giggled again, unnerving Sarah to no end. "Then we heard a knock on the door. Romero didn't even wait. He came right in. I grabbed a DVD off the shelf and ran out of there."

Exciting?

Sarah fanned harder. Valerie looked at her weird and turned the air on. Sarah welcomed the cool air. She was beginning to perspire.

"Did Romero say anything to you?"

"No, he just stood there speechless. You think he'll say anything?"

"I don't know."

She honestly didn't. This was out of control. She wished she could tell Sofia to please not tell her anything more. She didn't want to know. It was bad enough she was already keeping something big from Angel. She wasn't sure which was worse. The thought made her shudder. But she knew Sofia was all alone with this.

Sarah wasn't sure if she should feel sorry for her or admire her. Sofia's world was full of overbearing cavemen. But it didn't seem to slow her down.

"That's Eric on the other line!" Sofia squealed. "I'll call you back!"

There was a click, and the call ended. Sarah put the phone down still completely stunned.

"What was that about?" Valerie asked.

"Trust me. You don't wanna know."

She was home by the time Sofia called her back. Eric had been honest but told Romero as little as possible, and Romero promised he wouldn't say anything, but he thought Eric was incredibly stupid.

Sarah was relieved to hear it and glad she wasn't the only one now that knew. But she still worried that Romero might get drunk and spill it somehow. Tonight would be interesting. Everyone would be there.

CHAPTER 18

As usual, Angel's heart raced at the sight of Sarah. He kissed her as soon as she got in the car. It was supposed to be a friendly hello kiss, but unable to restrain himself, he kissed her passionately until someone in the back seat cleared his throat. Sarah pulled away immediately and turned around. Romero, Eric, and Sofia were crammed in the backseat.

"I didn't see you guys." Her scandalized expression when she saw them surprised him. This wasn't the first time he was ravenous for her in front of them.

"My bad." Angel smirked, pulling out of the driveway. "I forgot anyone was back there."

"I was just talking to you before she got in the car, ass," Romero protested.

Angel chuckled, lacing his fingers into Sarah's and placing their hands together on his lap. Sarah stared straight ahead, a bit too rigid. He wasn't sure what to make of it. He hoped she wasn't mad.

The ride to the bowling alley was a fairly quiet one, except for Romero protesting about the music. Angel hit the off button to shut Romero up and glanced in the rearview mirror for his reaction. What he saw was Sofia resting her head on Eric's shoulder.

"You tired, Sofie?"

She sat up immediately. "No."

Angel glanced at the clock on the dash. It was only eight. "She falling asleep on you, Eric?"

Sarah shifted in her seat, brought his hand up to her lips, and kissed it. He immediately forgot about Sofia and smiled instead. He was glad she wasn't mad. He had to remember just because he could care less what anyone thought about the crazed way she made him feel, Sarah was a bit more modest.

When they got to the bowling alley, Angel took Sarah aside. He put his arms around her waist and pulled her to him. "You mad?"

Her confused expression relieved him. "About what?"

"Nothing." He kissed her, feeling kind of dumb. "Never mind."

He should've known something like that wouldn't have made her mad. Whatever it was, she was over it now. She looked at him weird but didn't ask anything else.

There were a lot more people there than Angel had expected. He knew Friday's were busy. They turned the lights down and played music, but this crowd was huge. Most of the guys from the team had showed up, and, apparently, Sarah and Sofia had invited the track team because there were a lot of them there as well.

Sarah and Sofia walked away to mingle with their friends from the track team. Angel didn't mind. He was still holding out hope her friends on the team would talk her into joining and she'd decide to stay. There were only a few more weeks before she was leaving, and it killed him. But he wouldn't dwell on that and ruin the night.

Romero handed him a soda and put his arm around his shoulder. "Happy birthday, big guy."

Angel sipped through the straw cautiously. He knew better. Sure enough, it tasted like gasoline laced with some soda. Angel coughed. "What the fuck?"

Romero laughed and so did the other guys standing around him. "It's your birthday, man. Don't be a pussy!"

Someone always snuck in something to pour in the soda. And he knew the guys were going to try to get him wasted because it was his birthday. But he had other plans for later that night. There was no way he was missing out on that.

These things were always the same. Everyone was underage, so the only chance anyone had of getting a buzz was to sneak stuff in. He was sure half the people there were packing. Angel didn't even like hard liquor. The only thing he'd ever go for was beer, and even then it was one or two at most. But he didn't want to disappoint the guys, so he pretended to keep drinking. He knew they were all drinking the same crap, and before long, no one would notice when he dumped it out.

They'd been there almost two hours, and Angel couldn't believe people were still arriving. The place was almost too crowded. Angel could tell Sarah was trying to give him his space with the guys. She'd come over and hang with him for a little bit then walk back to mingle with her girlfriends.

He didn't have a problem with her staying by his side the whole night, but he knew Sarah. She wasn't having it. Giving him his space for some inane reason had always been important to her.

Alex showed up late, but Angel appreciated it. He knew this kind of party didn't even compare to the parties he was attending now that he was in college. Yet here he was, looking happier than ever to see him.

"Happy birthday, little man." Alex shook his hand then pulled him in for a bear hug. Angel groaned when Alex purposely squeezed him hard. Only Alex could make him feel small. He cut him loose and looked around. "Damn, this place is packed." Alex looked pleased.

There was too much alcohol floating around. That was never good. He'd already noticed some of the employees' stern expressions. There was only one security guard. An older guy in his fifties, and he had had a hard enough time breaking up a verbal altercation earlier between two girls. Of course, it didn't help that there were a bunch of idiots around yelling, "Fight! Fight! Fight!"

Angel had kept his eye on Sarah most of the night, but when Alex got there, he lost her in the crowd. Romero walked by and Angel tugged his shirt. "You seen the girls?"

It was obvious Romero was already lit. "Yeah, I've seen lots of girls."

"I mean Sofie and Sarah, stupid."

Romero struggled to lift his eyebrows. Angel could tell he'd be no help. "Not sure about Sarah, but Sofie's with Eric."

"Where's Eric?"

"I don't know."

Angel frowned. Why the hell did he bother? Just as he gathered his thoughts, there was a commotion behind him. He turned around and fists flew. He backed up and before he knew it, there were cups and food flying through the air.

Everyone scrambled, girls screamed, and more got involved in the fight. Angel searched frantically for Sarah and Sofia. He felt a hand on his shoulder and jerked it off defensively, but it was Alex.

"Where's Sofia?" His concerned expression matched what Angel was feeling.

"I don't know." Angel was pissed he'd let the girls out of his sight. It was chaos. People were being shoved around. Angel and Alex pushed their way through the crowd.

"There's Sarah." Alex pointed.

Angel saw her and rushed to her. She was with Valerie, but Sofia was nowhere around. Sarah's alarmed expression eased up the moment she saw him. He took her hand as soon as he reached her. "Where's Sofie?"

She shook her head. "I dunno. We got split up when everyone started pushing."

"Keep moving people!" The security guard and a couple of the bowling alley employees were making everyone exit.

They had no choice but to go outside. They all stood in the parking lot anxiously, watching the flood of kids continue to pour out of the exit.

What the hell was he thinking bringing Sofia tonight? Angel felt Sarah squeeze his hand. He spotted Eric in the crowd coming out the doorway but no Sofia. He noticed Eric held his arm out behind him, and as the crowd thinned out, he saw Sofia was on the other end of his arm, holding his hand. Angel exhaled as blissful relief set in.

"There they are!" Sarah lifted her hand in the air to get their attention.

Eric saw them and walked through the crowd toward them, never once letting go of Sofia's hand. When Eric reached them, he clapped Angel on the shoulder with his free hand and a fat grin. "Dude! Is this a birthday or what?"

Angel shook his head, and they made their way back to the car. Alex and Valerie were already there. "Where to now?" Alex asked.

The group party was over as far as Angel was concerned. He had his own plans. They were—after all—celebrating *his* birthday. "I've had enough action for one night," Angel lied. "I'm gonna take these guys home."

"What?" There was a note of disappointment in Eric's tone.

"It's not even eleven," Sofia added.

Angel pulled Sarah closer to him by the waist, and she leaned her head against him. "Yeah, Sarah's tired."

Sarah's head jerked up, and she punched him playfully on his side. "Don't lay this one on me!"

Angel tried but couldn't hide a smile. "Sarah, babe, you're supposed to play along."

Alex pulled the keys out of his pocket. "Here." He tossed them at Eric. "Take Sofie and stupid over there home. Valerie has something to show me."

He flashed a wicked smile, and Valerie elbowed him. "Don't make it sound like that."

Romero walked up to the crowd. "Hey! Where's the party?"

"You better not throw up in my car," Alex warned and walked away with Valerie.

Romero looked confused. "Your car? I'm going with Angel. Right?"

He turned to Angel.

"You're over there." Angel pointed to Eric and Sofia who had started walking away. They were walking toward a still rowdy crowd in the parking lot. "Be careful, Sof."

Eric took Sofia's hand again and showed Angel. "Don't worry. I got this!"

"You okay with that?" Romero said, pointing at Eric.

"Don't be stupid," Angel frowned. "Go catch up before he leaves your ass."

If it were anyone else, Angel would've felt weird about it. But he knew Eric had Sofie's back as usual.

Romero took off after them. "Hey, wait up. Hold my hand too, Eric!"

Sarah laughed, and Angel turned his attention back to her.

Sarah's grin teased and challenged him at the same time. "So, what about me, Birthday Boy? Where are you taking me?"

Angel's heart thudded. He knew exactly where he was taking her.

As soon as they entered the restaurant's back room, Angel pulled Sarah into a long passionate kiss. He was ready for her. Hell, he'd been ready for her all night.

After a few minutes, Sarah pulled away for air. "Wow," she said breathlessly.

"Yeah, wow." Angel smiled.

He was about to kiss her again when Sarah put her hand on his chest. "Wait." She pulled away and hurried to her purse sitting on the counter. "I have something for you."

Angel wasn't happy. He'd told her not to spend any money on him. He knew whatever small amount she was making from babysitting she was saving for when she went back to Arizona. "Sarah, babe, I told you—"

"Shush, I wanted too." She held out a small box with a silver ribbon around it.

Angel grinned sideways and took the box. She grabbed his hand and pulled him back toward the bed. They sat down, and he began to open it. Sarah shifted next to him. Her excitement amused him.

He opened the box and pulled out the silver chain. He could tell she was anxious for a reaction, but she looked so cute he wouldn't say what he really wanted to say—she shouldn't have spent this kind of money on him. "I like it."

He kissed her again. "Read the engraving."

Angel flipped it over. *Forever yours ~ Sarah.*

"I wanted you to have something to remember me every day when I'm gone."

When I'm gone. Damn, he hated the sound of that. She was crazy to think he needed anything to remind him of her. The thought of her never left his mind anymore. But he smiled anyway and took her in his arms. It was time now for the gift he'd waited for all night.

CHAPTER 19

Sarah was alarmed when she saw the time on her clock. Her cell phone was ringing, and it wasn't even 6 A.M. Who'd be calling this early? She reached over and looked at her phone. It was Sydney. She flipped it open not sure what to expect.

"Hello?"

"Hey, Lynni." He sounded calm enough.

"Everything okay?"

"Yeah," he said. "Sorry for calling so early. I couldn't sleep."

"Why? What's wrong?" In all the years she'd known him, she knew the only times he couldn't sleep were when he was stressing about something. She sat up and plopped a pillow behind her.

"Nothing's wrong."

Sarah knew that tone. "Sydney, you're stressing about something. You should know better than to try and hide it from me."

There was silence on the other end then a sigh. "I can't stop thinking about you and Angel," he said. "Are you sure you're going to be okay coming back here?"

Sarah frowned. It had been over two weeks since she and Angel had made love for the first time. She kept it from Sydney for a while, not wanting to betray Angel by sharing something so intimate with anyone else. But about a week ago, she hadn't been able to keep it to herself anymore.

Angel told her how much he loved her every day now. It was killing her that she couldn't say it back to him. So, she'd broken down and told Sydney, crying in the process. Ever since, Sydney had been beside himself, skeptical about her being able to come back to Arizona. But she'd been trying her best to convince him that she could and would. There was no way she'd let on that just the thought devastated her.

But she had to go back, no matter how much she wanted to stay now. She just wouldn't be able to live with herself. How could she tell him she was turning her back on him now because of a guy that she'd known for just four months? Albeit they'd been the best four months of her life, she just couldn't do it.

She'd never forget the way Sydney cried that awful day she found out she was going to have to move. She'd cried for him almost as much as she'd cried for herself.

"Sydney, I already told you. I can do this. Me and Angel are still going to be together, even once I move back."

"Are you sure?" He asked. "You two haven't been apart for even a day since you started going out."

Sarah squeezed her eyes shut. She knew he was right. It was going to be hard, harder than when she'd left Sydney. Still, she had to do it.

"I'll be okay, Syd. I made it this long over here, and remember how I didn't think I could?"

"Yeah, you've been fine—more than fine—because of *him*."

"Well, I'll have you when I get home to help me through this."

There was a strange silence for a few long moments. "Lynn, in all the years I've known you, I've never heard you so happy. I'd hate for you to come back and be miserable."

"Impossible," she said. "As long as I have you there for me, I'll be fine."

She couldn't help but let a yawn escape. She was so tired. The lustful stop at the restaurant had lasted much longer than they intended. She'd gotten home way after curfew. Luckily, as far as she knew, no one had noticed. Everyone was sound asleep when she snuck in.

"You should go back to sleep," Sydney said. "You sound really tired."

"I'm okay." She yawned again.

"No, you're tired. Go back to bed. We'll talk later."

"You sure?"

"Yeah."

"Okay," she said. "Stop worrying about it, Syd. Everything will be just like before. It'll be like I never left."

After she hung up and went to the restroom, she thought of the day ahead of her. Ever since the night she'd given herself to Angel and they'd agreed to continue the relationship even after she went back to Arizona, she'd been riddled with guilt. She had to tell Angel the truth about Sydney, and she almost had that same night. But she chickened out, not wanting to ruin the night. Sarah shook her head, remembering how she'd shamelessly used her mom to change the subject.

Ever since, she'd made one excuse after another to not tell him. But she wouldn't allow herself the pleasure of telling Angel she loved him until she came clean and told him the truth. And not being able to say it was killing her.

It was going to be tense, but if he really loved her like he said he did, he'd understand. She fell back asleep as soon as her head hit the pillow again. Being an early bird, it startled her when her phone rang again, and she realized she'd slept for almost three more hours. It was Angel this time.

"Hello?"

"Hey, babe, did I wake you?"

"Mmmm." She stretched her arms out. "Yeah, but it's nice that it's your voice I'm hearing."

"Don't make that noise, Sarah," he said. "It's gonna drive me crazy all day until I can be with you."

"All day? Aren't you picking me up early?"

"No, babe. We're short staffed today. It's so bad, me and Sofie got stuck dropping off the morning catering, and then we gotta go back to the restaurant. I won't be able to pick you up 'til at least seven tonight."

"Hi, Sarah!" She heard Sofia in the back.

Sarah frowned, upset with herself that she'd slept so late. She could've helped them with the catering. "You need me to help in any way?"

"Nah, Eric's gonna help out. We're picking him up right now." His voice got lower. "Besides, I kept you up late enough last night. I want you to rest up for me—for tonight."

Sarah beamed. Who needed rest? Her entire body felt great. She was ready for him now.

"I hope *you're* rested," she said, "because I'm ready *now*."

"Stop it," he whispered. "Shit, if I can get off earlier than seven, I'll call you, so be ready."

"Okay." She giggled.

"I love you, babe."

She felt her heart being held hostage, unable to say what she wanted so badly. "Okay, bye."

That's it. She absolutely was telling him everything tonight. Sarah dreaded it with every ounce of trepidation in her body, but she had to. She couldn't go even one more day without telling him how much she loved him.

Deciding that as long as she was coming clean, she'd also let Sydney in on the whole convoluted lie as well. Maybe he'd have some advice on how best to break it to Angel. She tried calling him, but it went straight to voicemail. She left a brief message only to say she needed to speak with him and was free of Angel for the day, so he could call her anytime.

The rest of the day was spent doing laundry and going over what she'd say to Angel. There was no backing down this time. She rehearsed it over and over again. Every time she looked at the clock, the knot in her stomach got bigger and heavier. She tried calling Sydney a few more times, but each time was sent to voicemail.

He'll understand. She kept telling herself. He had to. She'd make him, and once she told him how much she loved him, he'd know he had nothing to worry about.

Sarah was looking through her closet when she heard, "Hey, you," and jumped, almost losing her balance. She turned and saw Valerie standing there with a smirk. "What's with you?"

Sarah closed her eyes and put her hand on her chest. "God, I've been so nervous all day, I'm a mess."

"About what?" Valerie walked in and sat down on Sarah's bed.

Sarah slumped her shoulders. "I'm telling Angel tonight."

"Telling him what?"

"About Syd."

Valerie eyes opened wide. "He still doesn't know?"

Sarah rolled her eyes. Valerie always had a way of making her feel worse, especially about this. "No, but he'll know tonight for sure. No buts about it. I'm telling him." She turned back around to look in her closet. "I'm just not sure where to start."

"Well expect the worse."

Sarah spun around and shot her a look. "Gee, thanks. That helps."

Valerie shrugged. "I'm just saying he's gonna be pissed, Sarah. You know he is. Shit, his brother still had the nerve to tell me he didn't like me talking to Reggie. I'm not even seeing him anymore, and he was never my boyfriend to begin with, but Angel has it *bad*. And he has a little more right to feel like you're his, *all* his. He is *not* gonna be happy about you going back to Sydney, your *guy* friend."

"I have to tell him though," Sarah said.

"Yeah, and you should," Valerie said. "Have you thought about what you're gonna say?"

"All freakin' day." Sarah plopped down on her desk chair.

"Maybe you should dress up really nice," Valerie said. "You know, do yourself up extra sexy. The distraction might make him a little softer, less mad."

"You think?" Sarah looked at her apprehensively.

"Yeah." Valerie jumped off the bed. "I have a really hot dress you could borrow. It'll be a little short on you, but you won't look slutty. I promise."

Sarah watched as Valerie ran out the room. She chewed her lip, thinking about it. It seemed so silly, but she was willing to try anything that might help.

Valerie came back in holding a black dress. It was low-cut in the front and had slits on the side of both legs. It looked like it might be about an inch or two above her knees. Sarah stared at it. "Am I gonna fit in that thing?"

"Try it on." Valerie shoved it at her and left the room.

Sarah tried it on, and it was a perfect fit but a lot tighter than what she normally wore and a heck of a lot more revealing. It really showed off her cleavage. They were supposed to be going to a party on the east side, a bit ritzier than their usual backyard parties. But she had a feeling that after seeing her in this dress, they may not make it there and instead head back to the restaurant, which was just fine with her.

She turned around to get a view from behind in the mirror when Valerie walked back in. Sarah turned to see her holding her hand over her mouth. "What?"

"Oh, my God, I'm a genius." Valerie laughed. "I doubt he'll even hear a word you say. Why didn't I think of this sooner?"

Sarah glanced back in the mirror. The dress was so unlike her. Angel was going to know something was up the second he saw her. "Is your dad even gonna let me out in this?"

"Ooh, good question," she said circling Sarah, still sizing her up. "What time is he picking you up?"

"Around seven."

"Oh, you're good." Valerie still had that evil grin on her face. "They're going to the show and dinner. But they're cheap, so they like catching the earlier show around five."

Sarah turned back to the mirror. That ugly feeling in her stomach was back, but dress or no dress, she was telling him tonight—no matter what.

She started getting ready just after five. Valerie helped her with her hair. Sarah's hair was fairly straight, but Valerie said straightening it even more would make it look extra sleek and super sexy.

Sarah watched Valerie through the bathroom mirror as she concentrated on the flat iron she held in Sarah's hair. "So how was it last night with Alex? You two looked real chummy."

Valerie glanced up at the mirror and shrugged. She continued concentrating on Sarah's hair. "Well I think he turned his phone off or put it on vibrate 'cause it didn't go off once last night. I tried to resist him as long as I could, but it's so damn hard. I didn't sleep with him though. I told him I'm not doing that anymore. So he asked if it was because of Reggie. I told him, 'No, it's because it hurts too much.' Then he made a stupid joke apologizing for his size."

Valerie's expression was disgusted, but Sarah couldn't help laughing. Alex was too funny.

"Stop," Valerie said. "You're gonna make me burn you."

Sarah controlled her laughter as best she could, and Valerie continued to tell her about the rest of her evening with Alex. Sarah couldn't help busting up several more times.

The way she saw it, Valerie was partly to blame for Alex thinking the way he did. She had given herself to him way too easily and with no strings attached. But Alex had no right to demand she stop going out with or even talking to other guys. He was, as Valerie put it, pretty ridiculous.

Valerie said he agreed to going out but no sex, and they were already going out again tonight. Sarah had to laugh at that too. If it was true that Alex was just like Angel only intensified times three the way everyone made it seem, Valerie was dreaming if she thought she'd keep that guy off her. Not that she thought Alex would ever force himself on her. But she was sure he'd find a way to manipulate the situation. If it were anyone else, maybe Valerie could find the willpower to stand firm. But with him, Sarah highly doubted it.

Valerie left to get ready herself, leaving Sarah to finish getting ready on her own. When she was just about done, she heard the doorbell ring. She glanced at the clock. It was only six-thirty. He said he'd call if he would be early. She continued working on her makeup, and then she heard Valerie.

"Sarah, it's for you."

Maybe he got off early and wanted to surprise her. Sarah was glad she was ready. She put all her things back in her makeup bag and stuffed it in her purse. She sprayed herself with a little perfume and grabbed her purse. She inhaled very deeply then took one last look at herself in the mirror. He was going to flip when he saw her.

As she rushed out, she glanced out the window and caught a glimpse of that unmistakable 1964 canary yellow Chevy Impala parked directly in front of the house. *It couldn't be.*

She turned the corner into the front room and went numb. There he was, all six feet of him, standing there looking at her from head to toe. For a second, she was unable to speak.

"Sydney!" She jumped into his arms.

He hugged her tight. The smell of his cologne brought back all the wonderful memories. When they pulled apart, she stared at him still in shock. "Oh my God, what are you doing here?"

"We gotta talk, Lynn."

***

Angel had taken off early, feeling a little guilty about leaving when the restaurant was still busy. But he hadn't seen Sarah all day, and he was getting antsy about it.

He'd gone home to change and was just pulling out of his driveway, when his cell phone rang. Glancing at the phone screen, he smiled, thinking she must've read his mind because he was about to call her.

"Hey, babe."

"Angel?" She sounded odd, and immediately it made him uncomfortable.

"What's wrong?"

"Nothing," she said. "Well, something's come up. The neighbors up the street. The uh … Gleason's, they had an emergency and they need me to come over immediately to babysit. They're desperate, Angel. I couldn't say no."

Feeling disappointment, but at the same time warmed by her sincere concern, Angel sighed. "Is it for the whole night?"

"I'm not sure," she said. "But I'll call you as soon as I know something."

"All right." He turned the opposite direction back toward the restaurant. "I love you."

There was a long silence, then he heard her again. "Okay, bye, Angel."

He'd been back at the restaurant for a little over an hour when his phone rang. He answered it immediately without even checking who it was, thinking it'd be Sarah.

"Hello?"

"Hi, Angel."

He was quiet for a second. "Dana?"

The only times she'd called him since the day he told her off were a few times to leave drunken messages, but he hadn't actually talked with her since. Now he regretted answering.

"Yeah, it's me."

"What do you want?" It wasn't his thing to be rude, but he wasn't about to get in hot water with Sarah. The last thing he wanted to do was encourage Dana.

"I'm not calling to rub it in or make you feel worse if that's what you're thinking. I'm just calling to tell you I'm here for you."

Angel rolled his eyes impatiently. He had no clue what she was talking about and, really, no interest. "Dana, I don't need you here for me, okay? I'm working right now. I gotta go."

"Angel, I know I pissed you off, but before anything ever happened between us, we were friends. I don't know what happened with you and Sarah, but I know you were really into her, so if you need someone to talk to now, remember I'm still your friend."

Her words were all over the place, and still Angel couldn't make anything of them. He decided to just humor her. "All right, thanks. I gotta go."

No sooner had he hung up with her when the phone rang again. He glanced at the caller ID a little annoyed, thinking it would be her again. It wasn't. It was Eric.

"Hey, dude. Where are you guys?" Eric asked.

"I'm working."

"Working?" Angel heard Romero in the background. *"Ask him. Ask him!"*

Angel smiled. "Ask me what?"

"Is Sarah with you?"

"No, she had to work. The restaurant was busy, so I just came back."

"Oh, so Sarah's not with you?"

Then Angel heard Romero again, "I told you! Didn't I tell you? That was her. I know it was."

"What's he saying?" Angel asked.

Eric told Romero to shut up. "Nothing, man, this guy's just tripping. He thinks he saw Sarah a little while ago."

Angel was undaunted. "Nah, she's babysitting." He stood there smiling, listening to their conversation. He couldn't tell if Romero had been drinking or was just being obnoxious.

Eric and Romero went back and forth for a few minutes, then Angel heard a struggle, the phone got muffled, and the horn honked. He chuckled. *Idiots.*

"All right, man," Eric said to Angel.

Angel laughed. "Is he *that* wasted already?"

"No," Eric said. "He hasn't even been drinking, but you wouldn't know it by the way he's acting."

Angel's other line beeped.

"Don't answer your other line. It's just dumb ass," Eric said.

"Answer it!" Romero yelled in the background.

"Hold on." Angel chuckled, clicking over to his other line. "Wadda ya want, ass?"

He stood at the hostess stand at the entrance of the restaurant, looking back in to see how many customers were left. It was early, but most of the guys in the kitchen were on overtime now, and his dad had told him if it slowed down enough to close early and let them go home.

"It was her, man," Romero said.

He walked back casually, sneaking a peek in the second dining room. It was empty. He knew Romero couldn't be right, but he went along anyway. "Yeah, where?"

"In a car—a fucking yellow Chevy Impala, one of those old ones, all cherried out—with a dude."

CHAPTER 20

Sarah was both shocked and overwhelmed with joy when she saw Sydney. She hadn't realized how much she'd missed him until she felt the emotion in his hug.

She had had so many questions for him she almost forgot Angel was going to be there any minute. She'd felt so rotten having to lie the way she had. But she knew there was no way Angel was ready to meet Sydney—not like this. It would be a slap in the face. She needed to explain everything to both of them before she could have them meet.

This whole mess was her fault, and now it threatened to blow up in her face. She was a nervous wreck all day, and now she felt on the verge of a meltdown.

Sydney said he wanted to talk to her, and she had a feeling it wasn't going to be a short conversation. The only places she knew were places Angel had taken her. All of which were frequented by everyone from school.

There was no way she was taking him to her and Angel's special place. So she decided to go to a place further down the beach where she'd never gone with Angel. She figured it was safe.

Getting there would prove otherwise. They got stuck in Saturday night traffic. It seemed everyone was out that night. She sunk in her seat several times when she thought she saw people from school—guys from the football team even.

When they finally got to the beach, Sydney dropped a bomb. She'd been expecting something big since he'd driven all the way out here, but she was still shocked and upset when she heard it.

"Lynni." He started. "I should've told you this a long time ago."

Sarah braced herself. As long as he wasn't sick she could take anything else. "What?"

"Remember Carina Santiago?"

Sarah thought for a moment. "The girl in orchestra who plays the cello?"

"Yeah." He took a deep breath. "Well, just before you left, me and her started talking—a lot. We actually started seeing each other. But you were going through so much crap and stressing out 'cause of your mom's problems that I didn't want to tell you about it."

Sarah shook her head. "Why?"

"C'mon, Lynn, you had so much stuff going on. Half the time you were almost sick with worry about your mom. How could I sit there and tell you about how good things were going for me? It didn't feel right, and even after you left, you were so miserable, and that's when everything really started to happen for me and Carina. I couldn't do it."

Sarah stared at him, almost sick to her stomach, feeling so self-centered. All this time she'd been going on and on about having to be there for Sydney, and now she was finding out that she'd been too busy wallowing in her own crap to listen to him. He'd been there for her, and through it all, he'd kept his own feelings to himself, never once able to share his own anxieties or excitement about his own brand new relationship. Unless he'd kept anything else from her before this, Sarah knew very well this was a first for him too.

"Oh, Sydney. I'm so sorry." She hugged him tight.

He pulled back gently. "What are you talking about? I'm the one that kept it all from you."

"Yeah, but you did it for me because I was such a whiny useless wimp. I dumped all my crap on you, time and time again, and never once thought about how hard it must be for you."

Without warning, the tears came en masse. She felt terrible, but when her eyes met his, he looked mad. "Don't you dare do this, Lynn." He wiped the tears gently from her cheeks but spoke firmly. "You've been the best friend that anyone could ever ask for. You think I'll ever forget what you did for me? If it hadn't been for you, I wouldn't have made it through middle school. I was the fattest, laziest piece of—"

"No, you weren't!" She stopped him, infuriated.

"I was, Lynni. But you were the only one that didn't think so. And just like right now, you were ready to kick some ass if anyone ever made me feel like I was."

"That's because I've always known what a beautiful person you are, Sydney. They didn't know you like I did."

"And I'll never forget that about you. But I keep hearing you talk about how much you owe me. You don't owe me shit. You got me through the roughest years of my life. If anything, I owe you—big time. If it hadn't been for you, I might have shot myself."

She stared at him, stunned.

"It's true, Lynn. I'm ashamed to admit it, but there were times I was thankful that things weren't perfect for you because I knew if your life had been just an inch more normal, maybe you wouldn't need me so much."

"How can you say that?" The tears burned in her eyes. "I would never turn my back on you."

"I know that," he said. "That's why I'm here. You have to stay, Lynn. You belong with Angel, just like I belong with Carina. Why do you think I accepted the scholarship to Columbia?"

Sarah stared at him blankly.

"She's going there," he said. "It's been killing me because I know you want to stay here with Angel. It's where you should be. If you came back to Arizona just because you felt you couldn't turn your back on me, how am I gonna feel when I leave for Columbia? What if because you insisted on coming back to Arizona, you lose Angel, and you're on your own? How am I supposed to live with that? I'll drop out of school, Lynn. I swear to God. I'll lose Carina before I abandon you."

"No!" Sarah gasped.

"Then stay here, Lynn," he said. "Stop being so damn stubborn, and tell him you love him already. Stay here and be happy. He looked deep in her eyes. "Me and you, nothing will ever break us apart, not anyone, not any distance."

Sarah smiled, feeling her heart swell a million times over. "This is why I love you so much, Sydney."

"I love you too."

Sarah hugged him tightly. Then they hung out for about another hour, with Sarah insisting he tell her all about Carina. Sydney didn't hesitate, telling her everything. To Sarah's shock, they'd been intimate for some time now. Sarah tried to shake the guilt off. He should've been able to share that with her. She knew it was huge. Then he hit her with yet another surprise. "She doesn't know I'm here with you."

"What?"

"Everyone at school knew how tight we were, Lynn. She did too. When we started going out, she was incredibly insecure about you. You're a pretty rough subject with us, but I'm trying to get her to understand. It's too soon though, and I know if she knew I drove all the way down here to see you, it'd be over."

Sarah chuckled. "Yeah, well, Angel thinks *you're* a girl." The expression on his face made her laugh. "He assumed when I told him about my best friend, Sydney, that you were a girl, and I never corrected him." She held her breath, not sure what to expect.

He smiled slowly. "Well, Lucy, we both have a lot of 'splaining to do."

Sarah giggled and slid her hand in his as she'd always done before. "I was gonna tell him today. My mind was

totally made up. Why do you think I'm wearing this get up?
But then you showed up."

Sydney checked her out from top to bottom. "You know
I was gonna say something earlier. Then thought I better
not." He shook his head, still taking it all in. "Damn, Lynni. I
almost didn't recognize you at first."

Sarah blushed. "It wasn't my idea, okay?"

"Oh I didn't say it was a bad idea. Just sayin', wow."

Sarah laughed feeling self-conscious. "Stop."

"All right, all right, but yeah, tell him as soon as
possible. And, Lynni, if you need me to talk to him, I will."

Sarah smiled. She just didn't think that would fly with
Angel. She just couldn't picture him listening to another guy
talk about his relationship with her, even if it was Sydney.

"I'm starving," she said.

"Anything good around here?"

Sarah didn't care about good. All that mattered right
now to her was being discreet. "We'll find something."

***

Angel stood still for a moment. He knew it couldn't be, but
Romero sounded so convinced. He took in what he'd just
heard, then shook his head and started walking again. "Nah,
dude," he said. "She's babysitting for her neighbors right
now."

"Call her then," Romero said.

Romero's dogged tone made him uncomfortable. He was
so sure. Angel stood quiet for a moment. "Did she see you?"
What was he doing? This was ridiculous. There was no way
Sarah would be out with another guy. He trusted her.

"No," Romero said.

"*I didn't see shit!*" Eric yelled in the background.

"Yeah, well, he would've if he didn't drive like a girl. By
the time we turned back, they were gone," Romero said.

They'd actually gone back to check? Angel picked up the phone at the hostess desk without mentioning it to Romero. "So what was she doing?" He dialed Sarah's cell phone number.

"Talking, I guess," Romero said. "I saw her as we passed the car, and I had to do a double take, but Eric was driving so fast and wouldn't slow down. She looked *different.*"

"'Cause it wasn't her!" Eric yelled again.

Angel listened to him with one ear, and waited to hear Sarah's voice in the other. But it went to voicemail.

"So she's supposedly working then, right?" Romero asked.

Angel didn't like the way that sounded. He knew Sarah wouldn't lie to him. He hesitated to answer.

"I'm just saying," Romero said. "In case we see her again. I'll go ask her, 'What's up?' If the asshole even thinks of saying anything, I'll pop 'em."

Angel chuckled, but he didn't feel the least bit amused. This was starting to feel weird. It wasn't like Sarah to not answer when he called. She always answered. Even when she did miss his call, she'd call back almost immediately. But then he *had* called from the restaurant phone. Maybe she didn't recognize it. He'd only called her from that line a few times.

"I'll call you back, dude," Angel said.

"Call her," Romero persisted.

"I will."

As soon as he hung up, he called Sarah. It went to her voicemail again. This time he left a message.

"Sarah, babe, it's me. Call me as soon as you get the chance, okay?"

Within a half hour, the restaurant was empty and clean. Angel double-checked the kitchen then closed up. On his way home, Eric called again.

"Hey, dude, you still at the restaurant?"

"Nah, I'm on my way home."

"What? You're not gonna meet up with us?"

"I'm tired, man," Angel yawned. "I've had a long day today."

"All right then. Hey, did you ever talk to Sarah?"

Angel frowned. "No, not yet." He glanced at the clock on the dash. It was just after nine.

"Well, don't sweat it, dude. I'm sure it wasn't her, but you know how Romero gets."

Angel smiled. "Yeah, I know. I'm not sweating it. I'm just tired."

He sat, staring at the red light. *Shit!* He was getting a headache. For some reason, Dana's call popped in his head. He tried remembering all she was blabbing about. Now he wished he'd paid attention.

She'd said something about being there for him. The light turned green, and it came to him.

I'm not calling to rub it in. I don't know what happened with you and Sarah, but I know you were really into her.

What was that about? None of it made sense. Well, hell, he'd never make detective. That was for sure. That was it. He was done. He didn't need this aggravation; what he needed was sleep. And he planned on getting some when he got home.

If he had never talked to Romero tonight, he wouldn't be questioning where Sarah was, even if he hadn't been able to get a hold of her all night. He knew exactly where she was: at her neighbors, babysitting.

He was almost home and exhaustion was really setting in. His eyelids were getting heavier by the second. He kept blinking hard to keep them open.

Just a couple of blocks from his house, his cell phone rang, jolting him back to life. He grabbed it from the passenger seat and frowned when he saw it was Eric again.

"Hey, man." Angel could hear Romero going on in the background, but Eric, or something, was muffling the phone, and he couldn't make out what he was saying.

"You home yet?"

"No," Angel said. "Almost."

"It *is* her, man," Eric said.

It took a moment for it to register. "Sarah?"

"Yeah," Eric said. "She's with a guy."

Angel's heart thudded to a standstill. He had to pull over, so he could think … breathe.

"Are you sure?"

"Yeah, it's her." Eric sounded almost apologetic.

Angel fell back in his seat but still squeezed the steering wheel. He swallowed hard, not wanting to believe. "Where?"

"Some greasy spoon off of Proctor," he said. "I'd never even seen this place before."

"She still there?" Angel sat up straight. It suddenly hit him that Eric wasn't talking about seeing her earlier. She was still there—with another guy.

"Yeah," Eric said. "They're in there eating. They were holding hands when they walked in, and I don't know how much longer I can hold this guy back. He's ready to run in there and explode on the guy now."

"No, no, no!" Angel put the car into gear. "I'm on my way. How do I get there?"

Angel's mind raced. How long had she been doing this? He thought of all the Saturdays she had worked and he'd never even questioned it. The rage ripped through his veins, and he welcomed it. It was a familiar emotion that he at least knew how to deal with, and it helped numb the pain.

She'd completely blindsided him, and he felt ready to tear someone apart. He stepped on the accelerator. He'd have his chance soon enough.

✳✳✳

Sydney and Sarah had driven for a while with Sarah deliberately directing him into streets she and Angel never frequented. She saw a small café in the middle of one of the small streets that was still open. "There." She pointed.

Sydney frowned. "Are you sure?"

She wasn't, but it seemed perfectly discreet. Definitely not somewhere anyone from school would be hanging out. "Yeah."

He held her hand as they walked in almost guardedly. There were only two other people in there, and they were sitting together, yet it still took a while for the elderly waitress to come around and take their order.

Sarah took advantage of the time to ask more about Carina. She was determined to catch up on all of it, every little detail. She was still feeling terrible that he hadn't been able to share anything about it with her. Even after their food came, she continued to grill him, at times feeling moved and holding his hand across the table. How had she missed it all?

Finally, they finished. Sydney insisted on paying. He put his arm around her shoulders as they walked out the door. She leaned on him, her eyes at the floor, and then she looked up. Her legs almost gave out when she saw Angel. The bitter revulsion in his eyes was undeniable. He glared at Sydney then very slowly turned until his eyes locked on hers.

"You been working, Sarah?"

CHAPTER 21

Even as Angel had driven into the parking lot and seen the yellow Impala parked in front of the café, he'd held out hope that this was all one big mistake.

He'd parked next to Eric's car where he saw Eric and Romero standing. Eric motioned to the window of the café as Angel approached them.

It *was* her. And she looked unbelievably seductive. She sat there gazing attentively into another guy's eyes. Angel had watched disgusted as she reached across the table and held his hand, and he noticed her cleavage was out there like he'd never seen it before in public.

Eric and Romero filled him in on how they spotted the car leaving the beach and followed them to this secluded hole in the wall. Sarah wasn't stupid. She just hadn't counted on dumb and dumber seeing her.

Now, standing here looking at her startled eyes, he searched for answers. Her once beautiful green eyes, that normally gazed at him so brightly and with such emotion, were almost gray. And all he saw in them was fear and what looked too damn much like guilt.

It felt unreal, like some kind of weird nightmare. He sized her up and down, taking in the provocative dress she was wearing. For a second he thought he was going to be sick. Then he heard *him* talk.

"It's not what you're thinking, man," the guy said.

Angel charged forward ready to rip him apart. His voice boomed. "How the fuck do you know what—"

"Stop." Sarah jumped in between them.

Angel stared at her; a red haze of pain and anger nearly blinded him. Was she protecting this guy? He squeezed his fists tight.

"Angel, I'm sorry, I should've told you this a long time ago."

Angel's heart sank. *A long time ago?*

"This is Sydney."

Angel's mind went blank. He stood there, heart hammering away. He took a step back. "Sydney?" He stared at her then back at the guy.

"Yeah," she said. "I meant to tell you from the very beginning, but you'd just assumed he was a girl, and I know it was stupid of me, but…"

Her words buzzed in his ears. There was only one thing he could hear. It was screaming in his head. *All this time, she had another guy waiting for her back in Arizona.* He shook his head and backed away.

"Angel, please."

He saw her tears, but it didn't matter. Something squeezed his throat, and he struggled to get the words out. "This is who you're going back to live with?"

Sarah stepped closer to him. He flinched, not wanting her to take another step. Romero and Eric stood behind him, speechless. As the reality of it settled in, the anger inundated him.

"This is who you've been talking to everyday?" He raised his voice with every word. "This is who you can't fucking live without?"

Sarah clasped her hand over her mouth for a brief second. "Angel, please, you don't understand. Let me—"

"So, what? He's been coming down here every Saturday, Sarah?"

"No!"

"Is this what you call *working*?"

He stalked away, again feeling like he was going to be sick. He didn't want her to see just how deeply she affected him—not anymore.

Through the corner of his eye, he saw her coming toward him.

Angel didn't need to hear anymore. Whatever she had to say didn't matter. It was all too clear.

"Angel," she said. "Hear me out, please."

"It doesn't matter, Sarah." He stopped and glared. "Unless you can tell me it's not true, that you're not going back to live with this guy, that he's not who you're leaving me for, I don't need to know anything else."

"I'm not leaving you for anyone—"

"Bullshit!"

Sarah froze, and he started to walk away again. He'd lost control and needed to get out of there before he charged at Sydney.

"He's my best friend, Angel."

The words felt like a blow to his stomach. He stopped and turned around. "Really, Sarah? 'Cause I thought I was."

He blinked hard in a desperate attempt to hold the tears back. He turned his face away, panicked that she'd see him cry.

"You're *more*, Angel." She tried to grab his hand, but he snagged it away. "He's just been my friend for so many years. Everything I told you about Sydney is true. We're like family. You have to believe me."

Angel clenched his teeth. He thought of the way she'd gazed at Sydney in the café and held his hand at the table. The way she'd leaned against him as they'd walked out. *That dress.* That dress, that screamed come and get me, and she'd worn it for Sydney. Like family? Did they really think he was that stupid?

He didn't want to ask, but he had to know. "You love him, Sarah?"

When she didn't answer immediately, he knew, and it tore him apart. It was all he could take without breaking down. He had to get out of there, fast.

"Go," he said. "You're free to be with him without lying and sneaking around."

He rushed toward his car.

"Angel, you have it all wrong," Sarah cried. "Please, don't do this!"

He hurried his step, barely making it to the car when the tears assaulted his eyes. Never in a million years would he have believed a girl could make him feel like this. He could barely see as he backed up. He zoomed past Sarah, who was still standing there crying, and onto the road. He wiped away at his eyes, annoyed that they kept coming.

It all made sense now. She'd been lying all this time, and she hadn't told him she loved him because she couldn't. Couldn't—because she was in love with Sydney. How could he have been so blind? *Had she slept with him too?* He jerked the car off to the side of the road, opening the door just in time to be sick.

✳✳✳

"I have to go after him!" Sarah pleaded, as she ran toward Sydney. An older couple walking to their car stared at her with concern. The tears streamed down her cheeks, and she knew her face was a mess, but she didn't care about any of that. She pulled her cell phone out of her purse and started dialing Angel's number frantically.

"I wouldn't, Sarah." Eric said as she walked by him.

Sarah turned to look at him and tried to catch her breath. "But I have to."

Eric shook his head. "I've known Angel all my life, and I've never seen him like that."

"Yeah, no shit," Romero said. "That was bad."

Sarah wiped her face and tried desperately to regain her composure. "But that's why I have to talk to him and explain. He just doesn't understand." She turned to Sydney. "Please take me to him."

"Whatever you want, Lynni." Sydney put his hand on her shoulder.

"Who the fuck is Lynni?" Romero asked, disgusted.

"Hey, easy." Eric frowned.

"I'm just wondering did she lie about her name too?" Romero started back toward their car without waiting for an answer.

Sarah wanted to scream. *I didn't lie!* But she had, and she deserved this—all of it.

"Hey, that's her middle na—" Sydney began to say.

Sarah touched Sydney's arm. "It's okay. It doesn't matter."

"Yeah it does. He's calling you a liar."

"It is what it is." The disappointment in Eric's eyes ran deep. He turned without saying good bye and walked to his car.

Sarah could feel another wave of tears setting in. "Let's go, Syd."

She broke down again as soon as she sat in Sydney's front seat. It was worse than when she'd cried earlier. Earlier she'd cried out of fear: fear of seeing Angel so out of control, fear of her complete inability to make him understand, but now she was crying out of anger—angry that she'd been stupid enough to let it come to this.

Eric was right, she decided. Now was not the time try to explain, especially not with Sydney there. She'd wait until the morning to call him. By the time they reached her aunt's house, she was drained emotionally and physically. She sat there, looking out the window at the moon not wanting to move.

Sydney squeezed her hand. "Let's get you inside."

Sydney spent the night on the living room sofa and left early the next morning. The next couple of days were torturous. Sarah called Angel at least five times a day and sent him endless texts, all with no response. She couldn't believe how unreasonable he was being. He didn't even want to try to talk it out.

Sarah sat on her bed, staring at her cell phone. It had only been two days since she'd last seen him, and she missed him horribly. Didn't he miss her too? If it was the other way around, she would've already given in and answered his call. Could all his talk about him loving her so much have been a lie? Or maybe he just realized he couldn't possibly love a liar.

There was a soft knock at her door. The door was open, and Valerie stood at the entrance, pouting. "How we doin'?"

Sarah shook her head and pressed her lips together, looking back at her phone. She was so sick of crying, but just looking at Valerie's sympathetic expression brought a lump to her throat. Valerie sat next to her on the bed and hugged her. She squeezed her tight for a second then let go and patted Sarah's leg. "All right, so he's being a jerk. Give him time. He'll get over it."

Sarah wasn't so optimistic. Valerie hadn't seen him that night. "No, I really think he hates me now."

"Are you kidding? I'm sure he's still totally whipped. But expect him to maybe want to, you know, play games."

Sarah looked at Valerie who avoided making eye contact. "What do you mean?"

Valerie stood up and walked over to Sarah's desk. "You know guys are stupid." She picked up a pad of paper and a pen. Then came back and sat down again next to Sarah. She kept her eyes on the pad of paper and began to doodle.

"You hurt him, and maybe you know, now he'll try to hurt you back. It happens. It's immature yeah, but—"

"Valerie, what are you talking about?" She put her hand on the pen, so Valerie would stop doodling. "Do you know something?"

Valerie's eyes finally met hers, and she took a deep breath. "Not really, but I talked to Alex."

"And?" Sarah could feel her insides tightening up.

"Well, just so you know, Alex is worse than Angel, so he really thinks you did Angel wrong. He had the whole story all mixed up, the idiot." She began doodling again. "He thinks you were cheating on Angel this whole time and Syd's been your boyfriend for years."

Sarah squeezed her eyes shut and braced herself. When she glanced down, Valerie was doodling furiously. "What else did he say?"

Valerie stopped doodling but didn't look up. "I just got off the phone with him. He said he was glad Angel was having lunch with Dana today."

It hit Sarah like a ton of bricks, but strangely, she wasn't totally surprised. She'd always known in her gut that there was more to Angel and Dana. No wonder he wasn't missing her.

Valerie touched Sarah's hand. "Hey, she's the most annoying person on the planet. There's no way he could be into her. It's so obvious what he's doing."

Angel wasn't that immature. Sarah couldn't see him playing games like that. But she could definitely see him being hurt and needing to reach out to someone. Someone that would make him feel better, and of course he'd picked Dana. Sarah stood up. She'd been thinking about it since yesterday. This just sealed the deal.

"I gotta get out of here." She pulled the suitcase out from under her bed.

"Where you going?" Valerie asked.

"Back to Arizona, where I should've been all this time."

CHAPTER 22

Angel waited impatiently for the light to turn green. He was already regretting having agreed to this. But he hadn't been able to stop thinking about Dana's call that night. Breaking up with Sarah was, without a doubt, the hardest thing he'd ever done, and he wanted to make sure he wasn't making a mistake. But when he called Dana this morning, she insisted she wanted to talk to him in person.

Alex agreed to cover for him at the restaurant, even telling him to take his time and enjoy—as if he'd be able to enjoy anything the way he was feeling. He hoped Dana would keep it short and to the point. He was in no mood for much more. He was so tired from the lack of sleep the last couple of nights, and just thinking about Sarah made him want to bang the steering wheel.

He picked Dana up, and she announced she wasn't very hungry, but she could go for coffee, so they went to Starbucks. She talked all the way there but not about anything he wanted to hear. As soon as they got their coffee, he cut to the chase. "So, let's have it. What were you talking about Saturday night when you called me?"

"Angel, I didn't know you didn't know anything. I'd hate to cause problems—"

Angel waved it off. "We're done. It's over between her and me. I just wanna know what you were talking about."

Dana seemed surprised. But suddenly her eyes were full of compassion. "I'm so sorry to hear it."

Angel fought the urge to roll his eyes. They'd been there all of five minutes, and he was already losing his patience. "Saturday, Dana."

"Oh, okay. Well, I didn't see them, but I got a call from Lorena, asking me if I knew what was going on with you and Sarah." She fidgeted with her napkin. "She was calling from Lujan Beach and said Sarah was there holding hands and making out with some guy."

Angel could feel it happening all over again. The rage seared through his veins. "Making out? Are you sure?"

"Well I think that's what she said."

Fuck. He should've known better than to think he'd get a straight answer from Dana, especially about Sarah.

"It's important, Dana." There was no masking the irritation in his voice.

"But I thought you said you two are broken up."

"We are." He raised his voice, then stopped to take a drink of his coffee, and give himself a second before speaking again. He decided to play nice. It might calm him down. He reached over and put his hand on hers.

He strained to speak calmly. "It's a pretty big detail, hon. I'm just trying to get it straight."

She smiled at his hand on hers. "Well, let me text her."

She pulled her phone out of her purse and began texting. When she was done, she set the phone down and reached across for Angel's hand again.

"Do you wanna talk about it?" She traced his fingers slowly. "I meant it when I said I'm here for you, Angel. You know that."

Angel forced a smile and sat back in his chair. "I know you did. But I'd rather not."

Just then, her cell phone beeped. She picked it up and read it. "All right, she says they were holding hands, embracing, and gazing into each other's eyes. She seemed really happy."

Angel tried to hide the wave of pain that jolted through him as she read the text. It made sense. Not once since he'd met Sarah had she hidden her affection for Sydney. After Saturday, he didn't think the pain could get any worse. Why was he doing this to himself? Why'd he come here? He already knew Sarah was in love with Sydney. Then he remembered. He needed confirmation. And now he had it.

Angel could tell Dana was annoyed that as soon as he'd got the information, he wrapped things up and herded her out of there. But he didn't care. He didn't even finish his coffee. After that text, he couldn't stomach anything.

He dropped her off and went back to the restaurant. Alex was on the phone in the back office when he walked in. He put his hand over the receiver and sat up when he saw Angel. "That was fast."

"Yep, just had coffee." Angel grabbed an apron from the shelf. He saw Alex hang up the phone. "You can take off now if you want. I got it from here."

"That was Valerie."

Angel slowed down for a second but didn't look at Alex. "Yeah?"

Angel hadn't even turned on his phone in the past two days. Told everyone he'd misplaced it and to just call the restaurant or the house. The last thing he wanted was to hear Sarah apologize for being in love with Sydney. He'd rather never speak to her again.

"Yeah," Alex said. "You won't have to worry about seeing Sarah around here anymore."

Angel stopped tying the apron and looked at Alex. "Why's that?"

"She's leaving for Arizona," Alex stood up, "tonight."

Angel's stomach roiled. He couldn't understand why that bothered him so much. He knew she'd be leaving soon. But she wasn't supposed to have left until Christmas, and that was more than a week away.

He finished tying his apron and shrugged. "Good for her."

He rushed past Alex and made his way to the office door. He didn't want to hear any more about Sarah, let alone talk about her.

"Hey, Angel," Alex said, "Valerie said Sarah and that dude are really just close friends."

Angel was still searing from what Dana's friend had said about them at the beach. Was it possible that Alex of all people was falling for this crap too? Admittedly, he'd thought about that possibility himself about a hundred times since Saturday. But it made no sense, and after today, he was even more convinced it couldn't be true.

Angel barked a laugh. "That's bullshit, Alex."

"Yeah, that's what I said."

In a killing mood, Angel turned on Alex, "Then why the hell are you telling me?"

Alex smirked at Angel's rising temper. "Because she made a pretty good argument."

Keeping his stony gaze on Alex, Angel didn't move. "She's in love with him."

"Did she tell you that?"

"She didn't have to." Angel charged out the door, leaving Alex behind in the office. He was done with this subject. But Alex wasn't. He followed Angel to the back door of the restaurant. Angel knew Alex was never one to meddle, but he had a feeling Valerie was behind his sudden need to pry.

"She's been crying for days, Angel."

Angel slowed his step a bit. He was beginning to feel sick again. The last couple of days had been hell for him, but he hated the thought of Sarah hurting. The image of her and Sydney assaulted his mind again, and he clenched his jaw.

"I don't want to hear about it," he snarled and continued toward the back door.

"I'm just saying." Alex continued. "If you ask me—"

Angel spun around. He was ending this now. "You're an annoying ass. And no one's asking you, so just drop it."

Alex laughed at that. But put his hands up in the air and walked away. Angel stormed through the hallway toward the back entrance of the restaurant.

Truth was he'd choked up a hell of a lot in the past two days himself. He was glad Sarah had left now because he sure as shit didn't know how he'd be able to handle seeing her at school. She might be in love with someone else, but his feelings for her hadn't changed at all. They were still every bit as profound as they'd always been. Add to that the raw emotional turmoil he was now carrying, and he knew seeing her again would be brutal.

The phone had been ringing the whole time he was walking. Anxious for a break from his thoughts, he answered the phone just inside the back door.

"Moreno's, Angel speaking."

"I, uh, just wanted to say goodbye." Sarah's voice was a whisper.

Angel felt his windpipe being squeezed. Could this day get any worse? He froze for a second. He said the only thing that came to his muddled mind. "You're leaving early."

He heard her take a deep breath. "Yeah, no sense in sticking around."

Of course not. That was the final blow. His heart could take no more. "Be happy, Sarah, goodbye." Enraged that his voice cracked on the last word, Angel didn't wait for her to reply and hung up.

Sarah stared out the bus window at the last California sunset she'd be seeing for a long time. She'd added yet another reason to be mad at herself.

Besides the fact that she'd never forgive herself for hurting Angel, she had topped it off by going against her better judgment calling him. She couldn't help herself when Valerie mentioned she'd just got off the phone with Alex and he said Angel had just gotten there. She knew she had a better chance getting a hold of him there than on his cell, and she longed to hear his voice just one more time before she left. She'd had the preposterous notion that it would give her closure. Instead, it only intensified the agony.

His voice was so icy and bitter, nothing like what it once had been. His distaste for her now was what hurt the most. He'd never look at her the way he once had, and the pain was devastating.

Sydney didn't know she would be in Flagstaff tonight. Sarah had asked him to meet her at the bus stop tomorrow afternoon. When she spoke with him that morning, he was still feeling terrible about the whole thing and thought maybe if he talked to Angel, he might get through to him.

Before today, she might've thought it a good idea. A tiny part of her was still holding on to the belief that Angel's love for her would help him accept her relationship with Sydney. But with the knowledge that Angel had moved on so quickly and was already meeting up with Dana, Sarah lost all hope. She'd obviously been in denial all this time.

Tomorrow was a big day. If Sydney knew what her plans were, he'd insist on going with her. But this was something she needed to do on her own. She'd already reserved a hotel room to stay in Flagstaff for the night.

She still had at least three hours before she arrived. She tried to nap but couldn't. Valerie lent her a book on the power of thought and positive thinking. She closed her eyes, put her head back, and tried to think of happier times.

She remembered the day she met Sydney, the heavy kid in the cafeteria at her elementary school. She'd seen him before that day, but she was so shy she would've never dreamed of talking to anyone that didn't talk to her first. Besides, by that point, Sarah had stopped wanting to make friends anymore. She never knew how long she'd be in the same school.

Sydney had sat across from her that day and just started talking. Sarah offered him her fries when she saw he finished his, and he took them. He claimed he had friends but he didn't care for the playground and it was too hot. So he preferred to hang out in the cafeteria instead.

It wasn't long before Sarah found out the real reason he had no friends. His weight was a big issue. The kids made fun of him relentlessly. He brushed it off like he didn't care. But she could see it hurt him, and now she knew even better. She was so glad now that she'd been there for him. In hindsight, it was as if something had brought them together. They needed each other.

Someone behind Sarah sneezed loudly and brought her out of her memory. She frowned. She'd finally been able to think of something other than her heartache. Valerie had been right. This was working. But the best part was she'd begun to doze off. She closed her eyes and tried to think of happy thoughts again. For the first time in days, Sarah got some sleep.

CHAPTER 23

The restaurant stayed busy all day. The week before Christmas always was that way with a lot of the local businesses holding their company Christmas parties there. It kept Angel busy though did little to jolt his ominous mood.

He never realized how many songs had to do with lost love and broken hearts until now. He'd found himself switching the channel on his car continuously—sometimes abruptly turning it off all together, thoroughly disgusted with the lump in his throat.

He'd finally turned his phone back on only to find it loaded with unheard messages and texts. Not all were from Sarah, but he cleared them all anyway. Angel wasn't about to chance inadvertently hearing Sarah's voice or reading a partial text of hers. Even that was too painful.

The brunch rush was over, and the restaurant was enjoying a very short break. The afternoon crew had arrived and was getting things ready for the dinner parties that evening.

Sarah's absence was glaringly obvious, so Angel had filled in his family about the break-up, briefly, some more than others. He told his parents they'd decided to call it off since she was going back to Arizona.

Sofia had taken it the hardest and to his surprise was mad at him for not understanding. What was there to understand? Sarah was moving in with another guy, and she'd known it all along.

He made it clear to everyone he didn't want to talk about it. The bitterness only grew stronger each time he did. Sofia must've seen something in him because she asked him not to hate Sarah. Angel had held in a laugh. Hating her would be a hell of a lot easier.

For the past ten minutes, Angel sat in the office, staring at the pencil he twirled through his fingers. Sarah's voice from her earlier call was still on his mind.

Sofia popped her head in. "Someone's here to see you out front."

Angel sat up. "Who?" Sofia shrugged and walked away in a hurry.

He got up and walked to the front of the restaurant. As he turned the corner, he saw his guest. Every muscle in his body tightened, and automatically he clenched his fists. Alex left the hostess desk and walked past Angel toward the dining room, oblivious as to what was going on.

Sydney glared at Angel "I got a bone to pick with you."

Maybe this wouldn't be such a bad Christmas after all. He'd felt like kicking someone's ass all week, and now here was Sydney, of all people, calling him out. Sydney wasn't a small guy, and he had a fairly good build, but either way, Angel felt certain he could take him. Hell, the way he was feeling, he had been ready to take Alex earlier. Angel smirked and leaned against the entry archway to the dining room

"I thought you and Sarah would be back in Arizona by now."

Sydney was still glaring at him. "Have you listened to any of her messages?"

Angel's teeth locked and swallowed hard. "I've heard all I need to know."

"Then you know she's a wreck?"

Feeling a dull ache in his heart, Angel shook off any thoughts of Sarah in pain. She was happy now. She was with Sydney, where she'd wanted to be all along.

"I'm sure you'll fix that."

Patrons were beginning to arrive in groups, filling up the front entrance, Sydney moved closer to Angel. "Is there somewhere else we can talk?"

Angel glanced at the hostess desk. Alex had already sent someone to cover it. He walked out the front door without saying anything, and Sydney followed.

The weather was considerably cold with many of the people arriving in coats and heavy jackets. But Angel felt hot.

The yellow Impala was parked across the street. Angel squeezed his eyes shut for a second, remembering that night. He leaned against Alex's truck parked just two cars away from the restaurant's front door.

"I don't have a lot of time." Angel crossed his arms over his chest.

"I'll make this fast."

Angel did his best to look bored.

"Sarah loves you, Angel."

Angel stared at Sydney, his expression shrouded. "Funny, she's never told me that."

"She couldn't. She felt too guilty saying it when she knew she was going to be leaving," Sydney said. "That's just the way she is."

Of course she'd felt guilty.

Angel chuckled. "She loves me so much she's dying to go back to Arizona to live with another guy?"

Sydney stared at him. "For someone who claims to love Sarah so much, you really don't know shit about her, do you?"

Angel pressed his lips together, making every attempt to remain calm. "I know she lied about why she really wanted to go back, and that she's been in love with someone else this whole time." His words oozed with bitterness.

"You have no idea, do you?" Sydney shook his head. "Sarah and I go back a long way, and yeah, she loves me. I love her too."

Angel felt the knife, already lodged deep in his heart, being twisted viciously.

"She's like a sister to me, always has been and always will be. But the thought of her being close to any other guy besides you has you so fucked up you're gonna lose her."

Angel's pulse rose. He stared at Sydney square in the eye. "She's made her decision."

"You made it for her."

"She made it the day she decided no one would stop her from going back to you," Angel clenched his teeth, "not even me."

Sydney glared at him in disbelief. "So, that's it? You're gonna let your insecurities come in the way of your feelings for her? You're letting her go, just like that?"

Angel didn't respond. It took everything in him to not bang his fist against Alex's truck.

Sydney looked disgusted. He shook his head and began walking away. After only a few steps, he stopped and turned around. Angel hadn't moved.

"You know, after all she'd told me about you, I expected a lot more. I was actually happy that she'd found you. But now I can see I was way off. I'm glad she's coming back to Arizona. You don't deserve her."

Angel felt the same sick feeling he'd felt that night he'd seen Sarah with Sydney. The same feeling he'd felt when he was sick the entire next day. He glared at his feet.

"I'm sure you two will be very happy."

Sydney turned around one last time before getting in his car. "Yeah, you would think that."

Sydney drove away, revving the engine loudly as he past Angel.

Sarah loves you, Angel. As much as he wanted to believe it, the thought of her undeniable attachment to Sydney made it impossible—the way she'd dressed for Sydney that night and the way she'd held his hand in the restaurant. It was clear how she really felt about him, and it stung like hell.

***

It took a moment for Sarah to realize where she was when she woke. It reminded her of when she was little and she and her mom lived in hotels for months at a time. She'd woken many times by herself, her mom already off to work.

Just like when she was little, she turned on the television. She didn't want to watch anything; she just hated the quiet. She sat for a moment on the edge of the bed and thought about the day ahead. She should've done this a long time ago.

After showering and having a cup of coffee from the small pot the hotel provided in her room, she was ready to go. She could've taken the transit bus, but she decided to walk. Sarah knew well enough to come prepared. She layered up and wore her boots and beanie. She drew in the crisp cool Flagstaff air and smiled, remembering when she and Sydney used to walk everywhere. The walk was only about a mile, and it helped lessen her anxiety.

Sarah arrived at the Coconino Women's Detention center just after nine. She'd called ahead, so she knew not to bring anything except her ID and money. After going through the security check and walking through the long sterile hallways, she signed in and was escorted to a big room that resembled her school cafeteria. There were other visitors there, sitting at tables across from inmates in blue jumpsuits.

It was all very somber. The only thing on the tables were boxes of tissues.

Footsteps and doors closing and opening echoed loudly, rattling her already overwrought nerves. Each time the door where the inmates were escorted in and out opened, she held her breath. It opened again, and out walked her mom. She looked small and frail. Her usually done up hair was in a ponytail, and her eyes were drawn with dark circles under them.

Sarah gasped but forced herself to smile. She wasn't here to make her mother feel worse. She was here because she missed her and desperately needed her.

Her mother's expression broke when she got close enough, and she hugged her tightly. "Oh, honey, I've missed you so much."

Sarah never wanted to let go. She hadn't realized just how much she missed her. Her emotions betrayed her but she didn't care anymore. She cried openly. "I miss you, Mommy."

Her mother held her for a little more then pulled away to examine Sarah's face. She wiped Sarah's tears with her fingers. "Come, sit down."

They sat down across from each other at one of the tables. Sarah had been worried her mother would be upset that she'd come to see her. She'd always said she didn't want Sarah to see her like that. Now Sarah understood why. But she didn't seem mad at all.

Her mother reached across the table for Sarah's hands. "Nobody told me you were coming."

"Nobody knows."

Her mother's eyes narrowed. "Who brought you? Angel?"

Sarah shook her head, glancing down at her their locked hands. "I came alone on the bus." Her mother's face grew more concerned. "Aunt Norma knows I'm in Flagstaff. I just didn't tell her I was coming to see you. I didn't want her to try to talk me out of it."

Sarah couldn't get over her mother's appearance. Many times when she was little and they were forced to move for reasons unknown to Sarah, her mother had often looked sad and worn, but never like this. She'd lost so much weight too.

"Are you going back today?"

That was the question Sarah had most dreaded. She knew her mother wasn't going to be happy about her moving back to Arizona.

"No, Mom." Her mother's weary eyes searched Sarah's face for answers. "I'm staying with Sydney's family for the holidays."

Her mother's expression didn't change. "What about Angel? I thought you two were so inseparable?"

The knot in Sarah's throat nearly choked her. All she could manage was to shake her head and look away before the tears escaped her eyes again. Her mom squeezed her hands.

"Tell me about it."

Sarah took one hand back to wipe the tears. She was angry at herself. This wasn't supposed to be about her. The last thing she wanted was to burden her mom any further, but her mother pushed.

"Talk to me, baby."

After composing herself, she breathed in deeply. Sarah reached out for her mother's hand again. Her mom took it and squeezed it, smiling. "He found out about Sydney." She knew her mom would be confused, and her expression was just that. "I never told him that Sydney was..."

Sarah felt foolish. She'd told her mom as much as she could about Angel. But their conversations on the phone were so short she always felt guilty about using up all their time talking about herself, so she'd left a lot of the details out.

"Was what, honey?"

Sarah glanced around the room and back at her mom. "Ever known anyone that doesn't believe a guy and a girl can be friends?"

In an instant, the look of confused concern on her mother's face was replaced with that of understanding, and she nodded.

"I messed things up bad, Mom." Talking to her mom felt really good.

"So, he didn't know about Sydney?" Her mom let go of her hand and reached over to the box of tissue on their table, handing it to Sarah. "Blow your nose."

Sarah did and then continued. "Not exactly."

She told her mom the entire sordid story about Angel assuming Syd was a girl, how she wanted to tell him the truth so many times, and how finally he found out the truth in the worst way. And then she told her how she'd called him to tell him she was leaving and how cold he'd been telling her to be happy.

"So he thinks you're staying in Arizona?"

Sarah bit her lip. "That's what I really wanted to talk to you about."

Her mother's eyebrow went up.

"Mom," Sarah's voice fell almost to a whisper, "I can't go back."

Her mom shook her head, but her expression was kind. Sarah looked away. "Honey, I want nothing more than your happiness. Look at me."

Sarah turned back at her mother's tired eyes. There was no way she would argue with her. When she first arrived in California, she was so bitter she didn't care how angry her mom would be when she moved back to Arizona. But after seeing her today, her heart yearned to give her mom any pleasure, no matter how minuscule.

"Listen to me, hon." She cupped one of Sarah's hands in both of hers. "I know right now this seems like the end of the world. And you'll never know how sorry I am that I wasn't there for you when it happened. But give it time. Things have a way of working themselves out. Angel will understand…"

Maybe it was Sarah's expression. She couldn't even pretend to believe that this would somehow get worked out, but her mother stopped mid-speech. She leaned over, a tiny smile rising from the corner of her lips. "I have good news."

"What?"

"Well, I wasn't going to say anything until I knew for sure, but you look so sad." Her mom pouted. "My lawyers found a loophole in my case."

For the first time since she'd been there, Sarah thought she saw a twinkle in her mother's eyes. "What does that mean?"

Her mom sat back with a cautious grin. "Well, I won't know anything until we go to court, and that won't be until after the holidays, but according to my lawyers, if everything goes well, I could be out by early spring."

Sarah jumped out of her seat, causing one of the guards to look at her funny. She gave him a crooked regretful smile and then hugged her mom. "Oh, my God, Mom! That's the best news ever."

Her mom beamed then went back to being serious. She motioned for Sarah to sit back down. "But you have to promise me you'll stay in California until then, Sarah. It's not that much longer."

Sarah felt an uneasiness settle in her stomach, but nothing could take away the joy of what she'd just heard. The smile was still pasted to her face, and she felt the lump in her throat again. This time it was joy that had her choked up, an emotion that had been so foreign to her all week. "Okay, Mom," she smiled "whatever you want."

Carina was a tall busty girl with blond hair, not at all what Sarah would have thought was Sydney's type. But the girl loved her music, and that alone could have Sydney talking for hours.

She didn't offer much at all for conversation but was polite. Sarah hoped they could become friends, especially if Sydney was in this for the long haul. But so far things had been awkward at best.

After just a few days of being around them, Sarah finally accepted it. Her and Sydney's relationship was one that was going to take some getting used to by *any* third party.

Sarah was so used to being completely uninhibited around Sydney. She *had*—after all—grown up with him. Around Carina, she had to catch herself before doing things she didn't even do around Angel. Like belch.

It was so easy to get right back to the way things had always been and start laughing and carrying on. It amazed her that although she could never get Angel completely off her mind, being around Sydney really helped.

Christmas Day at Sydney's was the same as usual. Mr. and Mrs. Maricopa were blasting the Christmas carols in the kitchen while they finished up dinner together. They were going to have a few family members and Carina over for dinner.

Sarah could barely hear the television in the front room over the music, but it didn't matter. She practically had the movie memorized; she'd seen it so many times.

Sydney walked out of the kitchen, shaking his head. "They're already hitting the eggnog." He chuckled.

Sarah barely looked up from the T.V. She sat on the floor using some of the pillows she'd used from the night before to plop against. Sydney turned to see what she was watching.

"Pride and Prejudice again?" He sounded disgusted. "Geez, haven't you seen that like a hundred times?"

Sarah ignored him, still staring at the television, but smirked. He sat down next to her and picked up the remote from the floor. Next thing she knew, there was football on the screen.

"Hey!"

"Now this is more like it." Sydney grinned.

"I had the remote first, and I'm your guest." She reached over for the remote, but he put his arm up, and she couldn't reach.

"I'm telling," she smiled wickedly. "Mrs. Maricopa!"

There was no way Sydney's mom could hear her over the loud music in the kitchen, and Sarah knew it. She got on her knees to try to reach it, but Sydney fell back laughing, and she fell onto him. She had her hand on the remote, and Sydney tickled her in the ribs. Sarah instinctively flinched and started laughing.

"No fair!"

She tickled him back, causing him to drop the remote, and she grabbed it, but he grabbed her by the waist, and she fell back, shielding the remote under her body. He pinned her down, trying to get the remote from under her. Sarah hadn't laughed that much in a while. She squeezed her eyes shut, trying to catch her breath between laughing. When she opened them and saw over Sydney's shoulder, Carina was standing in the middle of the living room, staring at them. She looked stunned, and Sarah pushed Sydney off her.

"Hi, Carina."

Sydney immediately turned his head. His body was still half on Sarah. He pushed himself away from Sarah.

"Hey, babe."

"I knocked but..." Carina's eyes went from Sarah, who was pulling down her blouse that had ridden up showing a bit of her midriff, to Sydney and then turned around and rushed back to the door.

"Carina, wait." Sydney jumped up. "Where you going?"

Carina walked out and Sydney followed her.

Sarah stood up and made her way to the window. She peeked out and saw them arguing. Carina appeared to be crying. Sarah couldn't believe how naïve she'd been. Angel would've had a much more violent reaction. Just because this was normal to them didn't mean it was to outsiders. It was like she had a brother, but she really didn't. They were out there for quite a while, but he finally convinced Carina to come back in.

Sarah had no idea what to say but knew immediately when they walked in by the look Sydney gave her it was better to not say anything. He got the chance later when Carina was in the restroom to tell Sarah everything was okay. But Sarah knew better. She'd almost ruined Christmas for them.

So when Valerie called a few days later to convince her to come back to La Jolla for New Year's Eve, she agreed. Originally she planned to stay in Arizona and spend it with Syd and Carina. Given what had happened though, she had decided to let them enjoy a romantic New Year's Eve without the third wheel.

Sydney wasn't happy she was leaving early, but he was glad that she'd decided to stay in California, at least until her mom got out of jail.

CHAPTER 24

Christmas had come and gone with no feelings of joy for Angel. The restaurant wasn't nearly as busy the week after Christmas as it had been the week before. His parents were gone for the week, visiting family in Mexico. Every year they left the week after Christmas and came back after the New Year. Angel and Alex had covered the morning shift at the restaurant, and since Sal was there for the week, he and Sofia covered the afternoon shift.

Angel was in no mood to celebrate New Year's Eve, especially knowing Sarah's birthday was at midnight and it wouldn't be him kissing her happy birthday. He slid his fingers over the chain Sarah gave him for his birthday, before dropping it back in the sock drawer and slamming it shut.

Alex poked his nose in his room. "What's with you?"

Angel glanced at him but didn't answer. He sat down to on his bed and began putting the socks on.

"I got people coming over, so get down here and help me clean this place up."

Angel's shoulders slumped. "Who's coming over?"

"None of your high school, rioting, crumb friends, well," he laughed, "except for Eric and Romero. But everyone else is grown up, so try to pretend."

Angel frowned. "What time?"

Alex had already walked away, but he yelled. "In about an hour."

Angel glanced at the clock. It was already close to nine. He had just worked out and showered. He was looking forward to a quiet night of shooting some pool and calling it an early one—not a damn party.

By the time he got downstairs, the kitchen counters had been transformed into a minibar. The music was blasting, and Romero was already there with a beer in his hand.

Sal and Sofia walked in just as Angel grabbed a beer from the fridge.

"What's going on?" Sal asked.

Alex walked back in from the backyard with an ice chest. "Party time, brutha."

Sal peered and Sofia grinned. Sal looked back at Angel. Angel raised his hands in the air. "Don't look at me. This is all him."

"Yeah," Alex said. "Don't worry. It's not any of his juvenile friends—except for Eric and Romero."

Romero pretended to be appalled. "I'm standing right here!"

Alex ignored him as he grabbed a bag of ice from the freezer. "It's just a few of my more refined friends."

Sal shook his head. "Good luck. This place better all be in one piece tomorrow 'cause I ain't taking the heat for any of this."

Sofia ran out of the kitchen and up the stairs. Alex stopped to watch her. "Where is she going?"

"Yeah, she's gonna be here around all your refined college friends." Sal smirked, examining the bottles of booze on the counter.

Alex didn't like that. "Well, no one invited her."

Angel chuckled. "What are you gonna do? Lock her in her room?"

Alex raised his eyebrow. "Now there's a thought."

"Oh, yeah," Romero smirked. "College boys are what you guys need to be worried about."

All three brothers stared at him. "What does that mean?" Alex asked.

Romero shook his head and shrugged. "I don't know. I just felt left out."

Angel who was closest shoved him.

They finished getting things ready and people started arriving. Angel hung out with Romero in the front room, his thoughts, as usual, miles away. Romero kept nudging him to get his attention. After a few annoying conversations with what Alex referred to as refined college girls, he'd had enough. He headed back to the kitchen for food.

He stopped dead when he walked in the kitchen. Sofia was wearing jeans and heels that made her look way taller, not to mention older, but it was the blouse he couldn't take his eyes off. It was the same backless one Sarah had worn at that very first party he had talked to her.

Alex walked in after Angel. "Sofia, what are you wearing?"

Sofia looked down at her blouse. "What? Sarah lent it to me a while back. What's wrong with it?"

"You look ..." Alex struggled to find the word.

"Hot?" she teased.

Alex's jaw worked. "You need to change."

"Why?"

Eric walked in the back door and froze when he saw Sofia.

Alex saw the way he looked at her. "Go change now, Sofia, before anyone else gets here."

Sofia stomped out of the kitchen and up the stairs. Angel felt bad. He didn't mind the way she looked, but he was glad the blouse would be gone. Just seeing it had brought back memories of holding and kissing Sarah for the first time. It was all too painful, and as much as he missed her, he was glad he wouldn't have to see her again.

The time went by quickly, and before long, they were counting down. Angel was outside with Sal, Alex, and a couple of the girls. Sofia had gone inside with Eric and Romero to watch the countdown on the big television.

When they were done with the hugs and happy New Year's, Alex took off to bring some more beer from inside. Angel followed, his mind still on Sarah and what she might be doing right at that moment. She was officially eighteen now.

Alex walked in the kitchen. "What the fuck?"

Angel couldn't see, but Alex was livid. He caught up in time to see Alex charge Eric. "You're kissing my little sister?"

"It was a New Year's kiss." Sofia said, stepping in front of Eric.

"I don't give a shit! You don't kiss my sister like that. What the fuck is wrong with you?"

"Like how?" Angel tried holding Alex back. What the hell had he seen? By then other people were sticking their heads in the kitchen, and Sal rushed in from the backyard.

"It was just for New Year's, Alex. Relax," Eric said.

Alex reached over Sofia and grabbed Eric by the shirt. "I know what I saw, fucker. Sofia move!"

But between Angel, Sal, and Sofia, they held him off. Eric began for the door.

"What the hell, Alex?" Angel asked. "Wait, Eric."

"No, I want him out," Alex barked. "I ever see you around my sister again, I swear to God I'll fuck you up!"

Sal winced. "Enough, Alex."

Alex hadn't seemed drunk earlier, but now Angel could only assume that he was. Eric left in a hurry. Angel turned to Sofia. She looked ready to cry. People had given them their privacy and left the kitchen, except for Romero who stood at the doorway.

Angel didn't even want to ask. It was too bizarre. But he had to. "How was he kissing you?"

"Your friend had his tongue down her throat!" Alex shouted.

Before Angel could wrap his brain around what he just heard, Sofia spoke up. "Maybe I had my tongue down *his* throat, ever think about that?" The tears streamed down her cheeks. She stunned them all momentarily. "I'm not a baby anymore, Alex. I'm tired of being treated like one!"

"You're sixteen, Sof," Alex's tone was much softer now, and Angel knew he wasn't drunk.

"I'll see him if I want to. You can't stop me!" Sofia rushed out, pushing Romero as she made her way out the kitchen.

"Like hell you will." Alex said, soft at first and then again louder. "You hear me Sof? Like hell you will!"

Alex turned and glared at Angel. "I don't want that asshole around her again."

* * *

Sarah was tired and her feet ached. The party showed no signs of dying down. Valerie tried to pull her into the circle of girls where she was dancing, but Sarah motioned that she was going to the restroom.

Valerie's friends lived in a gated community. They had a recreation center, and that was where the party was being held. It was about the size of a small banquet room with a pool just outside.

Sarah passed the restroom and went outside. It was chilly but felt good. She sat down on one of the picnic tables by the pool and searched her small clutch for her compact. Her cell phone was lit. She'd just missed a text. Sydney had already called her to wish her a happy birthday.

When she flipped it over, she noticed she also had two missed calls. They were both from Sofia. Sarah smiled. Since the break-up, Sofia had called her a couple of times: once to tell her how sorry she was about them splitting up, and another just after Christmas to tell her she missed her and wished she was still in California. Both times Sarah had choked up.

She didn't remember if she'd even mentioned her birthday being on New Year's to Sofia. She clicked the envelope and read the text.

I hate my brothers. I'm so mad I'm crying.

Call me please. I need to talk to you.

Sarah thought of the cavemen and couldn't help frowning. What had they done now? She called Sofia, and she picked up right away. She was hysterical. Sarah could barely make the words out. The only thing she could make out was that Alex had ruined her life.

"Sofia, slow down. Take a deep breath." Sarah did her best to speak in a soothing voice. She remembered her mom doing that to her when she was little and she was crying. "I can't understand you."

Sofia breathed heavily, but Sarah could tell she was trying to calm herself. She sounded like a little girl, and Sarah wished she could be there to hug her.

"Alex told Eric to stay away from me."

Sarah dreaded asking why, but she did anyway. She listened quietly while Sofia told her the whole story, at times breaking down and crying again. After she'd calmed though, she sounded more determined and angry than anything.

"It's not fair, Sarah. Eric's been nothing but a gentleman with me. It was all me, and I told them."

"You did?"

"Yes." She sounded pleased. "I told them it was *my* tongue down *his* throat."

Sarah let out a gasping laugh. "No, you didn't?"

Finally, Sofia didn't sound so sad. Sarah even thought she heard her laugh. "It's the truth. Eric always holds back. He's so gentle with me." She sighed. "It drives me crazy, so then I become the aggressor."

Sarah still couldn't believe Sofia would say such a thing. In some ways, she wished she'd been there, but good God, of all the brothers to catch them, it had to be Alex? Knowing she would've felt terribly uncomfortable, she was relieved she hadn't been there. "What did Alex say when you said that?"

Sofia told her about how they'd all been speechless, even described the stunned look on Angel's face. For a moment, it seemed Sofia had escaped her dejected mood. But when she got to the end, she started sniffling again.

"Eric texted me, but only to see if I was okay. He said he didn't want to chance my brothers checking my phone. I told him I wanna try to talk to Angel about this. He didn't think it was a good idea and made me promise I'd tell him before I did."

Sarah tried to concentrate, but just hearing *his* name had rattled her. Angel wasn't the most reasonable person she knew. But under the circumstances, she didn't see how it would hurt.

"What would you say? You can't tell him you guys have been keeping it from him all this time. He'll be furious. Trust me."

Sarah had already begun to worry about how Angel might be feeling right now. She knew he felt completely betrayed by her, and now this? Eric was one of his closest friends. Her heart ached for him.

Sofia said she would think about it and run it past her before she did to see what she thought. They talked for a little while longer, and Sarah fought the incredible temptation to ask about Angel and if Dana had been at the party. But she decided not to torture herself. The fact that he hadn't bothered to even send a generic happy birthday text said it all. He was done with her.

CHAPTER 25

As usual, Angel hadn't gotten much sleep. He was up early and walked over to Sofia's room, careful that he didn't wake Alex. He needed to get to the bottom of this whole Eric thing, and he didn't want Alex there riling Sofia up to the point where'd she say something absurd like she had last night.

He'd known Eric too long and trusted him completely. There had to be more to the story. This wasn't a conversation he was looking forward to. He wouldn't even know where to start, but he had to do it fast before Alex was up.

He knocked softly on Sofia's half-opened door before peeking in. To his surprise, she was already up and on her computer. She minimized the screen she was on when he walked in.

To his relief, he didn't have to think of something to say. She spoke first. "Are you mad at me?"

Angel lifted a shoulder. "I don't know."

She stood up and closed the door behind Angel. The expression on her face reminded him of when they were kids. Sofie had always been handled with care. It's what they were taught for as long as he could remember. And it stuck real well. *No one messed with Sweet Sofie.* Not then—not now. Angel sat on her bed, and she took a seat back at her desk.

"Look, what happened last night was my fault. I take complete responsibility." She spoke in a hushed voice, and her eyes seemed to plead. "Angel, he gave me a New Year's hug, and I kissed him."

Angel stared at her. "Why?"

She looked at him then away. "I like him. I always have."

This was not what Angel had wanted to hear. He shook his head. Eric was like family and Sofia was ... well, his baby sister, damn it. He stood up, not sure what to say.

"No."

"No, what?" Sofia stood up in front of him.

"You can't."

"Why not? Jesus, you guys act like I'm a baby. I'll be seventeen this year—Sarah's age when she started dating you."

Angel's jaw locked. "That's different."

"How?"

"It just is, Sof."

Angel tried to walk around Sofia to leave. This conversation was over. Alex was right. Eric would just have to stay away. But Sofia didn't let him by her. She put her hand on his chest and looked him straight in the eye.

"You and Alex are going to have to face it sooner or later. I'm not a little girl anymore."

Angel wasn't used to her being so dauntless, and he didn't like it. "Dad won't have it either."

"I'll handle daddy, Angel. Just promise me you won't be mad at Eric. It really wasn't his fault."

Angel nodded and she let him by. That hadn't gone exactly as planned, but he was relieved he wouldn't have to be mad at Eric. Alex was a different story. The image of Eric kissing his baby sister would be branded into his hard head for a while. But he'd have to get over it eventually. Unless he wanted Sofie reminding him over and over that she was the one who initiated the kiss. Angel shuddered just thinking about it.

He didn't want too much time to go by and make things weird when he finally talked to Eric. Not only that, the conversation he had with Sofia had left him uneasy. He needed to get a few things straight with Eric. He planned on calling him later that day, but Eric beat him to it. His phone rang just as he walked into the restaurant.

"Hey, Eric, what's up?"

There was silence for a brief moment, and Angel smiled. He knew his cheery hello would throw Eric.

"Hey ... how's everything?"

"You mean with Alex?" Angel chuckled. "That's gonna be the same for a while. But Sofia told me what happened. And it's cool. I'm sorry Alex went off on you like that, man."

Eric cleared his throat. "Nah, it's all good. I know it could've been a lot worse."

Angel laughed. "Yeah, you got out of there in one piece."

"No shit. I had to change my pants when I got home though."

"Ha! Romero said you would."

"Yeah, I'm sure that ass had a lot to say."

It was actually a surprise Romero didn't say too much that night. The party was pretty much a wash after that whole mess. Alex was too wound up to relax, so they just started cleaning up, and everyone took off.

Angel lowered his voice when he walked by Alex who was sitting in one of the booths, looking over the restaurant mail from the week before. He was in charge of it while his parents were gone and, of course, he was just now getting to it.

"Listen, I guess it's not unheard of for a little sister to have a crush on her older brother's friend, right?" He paused, but Eric didn't say a word. Angel wasn't sure how to get the rest out without sounding awkward. He never imagined having to have this discussion, but here he was. Awkward or not he was getting it out. "You can't let anything like that happen again, all right?" That was a little lame, but he'd gotten to the point, and he felt satisfied.

"Angel, she's almost seventeen."

Angel stopped in his tracks and actually looked at his phone. "Are you shitting me?"

"I hear what you're saying," Eric added quickly. "And yeah, you got it, man. But c'mon, how long do you think you can keep her from dating anyone?"

Angel was walking again but could feel the agitation set in. He got that his sister was almost seventeen, but you couldn't measure maturity with a number. Sofie was different. "Don't worry about that. Just promise me you won't give into any of her silliness, will you?"

He heard Eric exhale loudly. "Yeah, yeah, you have my word."

"Thank you." Was that too much to ask for? But Angel couldn't help thinking this was another conversation that hadn't exactly gone his way. This year already sucked, and it had just gotten started.

✳✳✳

When Sarah had gotten back from Arizona, she made Valerie promise not to mention to Alex that she was back. So when he called her New Year's Eve to invite her over for his party, Sarah felt bad that Valerie turned him down.

She'd offered to stay home. She wasn't feeling up to partying anyway, but Valerie was actually kind of pissed about Alex asking her at the last minute. She said he insisted he planned it at the last minute, but she told him she wasn't canceling the plans she'd already made.

"No one plans a New Year's party last minute," she fumed. "He must think I'm pretty stupid."

Sarah knew her stay in California was only for a short while. Her mother had called her on her birthday and told her she'd spoken to her lawyer and things were looking even better.

Things between her and Angel were completely hopeless. Sydney had called her on the day after her birthday and confessed he'd driven out to see Angel just before Christmas. He hadn't told her sooner because he didn't want to make the holidays any harder for her than they already were. But he told her of Angel's refusal to even try to hear her side of it.

At first, she was hurt, but since then, anger had set in. She was sure Dana had something, if not *everything*, to do with Angel's unwavering frame of mind.

She'd see Sofia soon enough when she showed up for track after school, but in the meantime, she only needed to take three classes. She made sure they were all scheduled at the end of the day. Her plan was simple: move quickly from class to class, and keep her head low. The last thing she wanted was to run into Angel and Dana.

It was only a matter of time before she'd see him. She knew this, but she wanted to postpone it as much as possible.

The second she walked into her physics class, she realized her planning was all for nothing. Angel was sitting in the back of the class, and their eyes locked. For a moment, she was frozen. She gathered her thoughts enough to know if she sat in the front, she wouldn't have to look at him. Not surprisingly, most of the front seats were empty and she sat down in the closest one to her.

She'd barely sat down when, Kim, a girl she knew from the track team leaned over.

"Oh my God, I thought you moved back to Arizona."

Sarah turned to see a face full of braces smiling big at her. She realized then she hadn't noticed who else was in the class. The only one she'd seen was Angel. Everyone else was a complete blur. Her breathing was going back to normal, and she forced a smile.

"Change of plans. I'll be here a little longer."

The class started, and she tried to concentrate on what the teacher was lecturing. She hardly heard a word. All she kept thinking of was Angel's expression when he saw her. She was trying to put a finger on it. He wasn't angry, but he certainly wasn't pleased.

When class was over, as much as she told herself to not look back, she couldn't resist. She glanced back to where he'd been sitting, but he was gone. He apparently wasn't planning on even speaking to her. She bit her lip. Though she felt it coming, she forced the anguish away. She was done crying for Angel Moreno.

The rest of the day was fairly painless. When she showed up to track practice, Coach Rudy was overjoyed to hear she was trying out for the team. He said it was a mere formality. She was already in.

No one was happier to see her than Sofia. Sarah had gotten a little choked up when she'd hugged her so hard she thought she'd never let go. Sarah explained briefly that she would be around for a little longer but told her she had every intention of going back to Arizona as soon as her circumstances changed.

The next couple of days were even worse. Angel didn't show up to her physics class, and by the end of the third day, his name wasn't being called during roll call. He'd obviously changed his schedule. It was a slap in the face, but she sucked it up. At least she didn't have to deal with seeing him in class every day.

Sydney was getting increasingly annoyed with Angel's continued inflexibility. That weekend, she told Sydney about Angel changing his schedule, and to her surprise, she broke down and sobbed. Sydney was livid.

"Fuck him, Lynni. He's an asshole."

Could she have been that off about Angel? It amazed her now that somewhere in her warped mind, she'd actually thought Syd and Angel could be friends someday.

"I'm just waiting for my mom to be out, so I can come home," she sniffed. "It's all I want."

"Don't put your life on hold though, Lynn. It may be a while. Enjoy yourself. Go out. Seriously, have fun."

Sarah couldn't even imagine having fun. She could barely concentrate on just getting through the day without having some kind of emotional breakdown.

*

Things took a turn on Monday during practice. As if her emotional turmoil wasn't enough, she now had to deal with physical pain. During a routine warm up run, Sarah stepped in a hole and went down hard. She felt her ankle crunch and knew it was bad. Sofia was immediately by her side, but Sarah barely managed to stand.

Coach Rudy came over as soon as he was aware.

"Don't try to walk on it, Sarah. You'll make it worse. We have to get ice on this fast."

Before Sarah knew what was happening, she was in his arms, and he was carrying her toward the gym. Sarah put her arms around his neck for support. Some of the kids snickered as they walked past them. She felt a little uncomfortable until she moved her foot the wrong way and the stabbing pain in her ankle made her forget everything. She squeezed her eyes shut and grimaced, willing the pain to go away.

When the coach was satisfied they'd iced it enough, he carried her to his car and gave her a ride home. Sarah was a little surprised he'd called practice early on her account but was glad she was going home.

Coach Rudy seemed really concerned about Sarah's ankle. He gave her some paperwork he had in his office on proper care of a sprained ankle and talked about the do's and don'ts on the way home. Then the subject turned to what Sarah had dreaded.

"So when will you know for sure how long you'll be here? I mean, can we count on you for the whole season?"

Sarah had always been very vague about her situation, but he never pried. She had a feeling he sensed it was a sore subject. Still she felt bad that he was so enthused about her being on the team and she couldn't give him a concrete answer. She didn't want him to think she wasn't taking the team seriously.

"My mom's in jail." She stared out the window afraid to see his expression. Aside from her family and Sydney, Angel was the only person she'd ever told.

"Hmm, I see," he said. "So you're waiting to see when she'll be out?"

His demeanor surprised her. She thought maybe he'd be uncomfortable and change the subject or something, but she may as well have said her mom was at the mall. She turned to look at him.

"Yeah, we won't know anything for a few weeks, so I really can't say." She glanced down at her hands. "I do want to be on the team though."

She really did. Since her mom had made her promise to stay in California, it was one of the things she'd focused on to stay positive. Running was her passion, and she planned on using it as therapy.

"Oh, I know you do. I can see it when you're running." He pulled into her driveway and turned the car off. "There's a skill for everything. A lot of people think in track you just run, but it's not just about running. It's about knowing when to turn the wheels on and when to save them. You have it, Sarah. I saw it the first time I saw you relay."

He was smiling at her with genuine pride like a big brother. It made her feel good. Her coach back home had said the same thing. She smiled back at him. "Thanks."

"Hey." He waited until she was looking at him again. His expression had changed. He was concerned coach again. "I have a brother that's been in and out of jail, Sarah. It's nothing to be ashamed of. It took me a while to understand that what he's done does not reflect on the person that *I* am."

Sarah thought about it. She'd never been ashamed of her mom, but the thought of anyone speaking badly about her enraged her. The less people knew, the less ammunition they had against her.

Sarah nodded. "I know. But some people just wouldn't get it. *I* don't even get it." She turned and made herself as comfortable as she could without moving her ankle. "All I know is she took money from her boss for years. She offered to pay it back. I didn't even know you could go to jail for that kind of stuff. You would think because she was a single mom, they could've just made her pay it back and given her probation or something."

Coach Rudy listened quietly without interrupting. He also turned his back against the car door and made himself a little more comfortable.

Sarah told him how she'd planned all along to move back to Arizona and finish high school at her old school. Then she told him about seeing her mom in jail and why she was back in La Jolla after all.

The coach never once appeared to be sympathizing or judging. But he did hang on her every word. He waited until she was completely done, then he took a deep breath and smiled again. "I didn't think I could have any more respect for you than I already did. You're very mature and strong for your age. A lot of girls your age would've taken something like this as the end of their life. But you've handled it with such grace. I would've never guessed you had all this going on."

Sarah's lips went up in a half smile. "You know, this is the first time I've talked about my mom since she's been in jail without crying. It feels good."

"That's 'cause it's almost over. You're almost there, Sarah. And you're doing a great job. Just one thing, next time you go see your mom, tell someone. I'm sure you didn't think it was a big deal, but if something had happened to you, it would've been a whole twenty-four hours before anyone would've even noticed."

Sarah made a mental note. She felt really good after her talk with the coach. She soaked her ankle in warm water while she talked to Sydney that evening. To her surprise, he wasn't as moved as she was about her conversation with the coach.

"Isn't that the one Angel called a pervert?"

Just hearing his name was enough to bring her spirits down, and she frowned. "Yes, but he also calls you my boyfriend. So, what's your point?"

"I'm just saying that's kind of weird that he'd take you home isn't it?"

"What was he supposed to do? I couldn't walk." Sarah tried moving her ankle a little and immediately regretted it.

"Uh, hello, he could've had you call someone to pick you up."

"Why? When he could just do it himself and it was faster?" Sarah couldn't believe Sydney was actually thinking like this.

"Maybe because he had a team full of kids waiting to practice?"

Sarah didn't respond to that. She was getting annoyed.

"Look Lynni, I don't know, but most of the times when there are rumors like that about teachers or coaches, there's some truth to them. Maybe some stuff gets added in for a little more flavor, but if you dig deep, the rumors started from something valid."

There was no way. Coach Rudy had never been anything but nice and encouraging to her. The people that started those rumors were idiots as far as she was concerned. Syd made her promise she'd be careful, but she knew she had nothing to worry about. Coach Rudy was not a pervert.

CHAPTER 26

Seeing Sarah had been worse than Angel could've ever imagined. It was completely unexpected, and he was in no way ready for the blow. He had sat in class that first day for all of twenty minutes before he'd ducked out the back door.

He almost went home but instead decided to go to the counselor's office and switch his schedule around. He didn't care what classes he got stuck with as long as he didn't have to see her every day. It would kill him.

Since then, he'd done everything he could to avoid her. Sofia told him the first night that all Sarah had told her was that there'd been a snag in her plans, but that it was only temporary. She was still going back to Arizona. She just wasn't sure when. Sofia wasn't happy that Angel had no intention of reconnecting with Sarah, much less hang out with her.

The whole week had been a nightmare. The more he tried to not think about her, the more nosey idiots asked him about her. It seemed the whole damn school was talking about it.

To top it off, Dana was at it again. She conveniently mistook their little coffee outing over the break as an invitation back into his life. She'd gone back to hugging him every time she saw him. And he knew she was behind the rumors that had quickly spread about Sarah cheating on him.

The weekend was uneventful, and he finally went a whole couple of days without anyone asking him about Sarah. Monday went by pretty fast, but Angel wondered if he'd ever get over that tense feeling he had the whole day, worrying about seeing her.

That evening he worked out with Alex in the backyard. They'd just finished when Sofia strolled out holding a bottle of water. Angel lay back down on the bench to rest.

"Sarah got hurt today during practice." Sofia sat down on one of the patio chairs.

Angel sat up.

"She's still here?" Alex asked.

"Yeah." Sofia turned to look at Angel. "You didn't tell him Sarah didn't leave?"

Angel shrugged. His thoughts were still on Sarah getting hurt.

"No shit?" Alex smirked. "No wonder you've been so uptight all weekend."

Angel ignored him. Sofia hadn't moved her eyes away from him. But he still couldn't bring himself to ask anything about Sarah. Turned out he didn't have to.

"She twisted her ankle during one of the runs. It was pretty bad. Coach Rudy had to carry her to his car."

Alex wiped the sweat off his brow and laughed. "The perv?"

Angel had a feeling Sofia coming out to tell them was not without reason. And if that reason was to piss him off, it was working.

"To his car?" Angel tried not to sound as disgusted as he felt.

Sofia took a swig of her water and eyeballed Angel. When she was done, she took her time putting the cap back on before she answered. "Well, yeah, she wasn't gonna walk home."

"He took her home?" Alex's bemused enthusiasm wasn't helping Angel. He was trying hard to keep his cool. He had a feeling what Sofia was up to. But even if it was all true, it didn't matter what she was up to. He was still incensed.

"Yeah, that's why I'm home early. He called the rest of the practice off."

Alex sat down cackling. "Oh man. This is rich. So now she's dating the coach?"

"Shut up, Alex." Angel finally snapped.

"Yeah." Sofia jumped in. "You see that's how rumors get started. He was nice enough to take her home, and all of sudden they're dating?"

"I dunno. The guy is slick. I know a few chicks that actually *did* date him."

"He can get arrested, you idiot. Lose his job." Suddenly, Angel was defending the pervert's intentions?

"Nah." Alex was still grinning. "He knows what he's doing. Sarah's eighteen, right? It's legal."

Angel was beginning to wonder if Sofia and Alex were in on this together. Between the two of them, they'd managed to irritate him to no end. He stood up.

"Sarah wouldn't do that," Sofia said and then added, "besides, she's still not over Angel."

Angel stopped and looked at Sofia. "She said that?"

Sofia's expression went flat. "No, but—"

"But nothing." Angel walked past her. "She's going back to Arizona because that's where she wants to be, Sof. I just don't know what the hell's taking her so damn long."

"Did you know her friend Sydney has a girlfriend?"

Angel stopped, but didn't turn around to face her. "Is that a fact?" With all the damn rumors going around, he didn't know what to believe anymore.

"Yep, a serious one. Sarah spent Christmas with them," Sofia walked around to face him. Her expression was hopeful. "Does that change things?"

Angel thought about it for a second, and that image that he'd finally been able to stop seeing every time he thought of her assaulted him again. That dress—that *damn* dress she'd worn for Sydney the night she lied about where she was. And the way she was all done up. He'd never seen her that way before. Angel clenched his teeth.

"No."

He took a long shower and took in everything Sofia had just dumped on him. Even if he did get past the dress thing, which he knew he wouldn't, he'd never be okay with Sarah having so much affection for another guy. Never.

*

Angel sat in his car, waiting for Sofia to finish practice. He'd gotten there early and from where he was parked, he had a perfect view of the bleachers. He chewed his gum slowly as a calming technique when he saw Sarah make her way up the bleachers with her crutches and sit down. It had been four days since she'd hurt her ankle and from the looks of it, it hadn't healed at all.

This was the first time he'd seen her all week. He'd picked up Sofia every day that week, except Monday when she got off early, but Sarah hadn't been there until now. Even from that distance, he couldn't keep his eyes off her. She wore her hair down. The wind had picked up, and she kept pulling strands of hair away from her face. She sat there, consumed in the team practicing without her.

He thought of how different things would be if Sydney didn't exist. He'd be sitting there with her now, no doubt, moving the hair away from her face and taking advantage of the moment to kiss her each time.

Something heated inside him when he noticed Coach Perv walk out of the gym. The coach's eyes were instantly on Sarah. He wrote something on a clipboard, glanced at the team a few times, then his eyes were back on Sarah again. Angel swallowed hard when Coach Rudy started walking toward her.

The coach took a seat right next to Sarah, and immediately his hands were all over her ankle.

"What is he a fucking doctor now?" Angel muttered to himself.

They talked and even laughed. The coach stood up a couple of times and yelled out a few things to the rest of the team practicing on the field but never once moved away from Sarah's side.

Angel pounded lightly on the bottom of the steering wheel over and over trying not to lose his patience. But the damn coach hadn't stopped talking to Sarah since he'd sat next to her.

Sarah shook her head to move the hair away from her face, and then the coach reached over and tucked a strand behind her ear.

Angel spit his gum out the window and got out of the car. He took a deep breath. The air was cool, and it helped him cool off a little—very little. He leaned against the car, his eyes on them the whole time.

Don't do it. Just stay here and wait for Sofia. She's not your concern anymore.

Angel glanced down at his watch. He couldn't get over the coach's blatant disregard for the team. The rest of the week when he'd picked up Sofia, he'd been out there riding them hard. Now he was so busy with Sarah he'd barely addressed them, and practice was almost over.

The coach said something that made Sarah laugh out loud. Angel looked around to see if anyone else had noticed their banter. Didn't she realize people would talk? No one seemed to notice, but when the coach put his hand on her ankle again, Angel started walking.

He had no idea what he was going to say or do, but even the voice in his head couldn't stop him. Angel had made no secret of his relationship with Sarah last semester, and the coach had seen them together plenty of times. Maybe just seeing Angel would make him back the hell off.

Angel had made it halfway to the bleachers when the coach called everyone in. That's when his eyes met Sarah's. The smile on her face dissolved when she saw him, and she looked away.

He took slower steps toward the bleachers now as the coach gave his speech on what he thought they needed to work on. What a joke. He'd spent the entire practice chatting it up with Sarah, and now he was going preach to them?

Angel reached the bottom of the bleachers when the coach was done. Everyone started on their way, and Sofia came over to meet him. Sarah's back was turned to him as she gathered her crutches.

The coach held her by the arm when she lost her balance. Angel concentrated hard on relaxing. Sarah laughed when the coach called her a klutz, and she almost lost her balance again.

"C'mon, Sarah, you're killing me," the coach teased.

"I got it now." She giggled as she stood up straight.

Her back was still to Angel. She hadn't seen him that close yet, and the coach hadn't noticed him in the crowd.

"You need a ride home?" the coach asked. "I can drop you off."

"That's all right, Coach. She's got a ride."

Both the coach and Sarah turned to look at him. Angel didn't feel like he was talking to a coach at his school anymore. He was big but young, and what Alex had said hit him in the gut. This guy was slick and Sarah *was* legal. The coach stared him down like a rival and looked back at Sarah.

Sarah peered at Angel. "Really? Funny I wasn't aware."

Her attitude surprised Angel, but he didn't back down. "Yeah, I'm taking you home."

Sarah stomped down the bleachers. Her crutches made every step louder than normal. The coach was steadfast behind her.

"I'd rather walk." Her eyes were ablaze.

But Angel noticed a slight break in the heat when their eyes locked and took advantage. "Why?"

She glanced away quickly and then stared at him again. Angel's heart raced. She was so close he fought with himself to not take her face in his hands and kiss her as he had so many times before.

"You haven't even said hello to me since I've been back." She stopped when her emotions betrayed her. Her rigid stare faltered. And when Angel saw her beautiful eyes well up, he knew he'd made a huge mistake. "Don't you even wanna know why I'm still here?"

Angel panicked when he saw the tears line the sides of her cheeks. This was the last thing he'd imagined would happen. He could think of nothing else to do but shake his head. "I'm sorry." Was all that he managed to get out.

She stared at him incredulously and then leaned on her crutch to wipe the tears. In an instant, she went from weepy to resolute. "Well, I'm sorry too."

She looked at Sofia. "I'll see you Monday."

Coach Rudy had backed away but was still close.

"Does that offer still stand?"

"Of course," the coach smiled. "You're on my way home."

Angel clenched his jaw but didn't go after her. The coach turned casually to look at Angel one last time. There was something about the way he smiled then reached out and put his hand on Sarah's shoulder as they walked away. Angel was sure of it this time. Rudy was challenging him.

✳✳✳

Sarah didn't think there was any part of her heart left to break. She was so angry at herself for crying. Why did he still have so much power over her? It was pathetic the way her entire body went into a frenzy from just seeing him.

Being that close to him had such an overwhelming effect on her. She couldn't hold in what she was feeling, but his obvious contempt for her now was undeniable. He didn't even care why she was still here.

She tried desperately to shake it off on the ride home. Talking to Coach Rudy about her mom was one thing, but telling him about Angel would be quite another. Sydney would be the first to point *that* out.

She was quiet most of the way, and he finally asked. "Are you okay?"

Sarah nodded but didn't offer anything.

"You don't have to tell me about it," he said. "Just hope you know, even though it feels like you won't right now, you'll get over him eventually. I promise."

He always knew exactly what to say. Sarah had always thought it was just a coach thing. On the field whenever she questioned herself, he always knew just when to say something that would make her feel better. But now even off the field, his words were so comforting.

"I'm gonna go see my mom again."

They pulled in her driveway, and he turned the engine off. "Really, when?"

"On Sunday, but I leave tomorrow."

"Did you tell anyone?" he smiled.

"Well, I'm telling you."

"Really? No one else knows?"

He leaned against the door, and for a moment, he seemed much younger than how she usually perceived him. The way he was looking at her reminded Sarah of Angel when they used to park in their place and talk. Sydney's words came to her. *The rumors started from something valid.*

"Something wrong?"

Sarah shook her head. "No, I'm sorry. My mind was somewhere else. What did you say?"

She felt stupid. Just because he was so young looking didn't mean anything.

"I asked if I'm the only one who knows you're going?"

Sarah chuckled. "No, everyone knows, even my mom this time."

"You taking the bus again?"

"Yeah, and my friend is meeting me there."

He frowned. "That's a long ride to take all on your own. Can't your aunt or cousin go with you?"

There was something about Coach Rudy. Maybe it was because she'd never had a father figure or any older siblings, but his kind words and his worrying warmed her. She liked it.

"Valerie gets car sick on long trips, especially in a bus. And my aunt has to work." She smiled. "But I'll be okay. I slept most of the way last time."

"I'd offer to take you, if I didn't have to work. It's a beautiful drive. And," he emphasized, "I've never been to the Grand Canyon."

Sarah scrunched up her nose. "You work on the weekends?"

"Not every weekend. I ref youth soccer."

"Really?" He was so big she never imagined him as a soccer player. "So, you play also, right?"

"Well, I used to, back in the day," he laughed. "Now, I just ref. Too old to play. But it's still fun."

"You're not that old," Sarah regretted the moment it came out of her mouth. It seemed inappropriate.

"I could've still been playing in college, but I rushed the books to graduate early. Couldn't wait to start teaching."

He smiled and again Sarah got that feeling that she wasn't sitting there with a coach or teacher. She felt so comfortable—like talking to Sydney.

"So, any particular reason you're going to see your mom? Or just because?"

Sarah nodded. "Yeah, after seeing her last time, I realized I should've been doing it a lot more often. Only reason I hadn't was because she'd made it a point to tell me she didn't want me to when she first went in."

"Well, maybe next time you go, I can take you."

Sarah knew that would sound weird to others. Maybe it was her long history with Sydney that made her believe you could actually care about someone with no ulterior motives. She decided he was a good guy. He showed genuine concern for her, and she trusted him.

Before she could respond, he sat up a little. "Hey, ever been running at the Canyon?"

"Yeah, the trails are awesome. I loved the work out," Sarah smiled, remembering all the times she'd raced Sydney there.

"Ever been to Mount Soledad?"

Sarah felt her stomach hollow as the memories of the picnic she had with Angel there and all the times they'd gone back later, supposedly to hike but always ended up sprawled out on a blanket somewhere. She managed a nod.

"The trails are spectacular there also. I take a few of my students up there every now and then. Talk about a work out. Maybe when your ankle is better, you can join us."

"Yeah." Sarah bit her lip. "That sounds good." It really did, going back to the park would be bittersweet, but she could see herself getting lost in a run in the beautiful trails.

When she spoke to Sydney that night, he surprised her again. She thought he'd be furious about Angel. Instead he played devil's advocate. "So, he didn't like that The Perv was gonna drive you home? He's Angel. Did his reaction really surprise you?"

"Okay, Sydney, first of all, can you please stop calling him The Perv?" Sarah walked around her room cautiously. Her ankle was feeling a lot better. "And second, that's not the point. The point is he expected me to just drop everything and jump in his car without so much as a hello or how've you been. Does he really think he has me that wrapped?"

She pondered on that thought for a moment. Who was she kidding? She could hardly believe even now that she'd passed up the chance to go home with him.

"Lynni, how many times have you seen Angel being über male? He's all nerves and will," Sydney chuckled. "The last thing on his mind would be formalities. I'm sure he would've asked you how you've been in the car."

"That's not what I meant."

Sydney laughed. "I know, I know. I'm teasing. All right so he handled it wrong. But isn't that what he's always done—react? Bottom line is his intentions were honorable, no? He put all his feelings about everything else that's happened away to get you out of a possibly dangerous situation."

"Dangerous? That's so ridiculous. Coach Rudy is harmless."

"So, what did Coach *Rudy* have to say about the whole thing?"

Sarah knew Sydney wasn't going to like how long the coach had hung around again when he was supposed to just be dropping her off. But she'd learned her lesson about half truths. She was never going to lie for the sake of not arguing again.

"He didn't ask, and I didn't tell him. He just said I'd get over Angel."

"Why did he say that?"

"I dunno. I guess he saw how sad I was and thought it would make me feel better." Sarah sat down on her bed and moved her ankle around in the air. It was definitely better. "I told him about going to see my mom again."

"Let me guess. He offered to take you." Sydney chuckled.

Sarah gulped, unable to believe he'd hit it on the nose. She didn't respond.

"Lynni?"

"Hmm?"

"You're kidding me, right?"

"He just said he thought it was a long drive for me to go alone, and that—"

"Oh, my God, this guy is too much!" Sydney's tone changed from playful to exasperated. "Please tell me you see it, Lynn."

"No," she insisted. "Because it's not what you're thinking. He asked if my aunt could go with me. He thinks it's a long trip to take alone. All he said was if he didn't have to work, he would've offered to take me. But he is, so he can't."

"Lynni."

"What?"

"Promise me something."

"What?" Sarah was so frustrated. Coach Rudy had gotten her through today, and now Sydney was turning it all around.

"You know that voice that tells you to not read too much into anything?"

"Yeah?"

"Ignore it. From here on, anything you think is kind of funny about this guy, question it. Okay?"

Sarah was so exhausted she didn't want to argue with Sydney. She agreed, even though she knew she had nothing to worry about.

CHAPTER 27

Playing pool with the guys always helped Angel relax. This was the first time Eric had come over since New Year's. Alex and Sofia were both working the restaurant but would be home soon. Angel wasn't too sure if having Eric there was a good idea. He had talked to Alex briefly about Eric not being to blame, but Alex was dead set against having him around Sofia when no one was around. Angel hoped that didn't mean he'd make a scene even if everyone was around.

It had been another slow bitter weekend for Angel. His mind was on the usual, and it was getting real irritating. Being that close to Sarah on Friday made him realize he wasn't even close to being over her. Her resentment toward him had confused him. He was the one that had gotten duped. Did she really expect him to just accept another guy in her life? That wasn't happening. Though being that close to her for the first time in so long made it tempting to accept anything just to be with her.

He knew better though. Having to deal with her being out of state would be hard enough. But knowing she'd be with Sydney would make it impossible. There was no way it would work.

As if things weren't bad enough already, the tension had been lifted full throttle with this coach thing. He hoped Sarah knew better than to fall for that guy's shit. The smug look on the coach's face was the new image imprinted in Angel's head, and he welcomed the challenge. Teacher or not, Angel had no qualms about taking him down.

Eric racked up the balls. "Your break, Angel."

Angel leaned over and took a shot. The balls scattered violently, and one flew off the table. Romero laughed. "Easy, killer."

"Dude," Eric bent over and picked up the ball from where it had rolled. "What are you doing?"

Angel ignored them and bent over to shoot again. Sofia and Alex walked in from the side gate. Angel noticed Eric stiffen. The ball he hit went in, and he took a moment to chalk his pool stick.

Sofia walked toward them instead of the kitchen door, and Alex followed behind her. She smiled brightly without a care in the world.

Alex sat on the barstool between Eric and Sofia. To Angel's relief, he acknowledged Eric but just barely with a nod.

"Sarah texted me." Sofia focused on Angel but kept glancing at Eric.

Angel feigned disinterest and walked around the pool table for a better angle. "Yeah, so?"

"She was worried I might be upset about Friday."

Angel closed his eyes for a second. This wasn't a conversation he wanted to have in front of the guys. They'd have a field day. But he did want to know if she'd said anything else. He continued shooting without responding to Sofia. He'd manage to go all this time without asking Sofia anything about Sarah; he wasn't going to start now.

Sofia put her hand on her hip, obviously annoyed that Angel wasn't biting. "She said she wanted to but couldn't and added a sad face."

Angel glanced up at her and finally gave in. "Couldn't? What the hell does that mean?"

"I don't know. That's all she said. I didn't respond 'cause she said she had to go." Sofia started back toward the kitchen door. "Her ankle's better in case you care."

Angel glanced at the guys and stopped on Alex when he saw him grinning from ear to ear. "What?"

Alex looked over to make sure Sofia was in the house. "I heard about Friday."

Angel rolled his eyes. "So."

"So things are getting pretty heavy with Sarah and Coach Perv. I told you he was slick."

"Sarah and Coach Rudy?" Romero asked. "No shit?"

"He just gave her a ride home." Angel gripped the pool stick a little harder. "Your turn."

"Twice," Alex chuckled. "And he doesn't just drop her off either. Valerie said they sit out in the driveway, talking for a while. Friday night he was there longer than the first time."

Angel glared at Alex. New tension cramped his muscles. "So what did Sarah have to say about it?"

Alex still had the stupid grin on his face. "Valerie told her she thought it was kind of creepy, but Sarah doesn't think so. She says she feels real *comfortable* around him." He shook his head. "I'm telling you. He's working her."

Something burned through Angel's entire body. Suddenly Sarah in Arizona with Sydney and his girlfriend sounded ideal. Why the hell wasn't she there already?

"Does she know about him, Angel?" Leave it to Eric to be the only one to show any concern.

Angel nodded but frowned when he thought of how Sarah just humored him whenever he'd gone off about what a pervert the guy was. She had her own preconceptions of the guy, and he knew they were favorable ones. Like Sofia, she didn't buy into all the rumors.

"I heard he left the last school he was teaching at because someone accused him of rape," Eric said.

"What?" Angel felt the hair on the back of his neck stand. "I thought he was a new teacher. Straight outta college?"

Alex grimaced. "Nah, he's not as young as he looks either."

"How old is he?"

"About twenty-six or twenty-seven." Alex grabbed a bottle of water out of the small fridge and headed back to the kitchen.

"I heard that rape story too," Romero said, bending over to take a shot. Then he added with a shrug. "But I've heard so much shit about him, who knows what really happened?"

Angel sat on one of the bar stools, for once interested in what Romero had to say. "So, what's the story?"

Romero glanced at Eric then stood up holding the pool stick straight up in front of him. "It's different every time I hear it, but basically someone actually pressed charges on his ass for either rape or attempted rape." He set himself up for an awkward shot. "There wasn't enough evidence, so the charges were dropped. But I guess everyone was so pissed about it, he had to transfer outta there. And lucky La Jolla, we got him."

Angel wondered why he'd never heard the story, or maybe he had. He'd just never paid attention to any of the details. All he knew for sure was the guy had a reputation for being overly friendly with the girls. And from what Angel had seen Friday, there was no doubt in his mind anymore he *was* working Sarah.

✳✳✳

Sarah's trip to see her mom went smoothly. Seeing her was still as emotional as the first visit. But things felt brighter. Her mom still hadn't been to court, but the lawyers were even more optimistic about her chances of getting out early, and Sarah could see the change in her mom's appearance. The dark circles and deep eyes were still there but not as pronounced as before. And there was a sparkle in her eyes that made Sarah feel very hopeful.

Her mom gave her something to really think about just before she left.

"Sarah, I want you to know that I think you've been through enough. When I get out of here, it's up to you where you wanna stay. I don't have a job here in Flagstaff anymore, but if this is where you want to be, I'll find a way to make it work. Otherwise, if you'd rather stay in California, your aunt has offered to let us stay there until I get back on my feet. You think about it and let me know."

The choice seemed obvious. The only reason she'd want to stay in La Jolla didn't want anything to do with her. In Flagstaff, at least she had Sydney.

She'd spent the whole day Saturday with Syd and his family. Carina hadn't made an appearance. Sydney said she was busy, and Sarah left it alone. Sunday after her visit with her mom, Sydney drove her to the bus station and dropped her off. Each time she came back to Arizona, she worried things would be different with her and Sydney, but as usual, it was as if she'd never left.

Maybe it was the trip over the weekend or the fact that she hadn't run in over a week, but Sarah felt off during her first run in practice. Coach Rudy had stressed the importance of taking it easy and had wrapped her ankle pretty tight before letting her run—possibly a little too tight. It was beginning to feel numb. She slowed to a walk and looked around for the coach but didn't see him. He'd been adamant about her wearing it, so she didn't want to take it off. But it was really bugging her, so she went into the gym to find him.

She didn't see him anywhere, so she walked towards his office where he'd wrapped her ankle. The door to his office flew open just as she reached it, and a girl in her cheer warm-ups almost collided with her.

"Sorry," the girl said with a nervous smile.

"That's okay."

The girl hurried away quickly. Sarah watched her as she rushed off, fixing her skirt. She opened the door to the office. Coach Rudy had a clipboard in one hand and tucked his shirt in with the other.

"Hey, Sarah. How'd the run go?"

His fly was half zipped, and Sarah flushed, hoping he hadn't noticed she was even looking there. "I, uh, think the wrap is too tight. It's making my foot numb."

He looked down at her ankle. "All right, have a seat."

Sarah sat down on the chair next to his desk, and he put the clipboard down and leaned against the edge of the desk.

"Bring it up here."

She brought her leg up, and he caught it against his front thighs. Sarah suddenly felt very vulnerable. He unlaced her shoe and smiled as he pulled it off. "Did you get around the track at all?"

"One time," Sarah gulped. "But I walked at the end."

Once unwrapped, he massaged the ankle a little and worked his way up to her calf. "Feel better?"

Sarah nodded. She had to admit it did feel a lot better. He moved her ankle in a circular motion and then back and forth. She glanced up from her foot and saw how engaged he was in working it. He began wrapping it again meticulously. And she felt silly about her unnecessary angst. She was letting Sydney and all the stupid rumors get to her.

"Tell me if it's too tight."

When he was done wrapping it, he put her sock and shoe back on tying the laces himself. "Stand up."

Sarah did. The area between the chair and the desk was extremely cramped. When she stood, her thighs touched his, and her face was close enough to smell the gum on his breath. Sarah flinched back and almost lost her balance. Her eyes locked with the coach for a second.

"Careful now," he grinned.

Sarah smiled, feeling her face redden. The second wrap was much better, and Sarah managed to get in a few laps before practice was over. She was feeling really stupid about the way she'd reacted in the coach's office. Even her thoughts about the girl that had walked out of his office had been unreasonable.

Sydney had told her to read into everything, but that was so unfair to jump to such ugly conclusions. Coach Rudy was good-looking and a very nice person as far she was concerned. What need would he have to get involved with high school girls?

She saw Angel waiting by his car as she walked back to the locker room, and her body reacted in the usual way. She concentrated on staying cool, but her heart raced, and she knew it had nothing to do with the laps she'd just taken. She'd already accepted that as long as she was here in California, she'd never get over him—not by a long shot. She would just have to do her best to avoid him until she went back to Flagstaff. But it was annoying how just seeing him still affected her so much.

Sarah was almost to the locker room when she heard someone call her name. She turned to see Coach Rudy walking toward her.

"Hey, you looked real good out there. Anything hurting?"

Sarah shook her head and smiled. "Nope, nothing at all. Good as new, Coach."

The coach glanced down at her foot, and then his eyes were on hers again. "Listen we're going up to Mount Soledad this Saturday. You wanna come?" His lips went up in a crooked grin. "I promise I'll give you a good workout."

Sarah's mind raced to remember if she had any plans for that weekend. But running in the mountain trails overlooking the ocean sounded exactly like what she needed.

"That actually sounds really good."

"Great, I'll pick you up at ten. Bring water." He tapped her behind with his clipboard and winked before walking away.

Sarah stood still for a moment and then shook it off. Lots of coaches patted the players on the behind, even guys. She saw it all the time. She was done jumping to conclusions.

CHAPTER 28

Friday morning Angel sat in the kitchen going over last night's Spanish homework. After switching his schedule around to get out of his physics class, he got stuck with the same Spanish teacher as the previous semester. At the time he hadn't cared. All he could think of was getting out of seeing Sarah every day. Now he was seriously regretting it. The amount of homework this lady packed on was unreal.

Alex was fixing himself a protein drink when Sofia walked in. "So, dad said if one of you can come into the restaurant for me tomorrow morning I can take the morning off."

"I'll go in," Angel said, without looking up from his homework.

"Where you gonna be?" Alex asked.

Sofia stuck her head in the refrigerator and said something Angel couldn't make out.

"Where?" Alex asked again.

"Running with the team." She poured herself a glass of orange juice.

Angel looked up. Sofia avoided looking at him. "On a Saturday?"

"Ah huh." She pulled out the toaster and plugged it in.

Angel frowned. She was being weird. Ever since she'd told him about her feelings for Eric and been so brazen about going through dad to get her way, he'd wondered how long it would be before she'd start to get sneaky.

"Why on a Saturday, Sof?"

Alex poured himself his drink from the blender and leaned against the counter. "Yeah, your track meets don't start yet, do they?"

"It's not a track meet. We're just going to go run the trails at Mount Soledad."

"So, it's a field trip?" Angel asked, feeling the tension release.

"Well, no." Sofia buttered her toast and spoke with her back to them.

"Well, what the hell is it?" Alex asked.

Sofia exhaled but didn't turn around to face them. "The coach is taking a bunch of us to run the trails. That's all."

Angel's eyebrows shot up. "You're going in his car?"

"Oh, hell no!" Alex scowled in Sofia's direction, but she still hadn't turned around.

"Sofie, what did I tell you about watching out for this guy?" Angel stood up.

Sofia finally turned around. "You said not to be alone with him. I won't be. There's going to be other people from the team there. Sarah will be there."

That only soured Angel's mood further. "So, he's taking a bunch of girls up to the mountains with him?"

"I don't know. Sarah's the one that told me about it. I figured if she would be there, it would be okay. We're just running."

"Forget about it." Alex's tone was final.

"But why?" Sofia looked up at the ceiling, frustrated. "You guys are *so* unreasonable. Dad said it was okay."

"Does dad know he's a pervert, Sof?" Angel demanded.

"Don't worry. I'm sure he'll agree with us when I'm done talking to him," Alex said on his way out the kitchen. "You're not going, Sof."

Sofia looked at Angel exasperated. "Don't bother going into the restaurant tomorrow. I'll be there." She threw her toast in the trash and walked out.

Angel was fuming. What the hell was Sarah thinking? He thought about what Eric had said. Maybe his warnings hadn't been enough. If he hadn't heard the rumors about the perv being accused of rape and he'd been at this school a lot longer, maybe she hadn't either.

His only consolation was that she wouldn't be alone with him. Sofia said there were a bunch of them going. The guy wouldn't risk doing something stupid after being chased from one school already, and not with a bunch of kids around. Sarah should be okay.

***

Sarah woke up late Saturday morning. She had waited until yesterday to tell Sydney about going to Mount Soledad with the coach. And as expected he wasn't thrilled. They stayed up pretty late talking. He gave her the usual warnings, but in the end was glad she was finally getting out with friends, even if the coach would be there also.

The coach had texted her late last night to let her know three of the others going had cancelled but that it would still be four of them all together. Sarah was fine with that but was kind of uneasy when Sofia told her there was no way she was going. Knowing that Angel was dead set against it made her speculate about what he must be thinking of her going. She'd seen the way he looked at the coach the day he showed up at her practice.

She'd just gotten out of the shower and was drying up in her room when her phone rang. It was the coach. Sarah glanced out the window as she answered.

"Are you guys here already? I didn't realize I was running that late."

He chuckled. "No, actually I was calling to ask if you still wanted to go, or if we should try this another time."

"Why wouldn't I?"

"Nobody called you?"

Sarah looked at her phone. She had no missed calls. "No, nobody called."

He was quiet for a moment then spoke again. "Yeah, looks like it's just you and me. The other two flaked out at the last minute. But if you're not okay with that, we can totally do this some other time when everyone else can go."

Sarah's stomach stirred. She knew what Sydney would want her to say, but she felt bad. "I um ..."

"It's okay, Sarah. We can try again next week with the whole team if that would be more comfortable for you."

Sarah felt silly. He could've just picked her up without telling her and not given her a choice. And she'd looked forward to it all week. "No, I'm fine. If you're still up for it, I am."

"Are you sure?"

Sarah smiled, feeling more relieved. "Yeah, totally. Just give me fifteen minutes."

Sarah went over all the possibilities while she dressed. She knew Coach Rudy was harmless, but something still gnawed at her gut. She was glad Valerie and her aunt had taken off early for a day of shopping. Valerie would've probably made her feel bad about going.

Last night's conversation came crashing in her mind again. One of the only reasons Sydney had finally been okay with her going on this run was that it was a group trip. She felt like a liar now somehow.

Maybe that's what was bothering her so much. If she didn't tell him now, it would bug her all day. She picked up her phone and called him. She'd learned a huge lesson about coming clean. Her motto now was no matter how bad it is, it's best to come out with it sooner not later.

"Hey, Lynni."

"Sydney, I don't have time to talk. The coach will be here any minute. Just wanted to let you know, it's gonna be just me and him today."

Sydney didn't say anything, then she heard the unmistakable censure in his tone. "What?"

"Everyone flaked out. He called to ask if I wanted to just reschedule for another time when everyone could go."

"So why didn't you say okay?" Sarah could almost picture his eyebrows furrowed.

"Because I looked forward to this all week, and it would be silly not to go. We're going to be in broad daylight at a park. What's there to worry about?"

"Lynn." He uncharacteristically raised his voice. "Isn't this the same park you said has a lot of abandoned trails and you could walk for miles without ever seeing anyone?"

Sarah sighed. "I'm sure we won't be running on those, Syd. I just called to tell you because I didn't want you to be mad later—not to worry you. I'll be fine. I promise."

"How did it just so happen that everyone else flaked out?" Sydney paused and then in an even louder tone said, "Are you sure he didn't plan it like this in the first place?"

"Will you stop?" Sarah saw the coach's car pull in the driveway. "Why would he plan it then call and ask if I would rather reschedule?"

"Maybe that was part of the plan?"

"He's here Syd, I gotta go."

"I don't think you should, Lynni. Seriously, I got a bad feeling about this."

"Sydney, please stop worrying." She blew a couple of kisses in the phone and hung up.

Coach Rudy waited for Sarah without getting out of his car. Sarah leaned in the open passenger window. "Morning, Coach."

"You look good."

Sarah looked down at her sweat suit and shrugged. "You know me, Coach. I got all fancy for the occasion." She got in and put her seatbelt on.

"Sarah, if you don't mind, I don't have a problem with you calling me Rudy." He pulled out of the driveway. "Up to you though. I'm just saying I'd be cool with it if you did."

He stared straight ahead as he drove, and Sarah took it into consideration. That wasn't so unreasonable. It would feel a little weird at first, but it was no big deal. She could get used to it.

"Okay, Rudy."

He turned to her and smiled. "I like that."

The ride to the park was cold. The clouds were really swallowing up the mountain. All the times she'd come here with Angel had been in the fall with beautiful blue skies and rays of sun shining up every angle of the park. Now it seemed so dark and ominous: a tribute to how she'd been feeling lately.

"Didn't figure on the weather being so bad," Coach Rudy peered out the front windshield at the sky. "Forecast is calling for rain later, but we should be out of here by then."

Sarah stared out her window. She focused on relaxing. She couldn't shake the unease she felt after hanging up with Syd. Everything about the day seemed wrong. Her gut feeling was telling her she should've listened to Sydney, but a huge part of her still wanted to believe that Coach Rudy was a good person.

They parked in an open area. Only a handful of cars were in the parking lot. She didn't really remember this part of the park, but it was so huge she was sure there was plenty she still hadn't seen. They got out, and he opened the hatch in the back. It was much colder up here than it had been when they left her house. He grabbed a small backpack and their water. He handed her a bottle, and Sarah flinched when his finger caressed her hand.

Their eyes met. "You okay?"

Sarah's face flushed. She felt like a goof. "Yeah."

"Is it too cold for you?" His words were gentle, and there was earnest concern in his eyes.

Sarah took a deep breath and smiled. "A little, but I like it. It's so crisp and clean."

They walked over to the grassy area near one of the trails. Coach Rudy put the backpack and water down and began stretching. He reminded Sarah to make sure she moved her ankle around enough.

After loosening up for a few minutes, Sarah felt more relaxed and cursed herself for being so damn jumpy. This was supposed to be a day to relax and forget about all her worries, and she was ruining it with her anxiety. She jumped in place a little more and shook her hands.

She glanced up, and Coach Rudy had a smirk on his face. "I've never seen you warm up that way."

"I'm trying to shake the cold." She smiled silly.

"You sure it's not gonna be too cold for you?

. Sarah shook her head and continued to jump in place a few more times. The coach finished stretching and picked up the backpack. He threw both water bottles in there and put it on his back. He stood and watched Sarah for a moment. His eyes moved up and down her very slowly, making Sarah feel a bit invaded. She stopped jumping, and he smiled. "You ready?"

"Sure am."

＊＊＊

Angel was supposed to just drop Sofia off at the restaurant but ended up hanging out and helping out. That happened a lot lately. He had nothing better to do, and the last thing he wanted was to sit around the house dredging up painful memories.

Eric and Romero stopped by to grab breakfast. They sat in the bar area that normally wasn't open that early in the morning, but the restaurant was pretty busy, and Alex told them he didn't want them taking up space in the dining room.

Romero had snorted that he was a paying customer but shut up when Alex told him to pay his tab.

After showing a few more patrons to their tables, Angel walked over to where Romero and Eric ate. They were talking about going to watch some extreme fighting later that evening. Romero's dad's friend was promoting it, and he could get free tickets. Angel considered it. He hadn't gone out since he'd broken up with Sarah.

He was trying to snap out of the nasty mood he'd been in lately, but knowing Sarah was spending more time with the perv as they spoke did nothing to help.

Alex slipped his head out the office door. "Hey, Angel, some guy named Sydney is on line one for you. Isn't that Sarah's friend?"

Romero chuckled, and his voice went high pitched. "Whoa, drama!"

Eyes closed, Angel pinched the bridge of his nose, muttering under his breath. "What now?"

He ignored Romero and didn't respond to Alex's question. Instead just walked over to the bar phone. "I got it."

"This is Angel." Both Romero and Eric were staring at him with stupid curiosity, so he turned his back to them. Through the mirror on the back wall of the bar, he could see they were still gawking, and he flipped them off.

"Sorry to call you at the restaurant, but I didn't know how else to get a hold of you." Angel couldn't be sure, but he sensed panic in his tone, and it unnerved him.

"What's up?"

"Not sure how much you know about this coach of hers, but from what Sarah's told me, he sounds like a real prick."

"She said that?" Angel almost smiled.

"Well, no, she told me about the things people say about him, but she's convinced he's a good guy."

Angel frowned, not sure what Sydney was getting at but immediately lost his patience. "Yeah, so?"

"I personally don't think it's a good idea for her to be around him so much, especially alone," Sydney paused. Angel thought he heard him grunt. "He convinced her to go running with him today on some isolated trails up in the mountains. I don't like it. I think he's up to no good."

Angel gripped the edge of the bar and gritted his teeth. "I heard about the run. But they're in a group."

"That's why I'm calling you." Angel definitely heard a door slam that time. "She called me this morning. Conveniently, everyone else cancelled at the last moment. So she's up there with him now—alone. I don't think he ever intended for there to be anyone else. I think he planned it this way."

Everything after the word *alone* was muddled. Angel hadn't heard a word of it. The tension he'd been feeling for the past weeks peaked, and he felt ready to explode. Every muscle in his body was on edge. He spoke through his teeth. "Did she say where?"

"No, only that it was the same park you took her to in the fall."

The park couldn't be too crowded on a day like this, and he knew the car that asshole drove. He'd find them, and when he did, Angel was going to relieve all the pent up tension he'd been building up since he broke up with Sarah. He felt ready to kill.

"I'll find her."

After hanging up, Angel stormed past Eric and Romero. He heard Alex ask them, "What's with him?"

He was almost at his car when Eric called after him. "Hey, Angel. What's up? Where you going?"

"Gotta go find Sarah." He reached for door handle on his car.

"What's the matter?" Romero asked.

Angel turned just before getting in the car. "That pervert Rudy has her up at Mount Soledad all by herself."

He saw Eric and Romero run to Eric's car just as he gunned the engine. The image of Rudy walking away with Sarah at school and the snide way he'd looked at Angel fueled his already murderous temper, and he stepped on the gas.

***

After running for about four miles, the coach slowed down and stopped near a grassy area. They'd been running along a trail that wound along the side of the road. At times the trail veered a bit far from the road, but they were always within eyesight of it. Sarah hadn't seen a car drive by the entire time they ran.

Coach Rudy grabbed the bottles of water out of his backpack and handed one to Sarah. In between heavy breathing, he reminded her not to drink too fast or too much. Sarah walked over to a giant boulder off the side of the trail and leaned against it. She was glad for the cold weather, now the cool air felt good in her nose.

He walked over and joined her on the boulder. His thigh touched her leg when he leaned on the rock. "How's the ankle feeling?"

"Good." Sarah looked down and wiggled it. "I was a little nervous, but it feels fine."

The coach took a sip of his water "Can I ask you something personal?"

Sarah put her foot down and turned to him. "Go ahead."

"Your boyfriend last semester—he seemed pretty crazy about you. Just wondering what in the world would make him let you go?"

He must've seen the hurt in her eyes because he put his hand on her leg. "Hey, I'm sorry. I didn't mean to bring you down. I was just curious."

Sarah shook her head and stared at her feet. "No, it's okay. It's just been hard, but I'm getting over it."

The coach patted her leg then rubbed it gently. "Was he your first?"

Sarah looked up at him.

"I mean first love."

She hadn't really thought of it that way. But he was. No other boy had even come close to the way she felt about Angel. And she had an aching feeling that no one ever would.

She nodded and turned her attention to her water. "It was my fault." She took a small sip. "I was really stupid."

Sarah stood up. The pain was still so raw she was afraid she might get all sentimental. But the coach grabbed her hand and pulled her back.

"Come here. It's okay." He spoke softly. His words were kind, and his touch felt warm. Except for the night of the awful scene and the day she went to see her mom, all the times she'd cried for Angel, she'd done it alone in her room. Sydney was usually on the other end of the phone, but she still couldn't help feeling alone.

She sat back down next to him. He kept her hand in his and spoke to her, looking directly in her eyes. "Listen, you don't have to talk about it. But you're a beautiful girl, Sarah, not just on the outside, and I hope you know that there are plenty of guys out there that would be dying to be with someone like you."

Sarah wasn't sure about that. She didn't care either. There was only one guy she wanted to be with, but she knew the coach meant well. The lump in her throat was getting heavier with every word he said. She could feel her eyes welling up. Damn it. That was exactly what she didn't want, especially not today—the day she was supposed to getting away from all the sorrow. She gulped hard, trying to hold it together.

"Can I hug you?"

Sarah leaned against his chest without answering, and he put his strong arms around her. She felt him kiss the top of her head, and somehow it felt right. It's what Sydney would've done. The tears ran down her cheek as she took in the clean smell of his shirt.

She pulled away a little to face him, and he wiped the tears from her face. "Do you have any idea how special you are?"

She wasn't sure how to respond to that. Sarah knew he was just trying to make her feel better, but it made her uncomfortable. The level of tenderness in his eyes had changed a bit. He kissed her forehead softly and then the corner of her eye.

"You have the most beautiful eyes," he whispered.

Sarah felt an icy shiver up her spine. He was just consoling her, she told herself. But his kisses continued down her face, and his strong body leaned a little heavier against her. He pulled her against him by the waist, and his lips caressed hers.

She put her hand on his chest. "Coach?" But he didn't even budge.

"Call me Rudy," he said and kissed her on the side of the mouth.

"What are you doing?" She pushed him harder but was no match for him.

"It's okay, Sarah. Don't fight it. I felt the attraction all along."

The heated craze in his eyes alarmed her. It was almost as if she were looking at a different person. The reality finally sunk in. "What are you talking about? You're scaring me!"

His grip on her loosened for just a moment. "C'mon, Sarah. We're both adults. This has been building between us long enough."

The panic she'd begun to feel spiked, and she used her foot to push him away. He stumbled back awkwardly but caught his balance and reached for her again. Sarah moved away. The sorrow she'd felt earlier was now replaced with anger and fear. She'd trusted him. "How dare you?"

"You can drop the act now, Sarah," he said coldly. "We both want this."

"What? You're crazy! I can't believe you would even think that." Sarah moved away from him cautiously, but he never backed down.

"Crazy?" He grabbed her hand and thrust her to him. In an instant, she was locked in his arms, and she squirmed with all her strength to get away. "Don't act stupid. Why else would you be up here with me?"

Sarah kneed him, missing his groin by just an inch, but it was enough to stun him, causing him to let her go. The second she was loose, she bolted back toward the parking lot.

"Sarah, wait!"

Without looking back or the slightest hesitation, Sarah was in the run of her life. She did what she did best and turned on the wheels. Her mind raced, and the tears streamed down her face. *How could she have been so stupid?* Even with all the warnings she had put herself in this horrific situation. She thought of the few cars in the parking lot and prayed someone would be around when she got there. She still hadn't seen a soul.

Halfway to the parking lot, she realized the coach was still running after her. He was yelling something, but her ear hummed with the wind, or maybe it was dread. Raindrops began to bounce off her face. The adrenaline thrashed through her body, and she picked up the speed.

When she finally turned the corner and saw the parking lot her heart sank. Of the few cars that had been there when they arrived, only two were left. Her heart pounded as her eyes searched around for anyone. She heard a car's engine and tried to make out what direction it was coming from.

The car sped around the corner up toward the direction she'd just come from.

"Hey!" She yelled, waving her arms in the air. But the car was going too fast. It was out of sight, and she dare not run back in that direction. She could barely catch her breath and didn't think she could run anymore anyway. Her stomach bottomed out when she saw the coach turn the corner.

"Sarah, wait. I wanna apologize."

He ran slowly, and Sarah could see he was just as exhausted as she was. She looked around for anything she could use as a weapon. There was nothing and still no one in sight.

"Don't come near me." Sarah could barely get the words out she was breathing so hard.

But her words did nothing to deter him. He charged at her with that crazed heat still in his eyes.

CHAPTER 29

Angel skidded to a stop when he realized it was the coach he'd just seen running up the trail. But he was alone. Where was Sarah? He looked down the trail. Maybe she'd fallen behind. Would the idiot really leave her alone?

Eric and Romero had eagerly volunteered to help him find Sarah and were driving around the park as well. He texted Eric to let them know he'd found them and where.

Angel peered through his rearview mirror and saw the coach turn into the parking lot he'd just passed up. The rain was beginning to come down harder now. He put the car in reverse and backed up fast.

The tires screeched as he turned into the parking lot and saw Sarah talking to the perv next to his car. He was too close to her, and her stance seemed defensive. Angel pulled up next to them, turned off the car, and jumped out.

Sarah's expression crumbled when she saw him, and she hurried to him. His fist tightened, and he was immediately between Sarah and the coach.

"What happened? What's wrong?" he asked her.

Her frightened eyes enraged him. The coach answered for her. "It was just a misunderstanding."

Angel turned away from Sarah's tearful eyes very slowly. His pulse throbbed in his ear. He spoke as calmly as he could manage. "*What* was a misunderstanding?"

The coach seemed to take it in stride. "We were talking, you know, about you and the break-up. She got a little emotional. I was just trying to comfort her."

Angel's jaw tightened. The word comfort had never sounded so obscene. He could hardly contain himself anymore. He looked at Sarah's frightened eyes. "Is that what happened? Tell me the truth."

Something in her eyes flickered when he said the word truth. Her trembling lips tore him apart.

She put her hands over her mouth then said it, "He attacked me."

No sooner had she said the words than Angel was lunging at the coach. "You son of a bitch!" he growled, landing a nose-crushing punch to the face.

The coach stumbled back, and his hands went immediately to his nose. His face was a bloody mess. Angel raged after him, landing another blow to the chin, knocking the coach against the car. Angel charged at him ready to pound him unconscious, but his arms were held back by Eric and Romero. He managed a hard kick that caught the coach right in the groin, tumbling him to ground moaning.

"Holy shit, Angel. You kicked his ass!" Romero stared at the coach writhing in pain on the ground.

Even as he watched the bloody trail from the coach's face run down the parking lot, he wasn't satisfied. He'd been enraged many times before but nothing compared to what he felt now. The bastard was lucky Eric and Romero had shown up, or who knows what may have happened.

Angel ignored Romero and rushed back to Sarah. He put one hand on her shoulder and searched her stunned eyes. "Are you okay? Did he hurt you?"

Sarah shook her head. "No, he just scared me," she sniffed. "He tried to kiss me and held me hard, but I got away and ran. He'd just caught up to me. Oh, Angel if you hadn't gotten here, I don't know what would've happened. He was crazy."

She threw her arms around his neck, and he held her tight. The smell and feel of her in his arms was the only thing that calmed the tornado inside him.

They left the coach there to fend for himself, but Angel drove straight to the La Jolla police. He insisted Sarah make a report immediately. He sat with her the entire time, holding her hand. They put out a warrant for the coach's arrest. The police woman warned Sarah that it would probably get messy being that he was a teacher but encouraged her to be brave and stick with it so he wouldn't be free to do this again to anyone else.

Angel would make sure of it. They walked out of the station. He'd seen her send her calls to voicemail the whole time they'd been in there. Angel was sure it was Sydney. Just as they put their seatbelts on, Sarah's phone went off again, and she finally answered it.

She greeted him, and then her voice broke. "I know. I'm sorry I was at the police station. No, I'm okay. Yes, I'm with Angel. I'll tell you about it later, okay?" She lowered her voice, but Angel heard it and wished to God he hadn't. "I love you too."

The blatant jealousy scorched through him. He stepped on the gas. Just a few hours ago, he was anxious to kill for her, and now he just wanted her out of his car—his life.

He sped into her driveway. The rain was really coming down. He didn't bother to turn the engine off or even attempt to soften his tone. "I hope you make sure that asshole goes to jail."

Sarah nodded and gathered her things and the plastic Ziploc bag the police woman had stuck all her paperwork in to keep it dry from the rain. "Thank you, Angel. You really saved me today. I don't know what else to say to you. I just wish…"

She didn't finish and opened the door in a hurry to get out.

He was out of patience. "Wish what, Sarah?"

"That I could understand how you got over me so fast." She got out and closed the door.

Angel let his head fall back on his seat. *Unbelievable.*

He turned off the engine, opened the car door, and jumped out. "You really think I'm over you?" he yelled over the hood of car.

Sarah didn't answer. She didn't even turn around; she was halfway up the walk.

Angel charged around the car toward her. He called her name again, and she stopped and turned around. Angel saw she was crying. "I can't even imagine being over you and moving on, Angel, but you're already with someone else."

"What?" He couldn't believe she was doing this. "Don't throw this shit back on me, Sarah. I'm not the one who—"

"I know you ran back to Dana two days after we broke up."

Angel could see she was furious, and his mind raced to think about what she'd just said. "I went to talk to her, that's all."

"Whatever, it doesn't matter. I hope you two are happy." She began to turn back toward the house.

"No, no, wait!" Angel took a few steps forward. He wasn't about to let her turn this on him. "Only reason I wanted to talk to her was because she had information on you."

Sarah spun around. "What the hell would she know about me?"

"Someone saw you that night. The night you and Sydney were holding hands and hugging on the beach." Just the image tossed his insides. "She called me that night to tell me, and it made no sense to me. I ignored it. But after finding out the truth, I wanted to confirm exactly what it was she had seen."

Thinking about sitting there and getting the confirmation from Dana made him relive the pain, and he started to walk away. He was so done with all of this.

"I'm so sick of crying over you, Angel," Sarah sobbed. "You'll never understand about me and Sydney, and he's always going to be a part of my life."

It killed him to hear her so upset. But she was right. He'd never accept it. He couldn't. He turned around to face her. She looked as broken as he felt. But it only made him angrier. She'd done this, damn it—not him. "What do you want me to understand, Sarah? You really expect me to be okay with you moving in with this guy? This guy you're in love with?"

"I AM NOT IN LOVE WITH HIM!" she yelled. "I love him. It's different."

They were both getting soaked, but it didn't matter. Angel had a feeling this would be the last time he'd ever talk to her, and he wasn't holding anything back. He laughed in disbelief. "Like a brother, Sarah?"

"Yes!"

He stalked forward but stopped a few yards away from her. "What about the dress?"

Sarah stared at him wide-eyed at an apparent loss. Angel was glad the storm was so loud or his booming voice might bring out the neighbors. He could see Sarah trying to make sense of what he was yelling about.

"That fucking dress, Sarah! You've never dressed like that for me, but you wore it for your *brother*? You expect me to believe—"

"It was for you!" she cried.

She was still lying. *Incredible!* Angel clenched his teeth but was unable to calm his voice. He was too riled up. "I wasn't even gonna see you that night!"

"But you were!" Her eyes lit up. "Remember? You were supposed to pick me up, but then Sydney showed up last minute. I didn't want you to find out like that, so I left with him and called you."

Angel thought about it for a second, still breathing hard. It didn't make sense. She never dressed that way.

Sarah dropped everything in her hands on the lawn hurried toward him. She stood right in front of him, and Angel looked into her flooded eyes. "This is gonna sound so stupid. I was gonna to tell you that night about Sydney. I swear. I worried about it the whole day. Valerie came up with the idea that dressing that way would distract you. I don't know, make things easier. I didn't have time to change when he got there. But the dress, the hair, all of it was for you, Angel, not him."

Feeling an enormous weight lift from his heart and being so close to her, he had to resist pulling her to him. But he did move the wet strands of hair away from her face. Her eyes searched his. For the first time since they'd broken up, he began to feel a glimmer of hope. If only he could get past her going back to live with Sydney. "So, when do you go back to Arizona?"

She sniffed and bit her lip. "I may not."

Angel's heart had just started to calm, and he felt it start up again. He lifted an eyebrow. "What do you mean?"

"My mom may be getting out of jail sooner than we thought—maybe a couple months. That's why I'm still here. I went to see her, and she asked me to hold on a little longer. But she also said it was up to me where we would live once she's out."

His eyes searched hers now. "So what are you gonna do?"

"That depends." She had that crinkle between her eyebrows.

Angel frowned. There was always something. "On what?"

"On you." She seemed to hold her breath.

It took a second for it to sink in. But when it did, he pulled her into his arms. She was startled but laughed. "Don't play with me, Sarah. You'll really stay?"

Her eyes welled up again. "You want me to?"

Angel smiled, bringing his hands to her face and touched his forehead to hers. He stared in her beautiful eyes before kissing her tenderly. He'd missed her scent, her lips, her taste so much. He was never letting her go again.

Sarah pulled away and gazed in his eyes. "I love you, Angel."

Hearing her say it for the first time choked him up. "Say it again," he whispered.

Her eyes sparkled and she laughed. "I love you."

"I love you too, baby."

CHAPTER 30

Sarah lay there, tracing the engraving on the chain around Angel's neck with her fingers. She glanced at her wrist and smiled at the charm bracelet. She'd taken it off and refused to even look at it the entire time they were broken up. She almost mailed it to him, when she'd lost all hope. Something in her heart wouldn't let her, and she was glad now she hadn't.

After a week of being back together, they still couldn't get their fill of each other. Angel had made sure he closed the restaurant every night ever since, and Sarah was right there with him each night. She wondered if his parents had any idea of the things they did in that back room.

Angel lifted himself up on his elbow and played with her hair. "How'd you get so close?" He stared in her eyes. "You and Syd?"

Ever since they'd been back together, Sarah made it a point to keep any talk of Sydney to a minimum, and up until now, Angel really hadn't asked too much. She knew once the dust settled it would be coming, and now here it was. She had prepared herself. She wasn't keeping anything from him again—no matter how uncomfortable.

"Well, I told you we moved a lot when I was little. So I never had any friends. As soon as I made them, I had to leave them. By the time we moved to Flagstaff, I'd given up making friends. Then Syd befriended me," she smiled, remembering. "He didn't have any friends either, though he didn't admit it at first. He was really chubby."

"Sydney was fat?" Angel seemed amused by that.

Sarah smiled, trying not to roll her eyes. "Yes, he got pretty big in middle school. I just never made many other friends 'cause I wasn't sure how long we were gonna be there. Then my mom told me her job was made permanent and we were staying put. By then, Syd and I had already gotten pretty close. Since my mom was always gone, I spent a lot of time at his place. It became my home away from home, and his family treated me like their own."

Angel's eyebrow lifted. "And he never made a move?"

Sarah shook her head. "Never. Like I said, he was real heavy for a while there and very self-conscious about it, and I was self-conscious about my teeth."

"Your teeth? You have beautiful teeth."

"Yeah, now, after three years of braces. They were a crooked mess before. So me and Syd were a couple of self-conscious misfits who leaned on each other for years." She smiled again, thinking of the memories. Angel was staring at her, so she went on. "Anyway, middle school is when I started nagging him about losing weight. That's when I started running. It all began to get him to lose weight. We started to run every day; that's when my love for running began. By high school, he'd lost so much weight. Then he stretched and that *really* helped. We joined the track team together, and now you'd never even know he was so heavy."

Angel chuckled. "Yeah, I would've never guessed he was a fat ass."

Sarah frowned but was glad Angel wasn't being uptight about it. Angel leaned over and kissed her sweetly. It amazed her how happy it made her just being with him.

He kissed her some more, and then it came, "Babe, I know he's your friend. And I'm gonna try my damnedest to be as understanding about this as I can, but I need to know everything. I can't have you keeping things from me again, especially when it comes to him. So if he ever calls you, I don't need to know everything you two talk about. I just don't want you keeping it from me."

He must've seen something in her expression or felt her tense up because he stopped then asked, "What?"

"You want me to tell you *every* time he calls?"

Angel's eyes narrowed. "How often does he call, Sarah?"

Just like that, the complete honesty thing went out the window. Sarah knew it was wrong, but with that look in his eyes and the tone of his voice, there was no way the truth was going fly here. Telling him their calls were daily was out of the question. "Well, he doesn't do the calling *every* time, but we talk a few times a week."

Sarah saw Angel trying to stay poised. He rolled his neck like he always did as if that would somehow release the tension. As far as she knew, it never worked.

"I'll work on it," she added quickly.

"What does that mean? I'll work on it? Is it really that big a sacrifice?"

"No, but you just don't understand—"

"I'm trying to." He lay his head back, putting his hand behind his head.

Sarah lifted herself onto her elbow. "Is once a week too much?"

He stared at her but said nothing, and now it was her turn to do the kissing. She leaned over and pecked his lips then kissed the dimple that formed on his cheek with his furrowed expression.

He put his free hand behind her neck. "Sarah, babe, I don't want you to think I'm being insensitive. I get he's your longtime friend and all. It's just gonna take me some time to get used to this."

Sarah kissed him a little longer this time. "I know it is. We'll make this work. We have to 'cause I don't want to be apart from you ever again."

Angel smiled and pulled her to him with both arms now. "I love hearing you say stuff like that." He kissed her long and deep then stopped to add. "And yeah, I wanna know *every* time you talk to him."

Sarah was just going to have to cut down on the talks with Sydney because lying to Angel was a thing of the past. She wouldn't be making that mistake again. They made love again, and then Angel took Sarah home without another word about Sydney.

✳✳✳

Angel's heart almost stopped when Sarah called him crying. He couldn't make out a word she was saying. But then he heard her laugh in the midst of all the crying. "She's getting out the day after tomorrow!"

For weeks, they'd been waiting on the date, and finally Sarah's mom was being released from jail. Angel couldn't be happier. Sarah's mom would be there for her during the coach's trial.

"I told you, baby, believe." It was late in the evening and a school night, but they still stayed up and talked. At first, Sarah had the insane idea that she was going to Arizona alone to pick up her mom like she had when they were broken up. There was no way Angel was going to let that happen.

Sarah's aunt couldn't take the day off on such short notice, so Angel made arrangements and drove Sarah himself. Her mom wasn't being released until late in the afternoon, and Sarah suggested they stop at Sydney's to visit for a little bit, saying Sydney had invited them. Angel wasn't exactly looking forward to it, but for Sarah's sake, he pretended to be fine with it.

When they reached Syd's place, Sarah turned to him. "You sure you're okay with this?"

Not really, but he may as well get it over with. As far as he was concerned, Sarah was a part of his life for good now, so if Sydney was part of hers, he had to get used to this. "Yep, I'm good."

She leaned over and kissed him before getting out of the car. Angel walked around and met her at the sidewalk. Sydney was already standing on his porch with a blond girl.

He met them at the bottom of the porch steps, greeted Angel first, and introduced him to his girlfriend, Carina. Then he turned and greeted Sarah.

"I missed you, Lynni."

Sarah let go of Angel's hand to hug him. "I missed you too."

Angel watched as Sydney embraced her long and hard. "God, you look good."

He focused on not grinding his teeth too hard and tried not to frown. Sydney looked up and met Angel's eyes even as he still held Sarah. "I guess happiness'll do that to you, huh?"

Sydney's mom made them lunch, and they ate in the backyard under the patio. Sarah and Sydney talked about the track team she'd left behind in Arizona, and she filled him in on the details of her mother's early release. Angel glanced at Carina who, like him, hadn't said very much, and he wondered if she was as unsettled about their relationship as he was.

They didn't stay too long, and Angel guessed it was because Sarah sensed his discomfort, even though he did his best to try not to cringe every time Sydney called her Lynni.

Sydney hugged her just as hard when he said goodbye. This time Angel turned away casually, not wanting to see the way Syd's hands caressed her back. He was thankful neither professed their love for one another, or he may have snapped.

Sarah squeezed his hand as they drove away. "Thank you for that. I know that couldn't have been easy." She brought his hand to her mouth and kissed it.

"Why does he call you Lynni?" Angel didn't want her to think he was angry, but he couldn't help asking.

She shrugged. "From the moment I met him and I introduced myself as Sarah Lynn, his first remark was, 'You look more like a Lynn than a Sarah.' After a while it turned into Lynni." She kissed his hand again. "Does that bother you?"

Angel decided to just be honest. "I hate it."

Sarah laughed. "Why?"

He turned to look at her brilliant green eyes staring at him. "Sounds too damn sweet."

Sarah told him about her mom not liking it either, but after years of trying to correct him, she'd given up. Sarah was Lynni to Sydney and always would be. Great.

When they got to the women's detention center, they were still early. Sarah's mom wasn't done being prepped and handling paper work. They sat on a cold hard bench in the lobby. Sarah leaned against Angel, and he put his arm around her. He could tell she was anxious, and he kissed the top of her head. "Almost done, sweetheart."

She nodded. A good hour later, her mom finally walked out, and they stood up. Angel was surprised at the lack of resemblance. Her mom's hair was light brown, and she had very dark eyes. The one thing that she did have was Sarah's smile.

Sarah rushed to her and hugged her. After holding each other for a few minutes, Sarah turned to introduce her to Angel.

Angel reached out to shake her hand, but her mother hugged him hard instead. When she pulled away, she examined him thoroughly. "She was right, kid. You are a doll."

"Never been called that before," Angel smiled.

He took the bags her mother carried, and Sarah's mom locked her arm in his then locked the other in Sarah's arm. All three began the walk down the corridor. "So what do you say, kids? Let's forget the past and go start our new lives in California."

Angel and Sarah glanced at each other and smiled. Yeah, Angel liked the sound of that.

EPILOGUE

The musicians made their way through the restaurant, taking requests. Sarah sat with her mom, aunt, uncle and Valerie in one of the bigger booths. Angel's parents had thrown a graduation party, so the restaurant was open to guests only.

Sarah's mom squeezed her hand, and Sarah smiled. Her mom looked nothing like what she'd looked like when Sarah first visited her in jail. She'd gained weight and looked healthy and vibrant.

Her mom had been right there for her during the coach's trial. After Sarah pressed charges, several other girls stepped forward to accuse him of the same thing. All in all, he was tried on several different counts ranging from sexual molestation to attempted rape. But many others testified that he'd acted inappropriately with them as well. It took the jury only two hours to deliberate.

He was found guilty, and after all the counts were added up, he'd be doing at least thirty years before he'd even be up for parole. Angel couldn't have been happier. But Sarah couldn't help feeling bad for the guy. He was so young, and his life was ruined. She'd kept those feelings to herself though and celebrated along with everyone else.

Sofia winked and smiled at her from where she was sitting with her parents, holding Eric's hand. After Sarah had helped convince Angel, Sofia and Eric doubled with her and Angel to the prom. When she turned seventeen a month ago, she was allowed to date. Of course, Eric staked his claim the moment he found out.

Angel and Alex had been doing their best to not give them a minute alone. Sarah winked back and giggled. They'd never know just how sneaky little sister could be.

When Sydney walked in with Carina, Sarah stood up to go meet them. She hugged Carina first then Sydney. His fingers ran through hers as they stood and talked. Sarah turned to see Angel walking toward them and quickly dropped Sydney's hand. Old habits die hard.

"How's it going, man?" Angel shook Sydney's hand and clapped his shoulder.

Then he turned and hugged Carina.

Angel asked them about the drive and pulled Sarah gently to him by the waist. He was getting better with the whole Sydney thing, but a lot had changed. It was inevitable. Sarah stopped calling Sydney her best friend—at least around Angel. The calls had been down to once a week ever since their talk. Angel's patience only went so far.

Sarah had only gone back to Arizona the one time when they had picked up her mom. But since then, Syd and Carina had come out to visit several times, and each time got a little better.

They walked over to the bar to get drinks.

"So is your mom finally getting used to California?" Sydney asked.

Sarah told him about her mom having a hard time adjusting. "Yeah, she is now, even got a job. Angel's parents said she could work here at the restaurant. She starts next week."

"She won't be doing the books though," Angel smirked, handing her a soda.

Sarah glared at him, appalled, and he kissed her. "I'm kidding."

Sarah rolled her eyes and continued. "We won't be at my aunt's very long though. We're getting an apartment real soon."

"Do you still babysit?" Carina asked.

"No. The restaurant has been real busy. I've been working here so much I just haven't had the time."

"That's right, Lynni told me business is booming." Sydney turned to Angel. "You guys ever think of opening up another one?"

Angel squeezed Sarah's hand. He still hated to hear Syd call her that but was beginning to accept that it wasn't going to change.

"Actually," Angel said, "that's kind of the plan. After school, Sarah and I want to open up our own restaurant. My dad already said he'd help us, but not until we finish school." He turned to gaze in Sarah's eyes. "The wedding's first though."

Sarah and Angel would both be attending San Diego State in the fall. She had been so close to going to New Mexico for a time that Angel had been beside himself. Just a few weeks ago, though, they had gotten news of her scholarship to San Diego, and now everything was perfect. She would stay in La Jolla and work at the restaurant part time.

Sydney smiled. "Lynni told me if it were up to you, you'd be married already."

Angel frowned. "Yeah, everyone jumped all over that one. It's cool. I'll wait 'til we finish school, but no longer than that."

The musicians started singing *Sabor a Mi*, a slow, romantic Mexican favorite. Sarah smiled at the sight of giant Alex next to petite Valerie. Those two were still going back and forth. Sarah didn't get it. Alex looked at Valerie very much the same way Angel looked at Sarah, yet he was still doing the disappearing act on Valerie all the time. They'd go for a good few weeks being inseparable, then he'd be gone with just a few short texts to check in with her, and Valerie was certain he was with someone else.

Some people got up to dance, including Eric and Sofia. Angel tugged Sarah's hand. She put her drink down, and he led her to the dance floor. Angel bumped Eric hard before putting his arms around Sarah.

"You're an ass," Eric chuckled.

Sarah rested her head against Angel's strong shoulder and closed her eyes. His grip tightened, and he kissed her head. Never in all her wildest dreams as a little girl could she have imagined being this happy. She was finally home.

ACKNOWLEDGEMENTS

I would like to thank my husband Mark for believing in me and giving me my space, so I could write for hours and hours. I would also like to thank my kids for their patience and understanding that mom's room is also her office and allowing me to hole up in it for days at a time. I love you all for your continued support!

Since Forever Mine was my very first book out, and at the time, I could not afford to have it professionally edited, I thankfully had several friends offer to go through it. I'd like to thank those of you who took the time to help out with that. Anthony Buccino, Stephanie Lott, Judy Devries and most recently my current editor and "Eagle Eyes," the awesome Theresa Wegand. Your hard work, professionalism, and thoroughness are greatly appreciated.

To my beta reader, it's hard to believe when I first wrote this I only had one! At the time, I didn't even know that's what I was supposed to refer to you as. But it's exactly what you were: my ex-coworker but still good friend Ivannia Alay. Thank you for taking the time to read through this and giving me your very honest opinion and feedback.

To my cover artist Stephanie Mooney, I'm so glad I found you and you were able to not only give the MB series covers a much needed facelift but have gone on to create the rest of my covers.

A huge thank you to my wonderful group of amazingly talented authors who have been such an enormous support. I honestly don't know what I'd do without you ladies. It's been a blessing to have met you all. Every one of you is truly an inspiration, and I'm honored and very humbled to be included in this wonderful group. I hope our friendships stay strong and we continue to be this close forever! I love you all!

And last but certainly not least, I thank the readers/bloggers/reading community who have welcomed me with such enthusiasm and showered me with love. You have and continue to make my dreams come true. All your comments, emails, and messages inspire me to write more and more. I do it for the love of writing but also because I can hardly wait to hear what you think! Much love to all of you!

ABOUT THE AUTHOR

Elizabeth Reyes was born and raised in southern California and still lives there with her husband of almost nineteen years, her two teens, her Great Dane named Dexter, and one big fat cat named Tyson.

She spends eighty percent of time in front of her computer writing and keeping up with all the social media, and loves it. She says that there is nothing better than doing what you absolutely love for a living, and she eats, sleeps, and breathes these stories, which are constantly begging to be written.

Representation: Jane Dystel of Dystel & Goderich now handles all questions regarding subsidiary rights for any of Ms. Reyes' work. Please direct inquiries regarding foreign translation and film rights availability to her.

For more information on her upcoming projects and to connect with her (She loves hearing from you all!), here are a few places you can find her:

Blog: authorelizabethreyes.blogspot.com

Facebook fan page:

http://www.facebook.com/pages/Elizabeth-Reyes/278724885527554

Twitter: @AuthorElizabeth

Email EliReyesbooks@yahoo.com

Add her books to your Good Reads shelf

She enjoys hearing your feedback and looks forward to reading your reviews and comments on her website and fan page!

Printed in Poland
by Amazon Fulfillment
Poland Sp. z o.o., Wrocław